He Was too breathless to talk, too focused on Winning.

She shoved her hip sideways and kicked his leg, shooting pain up the length of it. This time she was able to roll to the side and gain her footing, jumping to her feet. He was right behind her and grabbed her again.

She was a fighter, and a practiced one at that.

He shoved her against the wall, hearing her breath whoosh out of her. He used his body to hold her, grabbing her flailing arms and anchoring them at her head level. Their heavy breathing was synchronized, and, with each breath, their bodies pressed tighter together. Her breasts, soft and round, sent heat pulsing through him.

Bloody fine time for that.

By Jaime Rush

DARKNESS BECOMES HER
BEYOND THE DARKNESS
BURNING DARKNESS
TOUCHING DARKNESS
OUT OF THE DARKNESS
A PERFECT DARKNESS

JAIME RUSH

DARKNESS
BECOMES HER

AVON
An Imprint of HarperCollinsPublishers

AVON BOOKS
An Imprint of HarperCollins*Publishers*
10 East 53rd Street
New York, New York 10022–5299

Copyright © 2012 by Tina Wainscott
ISBN 978–0–06–201892–2
www.avonromance.com

First Avon Books mass market printing: June 2012

Avon Trademark Reg. U.S. Pat. Off. and in Other Countries, Marca Registrada, Hecho en U.S.A.
HarperCollins® is a registered trademark of HarperCollins Publishers.

Printed in the U.S.A.

10 9 8 7 6 5 4 3 2 1

Dedicated to Dave Deslandes

ACKNOWLEDGMENTS

Thank you to Barrie James; it was your voice I heard when Lachlan spoke. Thanks for introducing me to the singular pleasure of British ales.

Nanine Case, I love our enlightening conversations while driving to the tube. I'll let you figure out which scene you inspired.

Louie Pastore, a researcher in Scottish martial arts, for your help in getting it right.

To David Schleifer, author of sci-fi adventure, who also helped with swordplay.

And to Crystal Adams-Clark, for giving me the great title for *Beyond the Darkness*.

DARKNESS
BECOMES HER

PROLOGUE

Fifteen years earlier

Wake up, Ally!"

Her daddy's voice, hands shaking her. Not a dream. Her eyes snapped open, finding his face, scared and desperate, hovering in front of her.

"You've got to hide now."

She tumbled out of bed, heart squeezing her chest. "What's happening, Daddy?"

"The man I told you might hurt me, he's here, Allybean."

She swiped up her penguin, the one with the special coin sewn inside it. She couldn't breathe all of a sudden. "Where's Mommy?"

"She's all right. He won't hurt her."

"But he'll hurt me?" The words squeaked out of her mouth.

"I don't know what he'll do. I just want to make sure you're safe."

He tugged her down the hall to the closet and shoved aside the coats.

"How will I know when it's safe to come out?" Fear made her voice a whisper.

"Either your mother or I will come get you. You'll be okay."

He didn't look as though he felt that way, and that made her even more scared.

"I love you, Allybean." And he closed the door, shutting her in the dark.

Daddy had always seemed overprotective and kind of worried. When she turned nine a year ago, he told her there was a man who wanted to hurt him: his own brother, Russell. Daddy had shown her a picture, trained her to be on the lookout for him. He had something called the Darkness inside him. Daddy had promised to tell her more when she was old enough to understand.

Now Russell was here, and she didn't understand, not at all. Minutes dragged by, each one so long, so painful. She squeezed her penguin and felt the coin her father had put inside. Through the fur, she could barely make out the raised cross on it. The symbol was supposed to protect her, to hide her presence from the man who was hunting Daddy.

A *thump* froze her. Like someone being thrown against the wall. Loud, harsh voices, two men . . . and Mommy. They were screaming all at once, their words crashing on top of each other. Another *thump*. Tears filled her eyes. *Please, don't die, Daddy*.

She tried to peer through the slats in the bifold door but could only see the hallway. What if she crawled out but kept the penguin with her? It would only be for a few seconds.

Her mom cried out, the same way she did when she dropped a heavy pan on her foot last year.

Mommy!

The men's voices got even louder, but nothing from her mommy. Her ears were buzzing, making it hard to hear more than angry voices. *Have to look.*

She stretched through the opening. What she saw froze her heart. There was blood everywhere, splattered on the walls and puddling on the floor. And her mommy, she was lying on the floor. Not moving. Ally stifled a cry.

"I can heal her," one of the men said in a voice so thick it was impossible to tell who was talking. "I can use Darkness to heal her, but then she'll have it, too."

"Don't touch her."

Those words, raw and hoarse.

The men moved into view, like two boxers, squaring off, punching, lunging like in the movies Daddy watched. She was in the dark, and she was pretty sure they couldn't see her. They fought, growling and shoving, moving in and out of her view.

The bad man said, "Does the child have Darkness, too?"

"No, she's normal. Leave her out of this."

The child? *Her.*

"My son inherited it," Russell said. "Your

daughter probably did, too. If she holds Darkness, she'll have to be . . . contained. Trained."

"The hell she does!" A loud sound, and a chair slid across the floor.

She'd stretched farther out into the hallway without even realizing it, and now saw Russell, his back to her, his foot on her father's chest. She wanted to burst out and save him but stopped herself. Anger and fear, it froze her, closing in her vision. No, not her vision. She saw blackness. Her father, turning into . . . she blinked. Couldn't be. He was now a black blob of smoke.

Russell stepped back, facing the dark mist. "You've been trying to suppress Darkness, just like before. But I've been working with it, mastering it."

He became the same smoke. The blobs took shape, changing to something solid again, to huge, mean wolves. Her daddy's wolf was gray, Russell's was black. The wolves fought, snarling, and then the black wolf spun like the Tasmanian Devil in the cartoons and wrapped itself around her father's wolf. Terror gripped her, making her eyes water and her throat dry. Was she really seeing this?

Go back in!

The shadows became men again, and one of them fell to the floor. The bad man! Her daddy was okay!

She got to her feet. Her legs felt so wobbly, and she hardly had breath. She took a staggering step toward the kitchen, her fingers clutching the penguin. Her daddy knelt by her mommy's body on the floor. "No. You can't be gone." Such pain in his words. Smoke snaked out of his hands as he leaned over her, sending . . . sending the smoke into her mommy.

"No!" The word roared out of her throat.

He turned to her and . . . his eyes were gray, not the green she knew. He wasn't her daddy. He looked like him, but she knew, knew in her heart, that he wasn't. Russell had gone into her daddy's body.

"There you are." He jumped up and grabbed for her.

CHAPTER 1

"What are you on to, checking up on me?" Lachlan narrowed his eyes as his brother sauntered into the kitchen.

Magnus managed to find a reason to come to the family's remote estate, dubbed Sanctuary, every few days for some lame reason or another. As usual, he surveyed the house, checking to see, perhaps, if garbage was piling up or if Lachlan had painted any of the walls black.

Magnus poured himself a cup of tea from the pot sitting on the counter, then opened the fridge to pull out milk and frowned. "If I *were* checking up on you, I'd point out the lack of quality food in the fridge." He closed the door and tugged on Lachlan's hair. "Or that you haven't cut your hair in months; it's as long as a girl's." Magnus pinched Lachlan's chin. "At least you shave, but next time use a mirror. You missed some spots."

"Considering you and the clerks at the stores are the only people I see, I have no need for a cut and style." Lachlan stroked the strip of hair that ran from the bottom of his lower lip to his beard. "I was bored, figured I'd try something different."

Magnus lifted the back of Lachlan's old T-shirt. "No lash marks on your back, at least. Saw a movie about those monks who beat themselves with whips in punishment."

Lachlan shoved him away, not that the big guy moved much. "Sod off. Thought you were busy, as you're so happy to tell me, living life, shagging women, and making up for lost time. Why are you driving all the way out here to check up on me? Making sure I haven't gone over the edge?"

Magnus dropped down into a chair and propped his big black shoes on the kitchen table. "Holing up here by yourself day in and day out, it's bound to make you mad. You're a pain in my arse, but you're all the family I got. You want to live like a monk, keep punishing yourself for the past, nothing I can do about that. But I don't want to come out and find your rotting body."

Lachlan smirked. "I didn't know you cared."

"I'm the one who's going to have to deal with it."

Lachlan leaned against the counter. "Ah, it's the cleanup you're worried about. I promise you, I'll not be doing myself in. That's a coward's way out. I'll live till I'm a hundred and deserve every wretched minute of it. Now you can move on."

Magnus tilted his head. "I do care. It's me and you, Locky. That's all we've got."

"Don't remind me, Maggie." Not that he could forget why their parents were dead.

"You're the only one who hates yourself, you know. It's time to ease up."

"'Ease up'? I killed our mum, for God's sake. Would have killed you, too, if I hadn't come to my senses. I'd hate me, if I were you."

"You made a mistake, a big one, but you had no idea that the outcome would be as horrific as it was. It's been almost a year, Locky."

Lachlan kept his expression passive. He didn't deserve forgiveness or release. Or the childhood nickname. "I'm happy working on my projects, being alone, and living vicariously through your exploits. Get any gigs?"

Magnus gave him an exasperated sigh, hopefully giving up on him. "I'm filling in for an ailing drummer Saturday for the Wee Willies. And I've got a date. Not that you'd know what one of those is."

"I know what a bloody date is."

Magnus's laugh came out a low rumble. "Oh, that's right, you learned all about that kind of thing in those chat rooms and from watching dirty movies." When Lachlan narrowed his eyes, Magnus raised his hands. "I'm not judging you. I watched them, too. We were hot-blooded teenage boys living a life in isolated areas, being home schooled. We had to get our jollies somewhere. But we're not boys anymore, not being hunted down. It's time to go out in the world and live."

He raised a thick eyebrow. "And touch women."

"I've no interest in either. I'll stick to my cars, thank you."

Magnus nodded toward the newspaper on the table. "At least you're keeping up with society. The girl I'm seeing, she's in there. Front page of the Living section." When Lachlan didn't move toward the paper, Magnus said, "Go on, have a peek."

She must be a number if he was eager to show her off. Or he was really hot for her. Maybe both. His brother always filled Lachlan in on the girl he was dating, a different one every time. Not to brag, but probably out of an attempt to draw him out into the world. Tempt him.

Dutifully, Lachlan turned to the section. The story featured a winter carnival to raise money for a local girl who not only had muscular dystrophy but had recently undergone a bone marrow transplant. An anonymous marrow donor had saved her life, but medical bills threatened to bury the family.

There, in the background of a photo of people setting up booths, was a petite, dark-haired woman, her shiny hair in a pixie cut that fanned over her shoulders. Unaware of the camera, she held up a large sign while two people hammered it in place. Her profile showed apple cheeks, tight-fitting jeans, and a sweater that molded a great set of knockers.

"Nice," he allowed.

"I haven't even pointed her out yet." Magnus jabbed his finger at the same woman. "Name's Jessie. I've fallen for her."

"That's what you said about the last four or five. Or ten."

Magnus's mouth turned up in a roguish smile. "Yeah, and I did, temporarily."

"What happens after you've fallen? You just get up? That's it, the feelings are all done?"

"Yeah, like the bubbles going out of a soda after it's been sitting for a while. But there's something about Jessie that I can't put my finger on."

"Well, she's hot."

"She is, but that's not it. Dunno. Anyway, you could come to the carnival—"

"No, thanks. Have fun with your girl. I hope you're using a condom."

Magnus smirked the same way he had. "I didn't know *you* cared."

"I was thinking of the lass, you horn dog. 'Twould serve you right, catching crabs or lobsters or whatever."

Instead of taking the bait, Magnus laughed, shaking his curls. Well, sure, he could be in a good mood. He was going to get laid.

Magnus pushed to his feet. "All right, carry on with your wallowing. Might help your mood if you got laid, too."

"Stop reading my mind. Invasive, meddling—"

Magnus chuckled as he headed to the front

door. "Nice job on the fifty-five, by the way. Sexy as hell. I'd say the sixteen coats of Marine Spar varnish did the trick." He let the door close behind him.

Lachlan knew that '55 Chevy truck was as sexy as his life was going to get. He carried the mugs to the sink but stopped short. The shiny, bloodred tile backsplash was wobbling. The floor shifted under his feet. Earthquake? He set the mugs on the counter, and the house started spinning. He grabbed onto the back of a chair at the small table, but it gave way. So did he.

Not the house, him. He broke out in a cold sweat, his body rigid. *Stroke? Heart attack?* Those words pinged through his head and seized his chest as he shivered on the tile floor. Then he was standing in a completely different place. He saw a Ferris wheel, booths, but everything was blurred. Over there, someone in the near distance. He stumbled toward him but his gaze went to the mound on the ground: Magnus, dead. Somehow, he knew his brother was dead. Standing next to him was a woman, petite . . . the woman in the photograph? No one else, just the two of them.

Then he snapped back to the kitchen, staring at the can lights in the ceiling. He patted his hands down his body. Here, alive. He got to his feet and grabbed the newspaper. Yes, the same woman. He slumped to the chair, feeling the same peculiar fatigue wash through him that he used to get after he astral-projected. Except he couldn't astral-project anymore. He'd lost that ability when his father had tried to save his sanity.

The carnival, that's what he'd seen. He grabbed his phone and called Magnus. "Get back here. Now."

Magnus walked in a few minutes later, concern in his eyes. For a second he reminded Lachlan of their mother. They'd both gotten her brown eyes, but only Magnus had her curls. A sharp pain stabbed him at the thought of her.

Magnus dropped into the chair next to Lachlan's. "What's up? I just left and you looked fine. Well, as fine as you can look. Now you look like shite."

"Something happened. I think I astral-projected." With shaking hands, he held out the newspaper, pointing to the lass. "She's going to kill you."

"What the devil are you talking about?"

Lachlan told him what had happened.

"You're serious?"

"You think I'd make something like this up?"

"You saw her kill me?" Not a small dose of skepticism in Magnus's voice.

"I saw her standing over you after she'd killed you."

"You were only able to project to the present and past. So you're telling me your ability's come back, and now you can see the future?"

"I'm telling you what I saw. So unless that's

happened in the past, then yes, I saw the future."

Magnus dropped the paper on the table. "You haven't had a glimmer of your abilities in ten months, and now, the moment I show you a picture of a girl I want to start seeing—"

"You think I'm making this up—or imagining it—because I'm *jealous* that you're interested in someone?" He rammed his fingers back through his hair, tangling in the strands. Yeah, a bit too long.

"It's either that or you're going mad again, in which case I hope it is jealousy. Jessie's sweet, shy, and she's not coming on to me. The opposite, in fact, which is probably why I'm so fascinated by her. So if she's a homicidal woman who picked me for her next victim, she's not doing a great job of luring me in."

"Maybe she is doing a great job. Play hard to get. Just like you said, that only makes you want her more. You don't think smart women know that will snag a play-around like you?"

Magnus rolled his eyes. "Why would she want to kill me? Do you know how many female serial killers there have been in history? Like, a handful. I hate to say it, but it's much more likely that it's your imagination. We don't know what the side effects of the antidote might be. It was something Dad worried about."

Was he going crazy again? What he'd felt when he saw Magnus dead . . . it shattered him. He couldn't take a chance that this wasn't real.

"It happened—it's going to happen—at the carnival. Are you planning to be there with her?"

"I'm helping her with last minute details tonight."

"Did she bat her eyes at you, tell you how much work there was to do, so little time to finish it?"

Magnus narrowed his eyes. "I offered all on my own, no eye-batting necessary."

"What do you know about her?"

"She just moved here, got a job at the music shop where I bought my kit. She won't let me pay for her coffee or lunch, yet I know she's tight on money because she wanted a large latte but settled for the small. She's volunteering her time at this carnival because someone in her life had muscular dystrophy. You can tell it means something to her when she talks about it. She's warm and playful with the kids who take classes. And you forget, if she had any murderous thoughts, I'd probably pick up on them."

Magnus could read thoughts, or at least pick up words here or there. He hadn't lost his abilities when he'd taken the antidote. Lachlan had been bitter about that, but he'd come to realize he didn't deserve abilities, not when he'd killed someone by using them. Now, though, something *had* come back. Something different than what he'd had.

"I'll go back earlier and see what happened." He had always been able to project at will, but nothing happened.

"So it's not back, then," Magnus said a minute

later. "You haven't gone all tense and twitchy."

Lachlan's eyes snapped open. "Humor me and stay away from the carnival."

"How did she kill me in this supposed vision? Knife in the parlor? Candlestick in the drawing room."

"Sure, joke around when I'm telling you your life is in danger. I couldn't tell how you'd died, only that you were dead. Everything around you was a blur, but I didn't see anyone else."

"Give me more, Locky."

Frustration swamped him. "I don't have any more."

Magnus got up and walked to the foyer.

Lachlan followed. "I never hallucinated. That wasn't what happened with mum."

"You saw something that wasn't there. By definition, that's a hallucination." He pushed open the door and turned back. "Last time you thought you had everything under control, and then you lost it. Don't do anything crazy."

Magnus left, and Lachlan stalked back to the table, staring at the picture of the girl. He had to find out more about her. He'd lost both his mother and father in the last eleven months. He wasn't about to lose his brother, not when he could prevent it. He could never live with himself if he didn't do something. Hopefully, Magnus wasn't in danger. But that meant his own sanity was.

Lachlan grabbed up the newspaper and walked to his room. The house was a square, like a fort, wrapped around a courtyard flourishing with flora, fauna, and fungus, his father's fascinations. The trek from one place in the house to another gave Lachlan too much time to think. He sat at the computer, booted it up, and waited through the process.

He'd been cut off from the world for so long, exposed to television more than to actual people. For the first half of his life his father had rented isolated homes. During the last half, they'd lived here in a house they owned, built in the middle of a large tract of land. Their social interactions consisted of brief forays into town.

Magnus made friends easily. He longed for the world, for contact. Lachlan had inherited the lack of need for others from his father. Dad could spend all day in his lab or out with the fungus. Lachlan did that with the old truck now, immersing himself in the process of restoring it. He'd done it several times before, resurrecting something old, rusty, and broken into something whole.

Something he could never do with himself.

He launched into a search for Jessie Bellandre, finding several mentions. One was a blog entry dated two years earlier in which her name appeared. The blogger was a sixteen-year-old with muscular dystrophy, talking about her experience at an MDA summer camp. Her counselor was Jessie, and the picture of the woman in a canoe matched the Jessie in the article, except she had blond, wavy hair. The camp was in Iowa.

After several more false leads, he found her again, this time in Nevada six months ago. Again, involved in a Muscular Dystrophy Association function. So she definitely had a connection with the disease. But what was the connection to the horror he'd seen? Why was she moving around the country so often, changing her looks? He kept digging.

He found three older mentions, all in the Boston area. In the two pictures, she had dark, long hair. At some point she started moving around and changing her looks. Why?

Given an age in one of the articles, he dug deeper and found something alarming: eleven years ago Jessie Bellandre, aged fourteen, died from a fatal form of muscular dystrophy. Someone had made a tribute page to honor children who had passed on, trying to drum up sympathy and donations. There was no picture. He went through several steps of finding the woman who'd put up the page. She no longer maintained it, having moved on to other projects, and all she could tell him about Jessie was that she had been a foster child, thus the lack of a picture.

Stymied, Lachlan stared at the tribute listing and then at the picture of her in the paper. They were the same age, or would have been. Both had lived in Boston. Now this Jessie—Magnus's Jessie—had been resurrected as a woman who was clearly living a lie.

He grabbed his cell phone to call Magnus, but

stopped. His brother would say it was a coincidence, even though it wasn't a common name, and that he was stretching things to match his crazy scenario. He needed more. He was going to have to hunt her down.

CHAPTER 2

Whenever Lachlan ventured out into the world, he felt like a vampire, pretending to be like the others he walked among. Jessie's current residence wasn't listed in the phone directory, but he had a piece of insider information: he knew where she worked.

He walked into the store located in Annapolis, Maryland. It was damned hard not to seek her out the moment the door closed behind him and appear only mildly curious. No woman in sight. Bells dinged against the glass. The bittersweet sound of a violin flowed from somewhere in the back.

A man walked out and asked if he needed help.

Yeah, tell me what you know about the girl working for you.

"Just browsing."

"I'm Glen, if you need anything."

Lachlan gave the man a nod and wandered over to an impressive display of electric guitars mounted on the far wall.

Her voice reached out to him, like a ribbon wrapping sinuously around his stomach. It was soft and sweet and full of her smile. He could tell even before he saw her.

"Look, you brought tears to my eyes, Charles. That was incredible."

Lachlan turned and felt a trip in his heartbeat at the sight of her. She was walking from the back with another woman and her young son, who was holding a violin case and beaming with pride. Smitten, too, judging by the way he looked at Jessie.

Her eyes were misty, all right. She knelt down to his level. "When you're a famous superstar, will you still remember the girl at the music store?"

The boy laughed and gave her a quick hug.

"Yeah, she has that effect on most of the males who come in here."

Lachlan turned to Glen, startled to see that the man was talking to him. Lachlan was about to deny the smitten part but laughed it off instead. He pretended to peruse the drum kits displayed in front of a wall of mirrors. Between the electric guitars that hung over them, he could watch her reflection. She was even prettier in person, her eyes glowing with sincerity and admiration. She wore slim black pants that outlined a luscious figure and a black top with grunge-style ruffles.

She died eleven years ago.

Or was pretending to be someone else. Either way, combined with what he'd seen in his projection, he didn't like it, despite her innocent appearance. Likely, it was all a show, along with playing hard to get.

He shifted his attention away as she began to look up. He imagined Magnus sitting behind the blue kit, as he had for the last few years at the Sanctuary, banging away in the basement. Curls bouncing wildly as he moved the sticks so fast they were a blur. Bliss on his face. Once, Lachlan had tried his hand at it, when no one else was around. Good thing, too, he thought now, as he had not a speck of rhythm.

He caught his own reflection in the mirror. Holy hell, was that him? His hair was long and mussed, button-down shirt hanging loose over faded jeans with a square, ragged hole in one knee. He hadn't looked at himself for a while, had avoided mirrors. Now he saw a stranger staring back at him.

"I'm going home for lunch," Jessie said, leaning behind the counter and pulling out an enormous dark purple bag. She glanced his way, their gazes locking in the reflection for a second. She paused for just as long before turning away and leaving.

The trick was to leave right behind her without looking as though he was following. He reached for the tag on the brass cymbal, noticing the calluses on his hands.

"I know your type," a man right behind him said.

Lachlan turned to face Glen, surprised to see a smile and not an accusation.

"Lives for the music, stays up all night playing the songs in his head. That was me, before the wife and kids and shop." He gestured to the place in general.

"You've pegged me, dreaming on my lunch break." Lachlan glanced at his watch. "Which, unfortunately, is over."

He knew she'd gone to the right, and spotted her as she turned the corner at the end of the block. Lucky break, that. He jogged down the sidewalk, slowing as he took the same corner. She got into a big SUV, and hearing the locks snick as he passed by, he again fought the urge to look at her. He got into his truck, which did looked damned good, though he still saw all the things that needed to be done yet.

Lachlan didn't take the time to revel in the purr of the engine, the only real pleasure he allowed himself. He was too busy watching the rear of Jessie's black Yukon as he followed her into an apartment complex some ten minutes later. He parked several spaces away and observed her jump down from the vehicle and take the stairs two at a time. She disappeared into unit 14B on the second floor.

Lachlan knew he would find the answers in her apartment. He tried to astral-project to her apartment but once again failed. Had the projection been a tease? His imagination? The thought tightened his chest. The picture of Jessie triggered the projection last time, but now that he was near her, he couldn't get it to work. He'd have to break in the old-fashioned way. He had done it before, every time his dad locked himself out of his lab, sometimes leaving not only his key in there but the backups as well.

Jessie remained inside long enough to eat lunch and then reemerged. He could understand why Magnus was smitten with her. Her hips moved eloquently as she walked to her vehicle. Interestingly, she scanned the parking lot, not paranoid exactly, but wary. When she drove off, Lachlan remained.

He carried a toolbox and appeared to be looking for an address. After knocking on her door, he identified himself as the handyman she'd called and pretended to converse with her through the door.

"The dispatcher said you can't get the door to open . . . Okay, no worries, I'll get you out of there."

He worked on the lock with the pick kit. When he opened the door, he continued the "conversation" as though she stood right there inviting him in to work on the knob.

The apartment was small and sparse, with generic furniture. Coupons littered the two-seater kitchen table's surface, each cut in a neat square and stacked in categories like food and household items. Several magazines lay on the counter, one open to a recipe for buttermilk biscuits. The one on top had the address square cut away. A To Do list had several bullet-point items scribbled all over it.

In the small living area, a sewing kit sat by the recliner, lid open to reveal spools of thread and a red heart-shaped pincushion. Juxtaposing the domestic ambience, a stack of well-read love novels on the end table sported covers with couples in provocative poses. So she liked the steamy stuff, eh?

Even further from the norm, a gymnast's mat filled a corner, a punching bag hanging above it. Several DVDs on karate were stacked by the television. Bars and a fine steel mesh reinforced the windows.

Ah, now he was getting somewhere. Someone had drawn a cross on the wall, four lines and a small circle in the middle. He looked around more closely. At the bottom of the stack of novels he found a hard-bound notebook, ragged with use. Sketches of demonic beings filled the pages, each identified as creatures like werewolves and shapeshifters. Many had X's through them. He took pictures of a few pages with his cell phone, then one of the cross.

He took a few steps into the only bedroom. Not a lot of personal effects here either. A framed picture, fuzzy blanket, a small stuffed penguin on the made bed that looked like it had seen years in the clutches of a child. The sight of it stabbed him in the chest for some reason. He saw no other signs of a child living here, so it had to be hers. He took a picture of that, too.

A key slid into the lock at the front door. Lachlan stepped out of view, watching as she dashed into the kitchen and grabbed some papers on the counter. The vision flashed through his mind again, this woman standing over his brother's body, and he reacted. He crossed the few feet, catching her eye with the movement, but he already had his arms around her waist before she could get in a kick. She pitched all her weight forward, throwing him off balance enough that she wriggled free. She spun, with a roundhouse kick to his side. Pain exploded, making him grunt. He regained his balance, finding her bouncing on her feet, fists raised, ready to attack.

Both fear and anger blazed in eyes a rich blend of green and chocolate. No sign of that sweetness now. A ruse, as he'd expected. She jabbed, and when he backed up, kicked. He grabbed her foot and sent her stumbling backward. She twisted, slamming sideways into him using karate moves she no doubt practiced on that mat. She was strong, and it hurt. It also felt good in a strange way.

He grabbed her arms, clamping them against her sides. She swiveled, shoving him against the wall and, with that split second of freedom, made to run toward the door. He grabbed her shoulder and yanked her back, intending to pin her against him. She twisted her ankle and pushed his foot enough to send him to the floor, her along with him. They crashed, both taking the brunt of the fall. His arms locked around her.

They ended up with her on top, her back plastered to his front. As she struggled to free herself, her ass ground against his pelvis. Of all damned things, the movement shot heat through him. This was a fight, not sex. But he was thinking about sex, which was crazy.

She brought her elbow down, but he blocked before she could dig the point into his side. He was too breathless to talk, too focused on winning. She shoved her hip sideways and kicked his leg, shooting pain up the length of it. This time she was able to roll to the side and gain her footing, jumping to her feet. He was right behind her and grabbed her again.

He shoved her against the wall, hearing her breath whoosh out of her. Didn't matter; she made to ram her knee into his groin. She was a fighter, and a practiced one at that. She hadn't hesitated to fight him. He used his body to hold her to the wall, grabbing her flailing arms and anchoring them at her head level. Their heavy breathing was synchronized, and with each breath, their bodies pressed tighter together. Her breasts, soft and round, nipples hardened, sent heat pulsing through him.

Bloody fine time for that.

She wriggled again, aiming a deadly look at him. The look didn't kill him, but it heightened the heat. He had the insane urge to grind into her but held himself in check. What the hell was wrong with him? He'd numbed himself to anything sensual, any desire, and here he felt it with this potentially homicidal woman.

She tried one last time to jerk up her knee, and his pelvis mashed even harder against her. Good God, he felt an erection, the first one since—

"I won't be an easy rape, you son of a bitch," she spat out at him, still breathless. "Is this what Russell's doing now, sending crazed rapists after me?"

Rape? Of course, his wayward cock. "I'm not going to rape you. I want to know why you're going to kill my brother, Magnus."

She blinked in confusion. "Magnus? *Kill him?* Are you crazy? I have no intentions of *killing* him."

"I am a little crazy, actually. I saw a vision of the future, you standing over his body." No need to go into any more than that.

"You saw a vision. As in a crystal ball type vision?"

"Don't look at *me* like I'm the strange one. You're obviously into some weird stuff. What's the symbol mean?" He nodded toward the sort of cross. "Are you a devil worshiper?"

Her laugh was hoarse. "No."

"Why didn't you scream for help, even when you thought I was a rapist? What are you hiding?"

Something happened. One moment they were there, him pressing her against the wall, and the next all he saw was a black blur and then he was thrown across the room. He hit the wall and slid to the floor. He blinked, stumbling to his feet even though every muscle in his body screamed in pain.

She stood where she'd been, eyes wide and

mouth trembling. "Get out of here. I would never hurt Magnus. Just get out of here."

The energy in the room had changed, sparking and electric. She was scared of whatever had happened.

Lachlan rubbed his shoulder. "What did you do to me?"

"Get out."

Or she'd do it again? No, she hadn't exactly said it as a threat. Still, it was a threat nonetheless. He glanced at the symbol and then at her. Her hands were clenched into fists at her sides. Now her whole body shook, as though she might explode. She took deep breaths, making her chest rise and fall.

He walked out, watching her the whole time. He had astral-projected into many different places and time periods, into battles and even one of the Holocaust camps. He had never felt this kind of energy.

She *was* dangerous. He got into his truck and drove directly to Magnus's new flat.

Jessie stood in her apartment for a long time, letting the trembles rumble through her body. Everything that had just happened washed across her mind, pulsing like a strobe. Fear of dying, of being raped, and then the bizarreness of the man's accusation. He had triggered her Darkness, which scared her as much as anything else.

She took a deep breath and looked around for

the papers she'd come back for. They were all over the floor. It hurt to bend down and grab them, and she winced. *Wince all you want now, because you can't when you get back to work.*

She walked outside, pausing on the landing to make sure the man was gone. No sign of him. She hadn't screamed. Couldn't scream. The last thing she needed was having the police dig too deeply into her life. She walked to her Yukon, taking calming breaths.

Her phone was beeping, signifying that some-one had triggered her security alarm. She might have known the jerk was waiting for her if she'd taken her phone with her. She was tempted to click on the link, but there wasn't enough time. A cluster of charms hung from her rearview mirror: an angel, rabbit's foot, horseshoe, four-leaf clover encased in plastic, and a Star of David, and they dangled back and forth as she maneuvered through traffic.

A quick fix of her face, a brush through her hair, and she looked as normal as she had when she left.

Glen looked up when she walked in. "Must have been a hectic lunch break," he said with a smile.

Damn, not exactly as normal. "Had to fit in a lot of errands."

"If you need a couple of minutes to defrazzle, go ahead and take them. I know you've got a busy weekend."

Glen and his wife Toni were great bosses, and even better people. The Tripps ran the store together. She was their only employee, running the storefront, handling calls and paperwork. She was good with numbers. They were stable, dependable, and impersonal. She liked working in small businesses where her employers wouldn't be bothered as much by her erratic work history. That also meant settling for menial jobs that didn't pay much.

Toni and the two grade-school Tripps came rushing in at mid-afternoon, as they did every weekday.

"Hey, Jessie!" the girls called as they gushed with enviable energy and innocence, dropping their backpacks on the floor. "Carnival's tomorrow!"

Toni rolled her eyes as she picked up the packs, as she did every day, and set them behind the curved desk where Jessie worked.

"Yep! You gonna ride the scary rides?" Jessie asked, bending down to their level.

"Will you ride with us?"

"Sure."

Both girls giggled and exchanged looks. "We might throw up, though," they said in unison, more like twins than girls who were two years apart.

"Ewww!" Jessie said, pinching her nose. "Then definitely do not ride the scary rides. I'd be tossing my cookies right along with you."

The girls commenced to making barfing noises until Toni shushed them. She set them on their homework just off the main desk. Jessie watched them asking their mom for help and felt a lump in her chest even as she smiled. When she was their age, she'd had a mom and dad, too. Thank God they didn't know how tenuous life can be, how all that matters can be ripped away in minutes.

Five other children came in for guitar lessons, and Jessie entertained them until class started. For a few minutes no one was in the front room. Glen was in the repair shop in back and no customers wandered in. Her head still felt light, as though she hadn't eaten for hours. She logged into the security software and clicked on the link for her system. It recorded any activity once it was triggered.

Her throat tightened at the sight of the man— Magnus's brother—walking into her apartment. He wasn't even creeping or sneaking, just walked in like he owned the place. Bastard. He looked around, taking pictures of a couple of pages in her notebook, walking to the doorway of her bedroom but not walking in.

The video quality wasn't good enough to see fine details. She realized she'd hoped to see his face again. He had dark, thick hair that fell past his shoulders and brown eyes with an exotic slant to them. He was good-looking, yeah, even though she felt pretty stupid thinking of him that way when he'd broken into her home and manhandled her.

Where have I seen him before? Oh, yeah, here! Right before she'd dashed home for lunch. He was stalking her! Her gaze went to the collection of signed pictures on the back wall. She remembered thinking he looked like one of those rockers from the eighties that Glen was so into, like Kip from Winger. The jerk probably followed her home.

Her attention went back to the monitor. She knew the moment the intruder heard her unlock the door; he ducked inside her bedroom doorway and waited for her. Even though she knew what would happen, watching it was odd, surreal, and scary. She didn't have this security system the last time she'd gotten a surprise visit.

She watched their fight. *I fought pretty damned good. Not good enough, though.*

He pinned her with his body, and she could feel all that muscle and hardness again, crushing her. Especially *that* hardness, which had thrown her, because she'd thought for sure he was connected to Russell, and the man's erection signified a different threat.

But he wasn't there for that. *Thank you, God.*

She glanced around to make sure no one had come in; she was engrossed enough to have missed it. Then she turned back to the screen. As her fear and anger had heightened, a smoky aura formed around her. But . . . there was something around *him*, too; not smoky, but a blurry form.

What the heck?

She paused the frame. Even studying him she

couldn't make it out. That nothing else had the same blur meant it was attached to him. Either he also had Darkness, or he was some other kind of weird. No matter, he was bad news.

Her abilities had taken the man off-guard. If he, or Magnus, were working with Russell, they would have been prepared. She would be dead. The supposed brother claimed he'd had a vision of her killing Magnus. That was all he seemed concerned about, wanting to know why.

When she continued the video, it hit her: she would see her Darkness for the first time. She steeled herself as she watched the black mass that threw him across the room. *Me, but not me. It just took over; I had no control over it.* She shivered and closed the program. What if the whole seeing-a-vision thing was true? Darkness could kill. Could she?

She picked up her cell phone and called Magnus. *Please let me go to voice mail.*

Relief when his deep voice said, " 'Lo, this is Magnus's phone. I hate that I missed your call. Don't make me hunt through the call log. Leave a message." Both men had a Scottish brogue to their voices. Magnus had told her he was born in the U.S. but got the brogue from his Scottish mother.

"Hi, it's Jessie," she said. "You're off the hook for tonight. I don't need any help with the carnival, and . . . I can't see you socially anymore. My life is too complicated in ways I can't explain. Take care of yourself."

Her mouth stretched into a frown. It wasn't like they'd done more than chat at the store, have a cup of coffee, and meet for lunch once. He'd kissed her cheek when he walked her back to the music store and said goodbye. She'd had the sense that he wanted to kiss her on the mouth, though, as his lips had lingered against her skin for a few moments. He probably would have, if the sensible part of her hadn't made her turn at the last second. She'd wanted the kiss, because she wanted to feel like the women in the romance novels she devoured, just for a little while . . .

You knew better. Why bother starting a flirtation when you're going to have to back away if it goes any further? Russell's going to find you eventually. You're either going to die or run again. No place for a man in that mess of a life.

Yeah . . . complicated. With a sigh, she deleted Magnus's number from her contacts list.

CHAPTER 3

Lachlan could hear the drums through the front door, which meant there was no point in knocking. So he turned the doorknob and walked into the small flat. He'd only been here once, when Magnus insisted he come check out his new digs. Lachlan followed the racket to the back bedroom where Magnus sat behind his kit in his skivvies, headphones on and eyes closed, lost in the music. He suspected Magnus escaped into his drumming the way he had escaped into astral projection back when they were bored and isolated.

Magnus was good, sounding every bit like the original version of Jet's "Are You Gonna Be My Girl." His singing was not quite as good as his drumming, but not bad, either.

Lachlan walked up and pinched the cymbal so that when his brother struck it, it went flat. He opened his eyes, blinking in surprise. He flipped his sticks, snapped them up in one hand, and set them on the top of his drum. The headphones, he hooked on the back of his chair.

He rubbed his eyes and stared at him. "Am I imagining things? My brother Locky, here in my flat?" The levity dimmed, though. "What'd you see now? My kit blow up?"

"Yeah, and all they found were your bloodied skivvies hanging on your cymbal."

Magnus came out from behind the kit. "Maybe I should play in the nude, then." He made to yank down the white briefs.

Lachlan held out his hand and walked toward the hallway. "Seen enough of your bare white arse growing up. Got any tea?"

"Nothing gourmet," Magnus called out. "If you came round more, I'd keep a stash of loose tea for you."

Lachlan went to work searching out a box of tea bags and set the kettle to boil.

His brother walked in a few minutes later, having pulled on a pair of sweats. He grabbed a can of Mountain Dew from the fridge. "This isn't a social call or the beginning of your awakening to life," Magnus said to him. "You look too somber and uptight for that. So this will have something to do with your vision or whatever you want to call it."

Lachlan faced him. "The shy girl you're sweet on swiped someone's identity, has a Satanic symbol on her wall, studies demons, and fights like the devil." He lifted his shirt to reveal an assortment of bruises. "This wasn't me thrashing myself. She threw me across the room like I weighed ten pounds. I'm no hulking beast like you, but I'm no wee thing either."

Magnus listened without expression, but his eyes hardened at the end. "Do I want to hear how you came to be in a physical altercation with her?"

"That wasn't my plan. I let myself into her apartment and looked through her things." He thought of the penguin. "But she came back unexpectedly, so I took the opportunity to question her."

Magnus slammed his can onto the counter, sending yellow liquid splashing onto the top. "You *broke* into her apartment?"

"You're going to quibble about that? Did you not hear anything else I said? She did something to me, something unnatural. Put it together, man. I see a vision of her killing you, and it turns out she's hiding under someone else's identity and has some ability that gives her superhuman strength."

"Bloody hell, Lachlan, you could have been arrested. Your imagination is making more of this than it is. Okay, so she can fight. Maybe she grew up in a tough neighborhood, used to dealing with thugs like you. You thought she did something unnatural, but women can be strong when they're proficient at martial arts. What did the symbol look like?"

"Here, take a look for yourself." He pulled up the picture on his phone.

"A cross? Not a goat's head in the center of a pentagram? Was there no blood dripping down the wall?" He reluctantly took the phone.

"Look at the next couple of pictures."

Magnus's eyebrows furrowed. "I can't see what's in the notebook."

"Sketches she'd done of creatures, with notes and everything."

Magnus handed him back the phone. "You've gone mad."

"I'm not the one blinded by my pecker. I'm going to find out who this girl is before she lays you low."

"Wait a minute. You said you questioned her? What did you say to her?"

"I asked why she was gunning for you."

Magnus slapped his forehead. "Now she knows I have a mad brother. Damn you, Lachlan, I'm no idiot. And no babe either. Or blinded by my pecker," he added in a low, menacing voice. "You're the only one blinded around here. Don't make me put you away, because if you become a threat to yourself or anyone else, I will. I've seen madness in your eyes." His shoulders shuddered. "I don't ever want to see it again."

He turned and stalked down the hall, returning a second later with his cell phone in hand. "I'd better call her—she called me. I can just imagine what she's got to say." He touched the screen and listened, his face tightening. "She's blowing me off."

"Good. Thank me for saving your arse, and I'll be on my way."

Magnus spoke, but his words were drowned

out by the kettle's harsh scream. It didn't look like they were words of appreciation, though, by the fierce look on his face. Or the way he grabbed onto Lachlan's sore shoulder and marched him to the front door.

"I save you, and you're kicking me out?"

"I told you there was something about her, and I intended to find out what it is. Now I may not get a chance. Go, before I add to your bruises."

There was gratitude for you, Lachlan thought as he left, hearing the kettle screaming behind him.

After one of the longest afternoons in her life, Jessie locked herself in her apartment and collapsed on the couch. An end table lay on its side, and a chair was still toppled over where she'd launched the intruder. She jumped up and righted everything so it looked like nothing had happened.

Like Darkness hadn't happened.

As though you could forget.

At least he had nothing to do with Russell.

The moment she dropped back into the cushions, a knock sounded on her door. The thought that it was Magnus's brother prickled through her, which was plain odd, because more likely it was Magnus, except he didn't know where she lived unless his brother had told him. She didn't want to deal with either of them right now.

A peek through her security lens showed a teenage girl with short pink hair, a little too much makeup, and the long, lean build of a colt. Hayley. She wasn't in the mood for her either, but she opened the door anyway.

"Hey, Hayley. What are you—"

The girl walked in, gave her a hug, and took a deep breath. "I took a cab here."

"Does your mother know? Are you all right?"

Hayley looked pale, worried, and Jessie's heart clutched. *Don't tell me you've had a relapse. Don't, don't, don't.* She couldn't take that, not on top of everything else. Her hair was just now growing back, her color a healthy glow.

"I'm okay, and I know you're really busy, but I need to talk to you."

Hayley sometimes came over for no serious reason at all. It was hard to push away a teenager, especially one she'd been paired with at MDA summer camp, and whose bones now held a touch of her own marrow. That scared her, because Jessie didn't know if Darkness could be transferred by blood. But with leukemia ravaging the girl and no matches for her rare blood type, she hadn't had a choice. Now she held her breath, waiting for Hayley to tell her why she was there.

Jessie nodded toward the couch. "Want to sit?"

Hayley shook her head, her spiky hair not shifting at all with the movement. "I know you're a private person. You weren't happy when I put your name in my blog, and now you're really going to be mad. Please don't be mad at me, Jess."

Now her heart tightened in a different kind of dread. "What happened?"

"'Cause you're so wonderful, and that's not only because you saved my life. You're the only person who doesn't treat me like I'm made of the thinnest glass in the world."

She hated having to push the girl away after they'd bonded in camp, but the whole thing with Magnus was a harsh reminder of what happened when she let people into her life. "Spill."

"Someone from the paper came over to do a story on me, you know, for the carnival. Which is great. You keep talking about getting publicity." She gave Jessie a fake smile. "I figured you'd be happy about that."

She waited until Jessie said, "Yeah, that's great," with as much reservation as Hayley had said the last bit.

"My mom accidentally said your whole name." She pushed the words out and let them drop on the floor. "She didn't realize it until later. She did call the reporter and left a message asking him to keep it out of the article, but she hasn't heard back from him yet. The story will run tomorrow. So maybe it'll be all right . . . Jess, why are you so worried about your name being in the paper? Are you, like, hiding from the law or something?" Another fake smile.

Jessie's hand went to her throat. She smoothed out her expression, even managed a smile that was probably as fake as Hayley's. "No. I don't want my family to find me. We don't get along."

Hayley plopped down on the couch. "Mom drives me crazy, but I can't imagine never seeing her again. What happened?"

Give an inch . . .

So she'd give her a yard. "My mom's dead. My uncle killed her, and now he's out of prison. I don't want him to know where I am."

There, that wasn't so bad. Except she'd left out the bizarre stuff.

"Ohmigosh, Jess, that's awful!" Hayley sprang up and hugged her.

"I don't want to talk about it, 'kay? I have to head down to the carnival grounds in a bit, go over some last minute details."

"Can I come? It's for me, after all."

She shook her head. "It'll be late, and you need to take it easy. Tomorrow's a busy day. Come on, I'll give you a ride home."

"So, are you totally not freaked about the article? I'm so sorry. We could call the writer and tell him why it's so important—"

"No!" The harsh order cut Hayley off. Jessie smiled to soften it. "But if I leave town suddenly, you'll understand why."

"Oh, Jessie, I'm—"

"Don't say it. And don't cry." That's all she needed. She had managed not to cry, not over any of her past. She reached out, and Hayley took her hand, painfully grateful that she wasn't angry.

Jessie walked out feeling fatigue and weariness weighing on her, heavy as her Yukon. The thought of packing up, leaving again. She blinked back the hot tears that threatened. *No crying!* Maybe it was time to change her name again.

He'll find you. Someday, he'll find you.

Lachlan pulled into the grass parking lot, staying at the outer edge. The Ferris wheel and other rides looked like dark, hulking monsters, the carnival grounds quiet. Only two other vehicles sat in the lot: Jessie Bellandre's SUV and Magnus's BMW.

"Bloody hell."

Earlier, he'd followed Magnus to a pub, then to his flat. He considered talking to him, but Magnus's surly expression didn't bode well. Afterward, he drove by the carnival grounds, seeing several vehicles, including Jessie's. Then he almost went home but decided to go to Magnus's after all. Only to find that he wasn't there.

"Yeah, there's something about her, all right. She's a devil worshiping demon-possessed killer . . . with a stuffed penguin. Who clips coupons. And gets misty at a kid's violin practice."

Hell, she made no sense to him.

Now, Lachlan looked at the fairgrounds and felt a stirring in his soul. Like a fire in the dark cave inside him. Did he sense the danger because it was there, or because he felt purpose for the first time in so long? He'd watched his mother die, knowing he inflicted the fatal wound. He had to leave his father locked in the cellar of a burning house. If Magnus was in trouble, he could do something. This time he could help.

He opened the door and stepped out, his muscles still groaning in pain. The air was whip-cold, becoming puffs of fog whenever he breathed. He pulled out his sword, in its sheath, and hooked it inside his long coat. The sword had been in his mother's family for hundreds of years. She'd given well-made replicas to him and Magnus when they each turned sixteen in a ceremony reminiscent of those that Scottish boys were honored with when they were deemed to be men. They were given a dirk under an oath that incurred supernatural penalties should it be broken. He and Magnus had been using the replicas in their matches ever since, preparing in case their father's enemy found them. Once in a while they used the antique swords.

Voices floated to him, echoing off the carnival equipment, winding and twining around the closed booths and over the stamped-down dirt. His hearing was keen, and he followed them.

"It has nothing to do with you having a psychotic brother," a voice said. Her voice. There was an edge to it, one he'd heard before.

"It's a wonder you didn't call the cops on him. You should have, you know." Magnus.

"No." The word shot out. "Look, you obviously have family issues. I have issues, too. I think it's better if we go our separate ways before things get complicated."

Lachlan spotted them on the other side of the tall fence at the corner of one of the booths, facing each other.

"Is that why you know how to fight? Lachlan said you kicked his arse. Are you in trouble?"

"I—"

A sound had them both turning to the side. Lachlan couldn't see who was there, but her expression froze in fear. She flicked a glance to Magnus. "Leave. Now." She said it the same way she'd pleaded with Lachlan to leave, but now she was terrified.

Something was wrong. No way would Magnus leave her there. His brother's body stiffened, shoulders broadened, and he took a step closer to Jessie as he faced the man who walked up to them.

The man was in his forties, brown hair, rough features, a big guy with blunt fingers. Lachlan always checked out an opponent's hands. No weapon that he could see, which meant nothing. He stepped to the fence and started climbing.

"Magnus, leave!" Jessie said in a strained voice, but she faced the man in the fight mode Lachlan had seen earlier.

"The hell I am. Who is this?"

The man's smile chilled Lachlan. "I'm her father."

"You are *not* my father," she hissed.

Lachlan dropped to the ground and started

heading over. Trouble. He knew it, felt it. That's all he could think before it happened.

The man became smoky black and then transformed into a shape that resembled a huge wolf.

What the hell?

Lachlan pulled his sword as he ran, the familiar sound of metal sliding against metal.

The thing lunged at Magnus, knocking him to the ground. Lachlan screamed as he charged, raising his sword, wanting to draw the creature's attention to him. Jessie threw herself at the wolf, clinging to his back with her arm in a choke hold around his neck. He shook her off, sending her rolling across the ground. The wolf, made of a blackness like thick oil, looked at Lachlan as he closed the distance. He raised a massive paw and raked it across Magnus's throat.

"Noooo!" The word tore from Lachlan's chest.

This was what he'd seen in the vision, only it wasn't the girl who had done it. This creature . . .

Jessie screamed in agony as she jumped to her feet. She shifted to black fog, too, though she didn't take a definite shape. She twisted, reared back, and slammed into the wolf, knocking him back from Magnus. Protecting him.

Lachlan felt as though he were slogging through mud, like a nightmare where you run and run and never get anywhere. The dark shapes fought, but the wolf turned to him when he finally reached them.

Lachlan swung the sword in an arc, slicing

through the thing. Bits sheared off. The wolf reared back, grabbing at his sword. Lachlan jerked it out of his reach, then rammed the blade forward. Could he even kill this man-wolf?

Jessie was human again, her terrified face glancing at Magnus before focusing on the two combatants. "Stop! He'll kill you!"

Lachlan felt something move through him, like an electrical current. The edges of his vision darkened, closing in. *No, not now.* This had happened before, on the battlefield of Culloden. He held on, focusing on the ridges in the handle of the sword, the cold air searing his lungs as he sucked in breath after breath. He held onto reality, and the darkness moved away.

He sliced, parried, cut, and all the while felt a strength, an energy moving through his arms, his whole body. It was . . . helping him. Making him stronger.

He grasped the sword handle with both hands, readying for a thrust, and saw—no imagined— the imprint of two hands over his. Not his hands, these were shorter, thicker, scarred and bloodied. Lightning sparked from those fingers and along the blade, arcing into the wolf's chest. With a horrific sound of pain, the wolf became a long stream of smoke and retreated.

Lachlan stared at the place where it had been, then at his hands, which now looked normal, and then at her. She wore the same shocked expression as he no doubt did.

"What the bloody hell?" Too much to ask, no time. He ran to Magnus, setting the sword down and kneeling beside him. His brother's eyes were open and unfocused but filled with shock and pain.

"Maggie! You'd better not die, you son of a bitch!"

Jessie dropped down on the other side of Magnus, gasping at the sight of the gaping slashes across his throat. Blood gushed out in a steady stream and he was having trouble breathing.

The smoky beast was solid enough to inflict this kind of injury. Lachlan jammed his hands beneath his brother's body, about to lift him. Too heavy.

"He won't make it," she said on a hoarse breath. "He's lost too much blood already."

"No, he will make it." He pulled off his coat, tossed it to the ground, then tore off his sweater and tied it around Magnus's throat to stop the bleeding.

She squeezed her eyes shut. "I promised I'd never do this again."

He took out his phone, intending to call 911. "Who are you talking to?" he asked.

"I can save him." Her gaze was on Magnus, pain and indecision wracking her expression.

"Then do it."

She turned to him. "The price is high. Maybe too high."

"You take on the wounds? I know a woman who uses her psychic energy to heal, but she hasn't died from it."

Her eyebrows furrowed at that and she shook her head. "It's not me I'm worried about. If I heal him, he'll become like me."

Like smoke. "And what are you?"

Her voice was tight when she said, "I don't know." The truth of that shone in her eyes. "I heard my father call it Darkness."

Lachlan gestured to Magnus. "That man who did this?"

"God, no. He's my uncle, Russell. He injured my dog, and I used Darkness to bring him back. Constantine was okay, for a while. Then another dog encroached on his territory and he went nuts. He had to be put down." She blinked rapidly, agony in her voice. "What should I do? We don't have much time to decide. I can't bring him back if he dies."

Magnus's face contorted in pain, his body shaking violently. Lachlan felt those gaping wounds in his chest as though he bore them himself. "Save him."

She nodded, removing the sweater and holding her hands over Magnus's throat. Before his eyes, she turned to smoke again, coalescing, but she kept a vaguely human shape. The smoke flowed from the tips of her hands into Magnus.

Lachlan put his hands on Magnus's thighs, keeping them from trembling so hard. "I'm here, brother. I'm here. Hang on."

The smoke covered those horrible wounds. Magnus's body stopped trembling, but Lachlan

didn't pull his hands away. His gaze went to
Jessie again. What in the bloody damn hell? Her
form began to lighten and she became wholly
human again. The smoke evaporated, leaving
Magnus's throat whole. Blood still covered his
ripped collar, but there were no wounds. Lachlan touched the smooth skin, stunned. Magnus
was alive, his chest rising and falling. He was all
right. They would deal with this Darkness. Relief
swept through him.

Her eyes were open, though struggling to stay
that way. "You have to get him out of here. I don't
know what you did to make Russell leave, but
he'll be back."

He hoisted his brother over his shoulder.
Magnus outweighed him by fifty pounds, and his
muscles screamed at the exertion. She held out her
arms, as though she could catch Magnus if he fell.
Hell, maybe she could.

"I've got him," he said in a strained voice.

"I'll get your coat. And"—she picked up his
half-lang sword, eyeing the long blade with wary
curiosity—"your *sword*." She grasped the leather-
clad grip with one hand, the disc pommel with
the other. "Follow me to the gate."

There would be no climbing fences with
Magnus.

She walked alongside him, vigilant of their surroundings, like someone who was used to being
under attack. "He'll probably sleep for a few days.
That's what Constantine did."

"Your dog?"

She nodded. "I have to go. I'll call Magnus's phone, check on him—"

"Like hell you're going anywhere."

Her eyes sparked with fear and rebellion. "There's nothing more I can do for him. And no way am I going with you."

He shifted Magnus's weight, wobbling as he tried to maintain his balance. "Still think I'm psychotic? This is what I saw, my brother getting killed. And even knowing it, I couldn't stop it." He let those words cut into him. "I assumed you'd done it, since you were standing beside him."

"Okay, I give you that; you did see a vision of the future. But that doesn't mean you're sane or safe. *You* even said you were crazy, back at my apartment after you broke in and assaulted me. Which isn't something reasonable people do, by the way."

"I didn't break in intending to interrogate you. I was trying to find out what you were up to, and you came home unexpectedly. So I took the opportunity." He could hear the strain in his voice. They walked through the gate, and she closed it behind her. Just a few more yards to the parking area.

"Look, it's better for all of us if I don't go with you."

He walked to her car. "Open the door."

She hesitated. "Why mine?"

"Your vehicle has more room, and I can't bloody

well lay him in the bed of my truck." When her mouth tightened, he pressed on. "You dragged him into this. Now I need your help to get him to safety." Yeah, he was using the guilt card. He saw the moment she caved, though reluctantly. She lunged forward and opened the back passenger door.

He held back the groan as he relieved himself of Magnus's weight. "We'll take him to Sanctuary. Our home. Follow me."

Her mouth fell open, but he headed to his truck. She would follow. Then he wanted answers.

CHAPTER 4

Jessie stood beside the bed, her gaze locked on the man across the room from her who had carried his brother through courtyards and doors that she opened for him. She'd hardly paid attention to the house, other than it was in the woods and down a long gravel road with signs warning against trespassing. People could do amazing things when they had to. When they loved someone. He cared about his brother, but he was no less scary than when he'd broken into her apartment.

Every muscle in her body twitched in preparation to run, escape. The brute had strong-armed her into coming here, but she owed him that because, dammit, it was her fault Magnus had been hurt. Her gaze drifted down to where he slept peacefully, unaware of what lurked inside him now. His brother had torn off his bloodied shirt and, while she looked away, his pants. Now sheets covered his lower body, leaving his chest bare. His brother had washed Magnus's body but missed some blood caked in his curls. She stared at Magnus's throat, with no trace of the fatal wound. It had astounded her when Constantine healed. Still did.

The room's blue walls were the color of a twilight sky. The bed's massive headboard had shelves filled with books, many about music or musicians. She saw one about Ginger Baker, and another called *Mad, Bad and Dangerous: The Book of Drummers' Tales*.

Mad, bad, and dangerous. Yeah, that about summed up the man who stood across the bed from her, his hands flat on the edge of the mattress as he, too, seemed stunned by the healed wound. She saw the same mixture of fear and anger that she felt. He wore only black pants, his bare torso long and leanly muscled. His long hair was tied back, emphasizing his square jaw and arched eyebrows. The trimmed beard made him look like a pirate or, seeing the sword he'd brandished leaning against the wall behind him, a primitive Highlander. The movie *Braveheart* came to mind, all those delicious men in kilts raging into battle for freedom. That same ferocity and wildness glowed in his eyes as they pinned her like that sword.

"Tell me about Darkness."

Those brown eyes told her she wasn't going anywhere until she laid out her soul.

"I don't even know your name." A hysterical hiccup-laugh escaped her mouth. "It's not like we've been properly introduced."

"I'm called Lachlan. What's in him?"

He knew her, of course, because he'd gone through her things, violated her space. "I'll tell you what I know." Her gaze flicked to Magnus. "But I want to wash the blood out of his hair. I . . . I can't stand to see it on him."

"Alright." He nodded toward the adjacent bathroom, inviting—or, rather, instructing—her to go first. He wasn't about to leave her in a position where she could run. He rinsed the washcloth he'd used earlier, squeezed out the excess water, and handed it to her. She settled on the edge of the bed and scrubbed out the blood.

Lachlan paced, jamming his fingers through his hair until they stopped at his ponytail holder. He wrenched it out and tossed it to the floor, shaking his head. As scruffy as he looked, his hair fell in shiny, clean waves down his back.

"Are you some kind of demon?" he asked. "I saw your notebook."

"*I'm* not this thing." She held herself, and the anger at his word *you*, back. "I'm a person, like you. It's something in me. Not me."

"Semantics. I saw you and that son of a bitch turn into something inhuman."

She wanted to convince him, but that would sound like begging. He'd seen her notebook, her own personal search for answers.

He jabbed his finger toward her. "That's how you threw me across the room. I thought something weird had gone on, but it happened so fast,

I couldn't tell. I thought *I* was mad. Then, back at the carnival, you turned to a black fog. What the hell are you?"

She heard the stretch of emotion in his voice. And the accusation. "I don't know. That's why I've been studying demonology, trying to find something that fits. I'm not evil. I don't want to go around killing people." *Way to sound like you're trying to convince him.* "I used it to save Magnus, after all."

"And now he's some kind of monster."

She bristled. "You had a choice."

"Some choice, that or let him die. But now I need to know, what's in him? Will he turn into smoke, too? Or some bloody wolf thing that'll eviscerate me the next time we have an argument?"

She wrapped her arms around herself. "All I know is what happened to my dog. Constantine turned to smoke, though not completely. I could see it blur his edges."

"And the man who did this to him . . . he turned into a creature. His *claws* were sharp enough to tear through flesh and muscle. Are you a werewolf?"

Keep calm, seem unaffected. "I studied the were-wolves' myths. They turn into actual wolves, with fur, so no, I don't think so. Plus Becoming Dark-ness has nothing to do with the full moon."

"You're not a vampire or a chupacabra or any-thing else I can think of. What you are doesn't fit with any of the supernatural myths, does it? But a demon, can't they do what they want?"

"I'm not a demon!" Now *her* emotion leaked into her voice. He'd touched on her biggest fear, that she harbored a demon inside. She took a deep breath, walked to the bathroom and set the cloth in the sink. "At least I don't think so," she added in a quiet voice, so soft she hoped he hadn't heard. She glimpsed her reflection, hair disheveled, eyes bloodshot, dirt smearing her face. That was the hell of it. No answers.

She splashed water over her face, needing the coolness of it as much as its cleansing. After drying off, she returned to the bedroom, keeping her gaze on Magnus and not Lachlan.

Not that he could be ignored. "Tell me about the man who turned to wolf, this Russell."

"He's my father's brother. He killed my mother and . . ." This would sound crazy, but he'd already seen Darkness. It wasn't much crazier than that. "He took over my dad's body."

"Took over?"

She didn't want to tell him everything about her life, but he wasn't going to let her leave until she told him enough. That was evident in the stiffness of his body, the way he looked like he would pin her with that sword if she tried. She supposed she owed him that much.

"It happened when I was ten." Every word about the events in the kitchen felt as though she had to wrench it from her chest. "Russell went to prison for fourteen years, two counts manslaughter. He got out two years ago, and now he's hunting me down for revenge, I'm sure. Magnus . . . he just got in the way, being a hero."

When she looked up, Lachlan was standing next to her, his hand on the wooden ball post at the foot of the bed. She took an involuntary step back. "It's my fault. He came into the music store and gave me that smile."

Lachlan nodded. "Aye, I know that smile. Melted you, did it?"

"No, it didn't melt me. I could tell he was one of those guys who flirts with every girl. Usually I shut out guys like that; shut out everyone, really."

"What made you change your mind about Magnus, then?"

She couldn't tell him that she'd so needed to feel like a woman . . . a woman who didn't have Darkness. "He hit me at a weak point." She shrugged. "There was something about him."

"He thought the same about you." His laugh was more like a bark. "He had that right."

That stung, even though it was true. "Your accusation that I was planning to kill him reminded me that I can't afford to bring anyone into my life. I left a message for him, called things off." Her voice fell to a whisper. "He was stubborn."

"Aye, it's in our blood. But now there's something else in his blood." His next question came out in a carefully neutral way. "Have you ever killed anyone?"

"No. What I became tonight . . . that's all I can do. I have no claws. No teeth."

"You can only toss a chap across the room, is that it?"

"Pretty much."

He rolled his right shoulder, wincing. "It's quite effective. You turn to smoke and kick arse. Russell turns to a wolf form with all the lethality of the actual creature. Anything else?"

She curled her fingers into the blanket. "All I know about Darkness is that, for me, it's triggered by high emotions, like fear, anger." The reason she kept such a tight rein on her emotions. "Tonight, or with you at my apartment, I didn't Become on purpose. I never have. The first time I Became was when Russell found me after his release. I felt my body shift, change. Like being superheated. I threw him, then Faded and ran."

"Faded?"

"Went invisible. That's what the cross on my wall helps me to do." She lifted the bottom edge of her shirt and pushed down the top of her jeans, revealing the symbol on her lower right stomach. He started to reach for the symbol but stopped himself just short of making contact. "A tattoo?"

"I had it scarified into me."

"Scarified?"

"Carved." At his horrified expression, she said,

"I wanted to feel it." She touched the raised edges, something she did a lot. "But Fading is the power of the symbol, not Darkness. I don't think Magnus will be able to do that."

"He can already go invisible."

She stared at the tips of his long fingers, hovering close to her cross. His words sunk in. "He can?"

He pulled his hand back. "It's more of an ability to blend in, to not be noticed."

"How can a guy like Magnus not be noticed?"

"I don't know how he does it, really. He's been able to do it since he was a kid. That's how I got blamed for breaking one of our mum's porcelain owls. How do you become invisible?"

"My father sewed a wooden coin carved with this cross into one of my stuffed animals and told me it would protect me. He said to call out the word 'Fade.' That's how I escaped Russell the night he killed my mom." His gaze was still on her symbol, more fascinated than disgusted. She yanked her shirt down, feeling self-conscious.

"Why did Russell kill your parents?"

"I don't know. My father was afraid of him. He'd told me his brother might come after him, but only said they had bad history. He showed me a picture of him, told me to be on the lookout. The coin, and ability to Fade, was something he'd taught me as a way to keep myself safe. The horrible part was, it was my dad's body and identity associated with the crimes, and I couldn't tell anyone that it wasn't my father anymore." That same frustration swamped her again.

He was studying her, an odd expression on his face. "Maybe that 'something' Magnus sensed about you was your vibration of living in fear. We spent our lives preparing for some bad man who was hunting us by living in remote areas and rarely going into society."

"Really?"

"Why do you think we live out in the middle of nowhere? We finally settled down here, where my dad felt safe for the last ten years."

"And was he?"

He shook his head, his gaze fading into the distance, the past. "No. Like you, both our parents are gone."

"Who was after you?"

"It's not important now. The bastard's dead, too." His focus homed in on her again. "Why do you bear the name of a dead girl?"

Her mouth opened, in surprise and immediate rebuttal. It closed when she saw that somehow he'd figured it out. "That's not important either." She started walking to the door. He blocked her way, his wide, sculpted chest a wall in front of her. "Move. I've told you everything that's relevant."

"*Everything* about you, and your past, is important."

She blew out a breath and took a step back. "I took another identity, that's all. To hide from Russell."

"That's why you volunteer at all these MDA events? You don't look like you have it yourself."

"Jessie's none of your business." She put her hand at his waist and tried to push him aside. He didn't budge. The feel of his warm, bare skin made her pull back.

"Where are you going?" he asked.

"I've got to leave town. *Again*." The word came out soaked in weariness. "I can take you back to Magnus's car, if you're comfortable leaving him alone. But I have to go. Now."

She ducked around him. In a flash he held the sword across the door's opening at her face level. Her throat tightened. He wasn't normal either, but no way did she want an explanation for what she'd seen on the security tape. Or while he'd fought Russell that night. Better not to know.

Lachlan's expression was calm, his muscles hard and defined as they held the sword. "You're not leaving."

Anger bristled through her. "And you can't keep me here. I told you what you needed to know. Magnus has my number. I'm sure he'll have questions for me. I'll answer them as best as I can, but I don't know any more than I just told you."

"Maybe you didn't hear me. You are not leaving."

"You're keeping me prisoner? Why would you do that? Russell will find me here. I don't know how, but he's found me three times now. Keeping me here exposes Magnus to more danger."

She patted his arm, a fake smile plastered on her face. "And being the dutiful brother, you wouldn't want that, would you?" There was *something* about Lachlan and Magnus, too. She'd felt a vibration like a soft electrical shock when they touched.

She ducked under the sword and stalked down the long hall. His footsteps sounded behind her, and then his arm went across her shoulders, spinning her around.

"You're going to just run away? Again."

She shrugged out of his grip. "Running is working for me so far. You make it sound like I've got a bevy of choices. I can't go to the police. They'd only lock me away in the loony bin, and besides, they wouldn't be able to help me anyway. Make nice with Russell? Not likely."

"You can throw him, and he can tear you apart. How long do you think you can stay ahead of the game?"

"As long as I can. What else can I do?"

"Kill him."

She laughed, especially seeing that he was serious. "I'm capable of fending off an attack, as you know. But that's a far cry from planning to kill someone, even with a good reason. He's stronger, and hell, I don't even know what I am, much less how to use it to defeat him."

He was shaking his head. "When Magnus wakes, I'm going to have to tell him there's some new supernatural essence in him. That's going to be bad enough. If I tell him I let you leave, a lamb sent to the slaughterhouse, he'll have my head, and rightfully so."

Part of her softened at the thought of not being alone. She had been alone for so long, holding her secrets, her pain. "I saw kids who were given a death sentence because of a disease that ravaged their bodies bit by bit. At least I won't die like that. If it comes, it'll be over quickly."

"How did you come to be in a place where children died?"

"I lived with a couple who fostered special needs kids."

He looked her up and down, searing her with his gaze. "You were ill?"

"Not like that."

He braced one hand against the wall, leaning closer. "When you watched those children dying, did it kill you, too, that you couldn't do anything to help them?"

His words cut into her. "Yes."

"Those diseases, they were monsters you couldn't defeat."

She shook her head.

"I watched people I love die, too, unable to do anything to save them. So you'll understand why I can't let you walk out there alone."

She took a deep, halting breath. "This is my war."

He gestured toward the doorway behind him to Magnus. "Now it's mine, too. Don't make me waste time and energy trying to convince you or find you. We're going to wipe this son of a bitch off the planet. First, we figure out what Darkness is." He studied her again, his head tilted. "Though Russell seemed hellish, you don't."

"Gee, thanks."

His mouth quirked in a grin. "What I mean is, I don't think what's in you is demonic."

She wanted to smile at that, to gush in relief, but checked the impulse. "Then what? I've run out of ideas."

He wrapped his fingers around her wrist in a gentle hold. An energy thrummed from where he touched her and set off an answering pulse in her body.

"You feel it, too, don't you?" he asked. "The *something* Magnus sensed." He gave a dip of his chin, as though she'd confirmed whatever he suspected.

She pulled her hand back. "What is that?"

"Were either of your parents in a top-secret government program back in the eighties? Did they live in the DC area?"

"Not that I know of."

He considered that for a moment. "You have to be an Offspring. I know someone who can probably tell for sure." He went back into the bedroom. "And I'm not looking forward to asking," he muttered to himself.

She knew she should leave now, while she had the chance, but her feet wouldn't budge. He had commanded her, and her body obeyed. Not only obeyed, but stirred at the sight of him coming back out to the hallway, cell phone in one hand, sword in the other. She had felt him against her, a crazy-assed moment for him to be aroused, and for her to be thinking about it now, when she should be leaving.

He was scrolling down a list on his phone, probably contacts, when he came to a stop in front of her. "There's the dodgy bastard." He touched the screen and put the phone to his ear while he turned the sword back and forth, throwing a reflection onto the wall. "Eric, I presume? . . . This isn't Magnus. It's Lachlan. I'm using his phone . . . Yeah, *that* Lachlan. Big surprise, I know. I've got an even bigger one. I need your help . . . Aye, but I didn't actually throw the wrench at you. I wanted to, but unlike your hotheaded self, I restrained my impulses."

She whispered, "You have an odd way of asking someone for help."

He narrowed his eyes at her as he continued to speak on the phone. "Look, I was . . . wrong to blame you for my father's death . . . Aye, you can take that as an apology. Now, moving onto the help part. I'm not asking for myself. Seeing as Magnus saved your arse, I figure you owe him one. I need someone to pick up his car and bring it to our place. He's out cold, and I don't want to leave him alone . . . He's all right, mostly, anyway, but I need to get him somewhere safe while he recovers. And I need to talk to the odd bloke from the other dimension. I've got a situation." His gaze met hers. "I don't want to involve you, any of you, but I need an idea of what I'm dealing with." He gave Eric directions to the carnival grounds and told him where Magnus hid the spare key.

"*We're* dealing with," she said when Lachlan disconnected.

"What?"

"We're dealing with this. You can't just take over."

Instead of responding, he went to a room at the end of the hallway and returned a minute later pulling on a red knit shirt. "I need a beer. You could use one, too."

The gall. "Now you're ordering me to drink?"

"Suggesting."

She followed him through the family room and eventually into the kitchen, because she needed answers, not because she was obeying him. That phone conversation had only spurred more questions.

"What's an Offspring? Who are these people whose help you're asking for? Obviously you're not all that friendly with the guy you were talking to. You threatened him with a wrench? He killed your father?"

He opened the stainless steel door of the huge fridge that contained large cans of beer, a few packages of chicken and lunch meat, a loaf of bread, and not much else. He held up two different cans, a black one and a yellow one. "Boddingtons or Guinness?"

"I'm not much of a beer drinker."

"Boddy, then." He pulled down two tall glasses, opened the can, and poured the contents into one. Bubbles sank through the creamy-looking liquid, a thick foam settling on top. "No, I don't exactly have a buddy-buddy relationship with these people. Eric can set fires psychically, dangerous because he has a habit of sparking first and then assessing the situation. I'm sure he wasn't thinking about my father locked in the basement when he set the bastard who'd been after us our whole lives on fire." He opened the black can and poured dark liquid into the second glass. "It's a long story."

"Oh, no, you don't get to drop something like that and wave it off. Who *are* you people? Magnus can go invisible, you have visions of the future—and God knows what else—and one of your sort-of friends can set fires with his mind? Are you freaking kidding me?" She thought she was the only one who had a screwed-up background filled with things that couldn't be explained.

He looked completely serious. "I'm not . . . freaking kidding you. But I'd rather wait until I can confirm my suspicions before getting into everything."

"No way. You already opened that door. You said the 'odd bloke from the other dimension.'

Bloke is a guy, but what did you mean by 'other dimension'?"

"Ever heard of string theory? Membrane theory?" He leaned against the counter. "Some quantum physicists theorize that there are many dimensions parallel to our own. Different beings live there, and every now and then one slips through cracks between our dimensions. This bloke, Pope, comes from one called Surfacia."

She watched him take a long drink of his beer, his Adam's apple bobbing as he swallowed. He set the glass on the counter and met her gaze, looking every bit as casual as if he'd just told her about his favorite sports team.

"And you expect me to believe this."

"If I were you, I'd keep an open mind. Because if my guess is right, what's in you isn't demonic . . . it's from another dimension."

That blew her mind; everything he was saying simply splintered it apart. She grabbed onto the pieces, desperately needing to pull it together. "Me . . . another dimension . . . people . . ."

He watched her, clearly amused. "I'd better start at the beginning. My father was fascinated by slime molds, unclassified blobs of biological material. He especially loved when he found *powdre ser* where a meteor had landed. One day he tracked what he thought was a meteor, collected the *powdre ser*, and brought it back to his lab here, where he accidentally ingested a bit of it.

"My dad wasn't only strange because of his affection for slime. He could astral-project—send his soul to other places—but after eating slime, he could go to the past, and even move things. The slime mold amplified his powers. Eventually, it fell into the wrong hands and was given to a group of people in the top secret government project I asked you about. The offspring of those people inherited their parents' enhanced psychic abilities. Magnus, Eric—"

"The woman you mentioned at the carnival grounds who can heal . . ."

"Aye, her, too, and others. We all have psychic powers beyond the norm. The man behind the project, he was the one hunting my father. He hunted the Offspring down, too, but now he's dead."

"The reason your father kept you in hiding." Things were clicking into place. "The thing he thought was a meteor, I'm guessing that has something to do with this other dimension."

"Aye. What my father saw wasn't a meteor; it was an aircraft from Surfacia that crashed here. What he found that day wasn't *powdre ser*; it was the pilot's Essence. His life force. That is in us. And maybe you."

She took a big gulp of beer. There were people like her, who had powers, who had been hunted. Were they good? Or evil like Russell? Magnus had fought to protect her. Lachlan . . . she wasn't so sure.

His phone rang, and he answered it. "Lach-

lan . . . You're here? Good . . . Sure, come on in . . .
Aye, come in that way." He disconnected and gave
her a curious smile. "Keep your eyes open."

Russell leaned against the bathroom sink,
clutching at the edges of the small counter,
and used Darkness to heal the slice the sword-
wielding intruder had inflicted. He let out groans,
throwing his head back, straining the muscles of
his neck.

The girl now known as Jessie had paired up
with two men, and one of them had a powerful
energy about him. That energy had arced down
his sword and electrified Russell. Cut into him.
There was little that could harm him while he was
in Darkness, especially by a human. The sword
should have merely sliced through his energy, ne-
cessitating a quick repair. This wound was painful, healing it more so.

He had retreated, not out of fear but sensibil-
ity. Wounded, he was not as strong. She had taken
him by surprise, having allies. Where had she
found these men? Well, one was dead. The other
would be soon.

Time was running out. He had to capture her
before all was lost. The thought of what he'd lose
hurt more than the wound. He would not lose, not
this time.

All those years in prison, he could only use
Darkness in private. Yes, he could have broken
free, killed numerous humans, but he would then

be a wanted man. That would not be the right life for him, for his plans. So he'd bided his time, behaving. The other prisoners left him alone, but he heard whispers that he was possessed of dark powers. He had encountered people who could sense it in him. During an altercation, he had started to Become, just enough to let his eyes darken and encourage the rumors that incited enough suspicion to keep even the most dangerous felons at bay.

No one was more dangerous than he was. Only one thing kept him from insanity, gave him a reason for being. But that thing was slipping away. Capturing Jessie was the only way to keep it.

The pain in his chest eased at last. He looked at his haggard reflection in the mirror. The strain of healing showed on his face, flushed with the effort. He looked at his chest, sculpted by years of working his body hard. His chest rose and fell with his heaving breaths. Those men with Jessie weren't normal humans. Not mere bystanders either. Any normal man would have run away screaming or been frozen in fear of his wolf. The first one had been prepared to protect Jessie. The one with the sword had charged in. He felt something in them. Not Darkness, but the tremor of a fellow Callorian—someone like him.

He trudged into the living room of the small house he was renting by the week and sat in the recliner. Only three candles lit the space. He flexed his hand, staring at his palm. He had been working with Darkness since his release, using it in new ways. It was only recently that he realized he could create minions, sending off bits of himself and focusing on what form he wanted them to take. Connecting to them so he could use them as scouts.

He flung out his hand, sending Darkness into a stream that pooled at his feet. He held an image in his mind, and the smoke formed into the shape of a Doberman pinscher. At a glance, it would seem like a normal dog. Only if one looked closely would they see the black substance, the lack of fur and fine details. He created two more. The three stood at attention, facing their master.

"Find her." He formed the image of Jessie in his mind, sending it to them.

Just like last time, they sped off, through the wall and into the night.

CHAPTER 5

Before Jessie could ask why she should keep her eyes open, two men appeared—*out of thin air*—in the courtyard. Lachlan pushed away from the counter. "Magnus told me about Pope doing that, but seeing it"—he shook his head as he headed to the door—"bloody wild."

He waved for her to join them after he opened the door for them. They exchanged greetings, obviously having met but not knowing each other well.

She downed the rest of her ale and set the glass on the counter with a thud. Bubbles tingled along her upper lip, and she wiped them off with the back of her hand. She walked over to the group, wondering if it was trepidation or all the carbonation that filled her chest.

One man had Native American looks, with dark wavy hair that fell to his shoulders. The other also had brown hair, though his was thick and roughly cut, his eyes a beautiful violet blue.

Lachlan gestured to her. "What is she?"

The Native American's thick eyebrow arched. "Is she a specimen?"

It seemed to take Lachlan a moment to realize he had bypassed manners. He gestured to her. "This is Jessie, Magnus's girl, and I need to know if she's an Offspring."

"I'm Cheveyo," the man who'd spoken up for her said, holding out his hand. When she took it, she realized he was analyzing her, despite his admonition. He nodded toward the other man. "This is Pope."

She felt that tingle with them, too, as she shook the hand Pope thrust her way. He didn't look different.

"She's not an Offspring." Pope's hand tightened on hers before letting go. "But I sense Callorian energy, yes. And something else." His expression tightened and he turned to Cheveyo. "Have you ever fought a being that morphs from human to black smoke that takes form?"

Her eyes widened. *He knew.*

Cheveyo shook his head. "I've never seen something turn smoky first. Usually they go right from humanlike to dog or creature."

This conversation was getting more bizarre, but she latched onto the fact that Pope knew, and that he took her in without disgust or fear.

"Darkness."

To hear someone else say the word took her breath away. She pushed out the words, "What is it?"

"The C—the government in the other dimension—tasked me, as an agent whose job it was to track down outlaws, to find two brothers who'd escaped here more than twenty-five years ago. All I knew was that they had something called Darkness, and it made them very dangerous. The C was desperate to get the men back. Darkness was nothing I'd ever heard of, and I knew a lot of classified information. The C would tell me nothing more, only that I was to destroy them or bring them back. I fought one of the brothers, and he turned into a smoky wolf and escaped. I never saw him again, nor could I find the other one."

Her chest tightened. "My father and his brother, Russell, they're from . . . this parallel dimension?" It sounded crazy just asking. "And you, too?"

"We are Callorian, yes."

"Callorian. Does that mean they—you're not . . . human?"

Pope said, "Most Callorians would emphatically state that they are not, but like the debate on whether humans evolved from apes, a similar debate exists among them that we all come from the same species. A long time ago a large population descended to live beneath the surface for reasons unknown. Some theorize that because we lived so close to the Earth's magnetic field, it changed the characteristics of our energy, and thus our bodies. We lost the density of the human form and became capable of manipulating our energy, all energy."

This was getting more and more bizarre. "So I have Callorian in me?"

"As we all do," Pope said. "But you also hold Darkness."

Cheveyo turned to Lachlan. "Eric said you needed help for Magnus?"

She answered. "My uncle mortally wounded him. I used Darkness to heal him, but now . . . now he has it in him, too." She told them about her dog.

Lachlan said, "I need him out of here. Russell may come, and I'll be waiting for him."

A fire sparked in Cheveyo's eyes. "I'll fight, too."

Pope put a hand on his shoulder. "You have a son now, and a wife to whom you promised you would not fight. It's only been three months. But I—"

"Your abilities haven't come back yet," Cheveyo reminded him. "At least not in a way you can depend on."

"I can handle him," Lachlan said.

She waved her hands, getting their attention. "This is crazy. None of you should fight. He's after me, only me. I can't put you all at risk."

Pope turned to her. "What abilities do you have?"

"I've never looked at it as an ability before. Only a disability. A curse. When I'm triggered, I can throw a man across the room." She looked at Lachlan, feeling like she could do that just about now. "But I can't turn into a beast."

Something sparked in Cheveyo's eyes. "That you know of."

That tripped her heartbeat. "I don't want to Become like Russell."

Pope nodded at Lachlan. "You lost your abilities when you took the antidote?"

"Aye, but my ability to astral-project has come back. That's how I knew Magnus was in trouble."

"You can astral-project, too?" she asked.

He pressed his palm against the glass, staring at the back of his hand. "Like my dad, I could send my soul to other places, even to other time periods. For a while I lost that ability, but it came back spontaneously, showing me a vision of the future."

What about the energy she'd seen when he fought? Did he not want these men to know about that? Maybe that's why he hadn't looked at anyone as he spoke.

"You feel you can deal with this man?" Cheveyo asked. "We can call in—"

"No, I don't want to involve any of them. All I need is for someone to take care of Magnus until he wakes. Russell will be history by then."

Lachlan gestured for them to follow him down the hall to Magnus's room. They stood by his bed, and Pope waved his hand over him. "I feel the Darkness in him."

Jessie dropped her head, pinching the bridge of her nose. She'd hoped, prayed, he wouldn't have it. "When he wakes, I'll tell him what I've done. And hope he'll understand."

Cheveyo said, "I only met him once, but he seemed like a good-natured guy."

"If he stays that way," she whispered, her eyes locked to Magnus. He'd been easy to talk to, with a quick smile and hearty laugh. How could he remain that way with something dangerous lurking inside him? He would be angry. Confused. She looked up at Lachlan, who didn't appear to smile much. He'd been watching her but now shifted his gaze away.

Cheveyo said, "Petra will take good care of him." His smile was warm. "She's just that way. We're staying in Annapolis, so we'll be close by."

Relief and gratitude suffused Lachlan's face, but he simply said, "Thank you."

"The car is out front, too."

"You brought the car?" Lachlan asked. "How?"

Pope smiled. "Whatever we touch, we bring with us. I've never brought something quite so large before, but it worked splendidly."

"Brought it with you?" She looked at the courtyard. No car.

"It's out front," Pope said.

"You just popped in, out of thin air."

"Teletransported, actually." Pope smiled. "Where astral projection is sending your soul to another location, I actually send my body.

After Eric told me what was going on, I 'ported to Cheveyo's and Petra's, explained the situation, and then he and I went to Magnus's car. We brought that here, then saved time by 'porting to the courtyard."

All these years she was an oddity, but these people . . . they weren't exactly like her, but they were definitely different. That they, and her father, came from another dimension, that was harder to believe.

"We'll go, then. If you need help, call us." Pope's gaze flicked to her. "Be careful."

Did he mean to warn Lachlan about her? Yes, because she was dangerous.

Cheveyo took a step closer to Lachlan. "I can put a psychic shield over this place. It helped when the others were hiding. Eventually the enemies who came directly from Surfacia did break through, but it should buy you some time."

"What does that do?" she asked. "Will it keep Russell out?"

"If he has abilities to remote view or psychically see or find you, he'll get stopped at the shield. It won't keep him out physically."

"Do it," Lachlan said. "Thanks."

Pope put his fingertips on Magnus's forehead, and Cheveyo put his hand on Pope's shoulder. They disappeared, all of them.

She rushed forward, running her hands over the flattened sheets where Magnus had just been lying. They were still warm, but he was gone.

Completely . . . gone. She met Lachlan's gaze. "This is crazy."

"Yes." He was staring at the bed, too.

"No, I mean all of this. You, astral-projecting, parallel dimensions—"

"Your father having Darkness."

That stopped her. She was part of the madness. "Yes, all of it."

"It's late. Get some sleep." He nodded toward the room in general. "You can stay here."

She sank to the bed, her legs growing rubbery. "This was Magnus's bedroom?"

He walked to the doorway. "For ten years. I'll be next door if you need me." He cleared his throat. "Like if you hear anything out of the ordinary. Even with the shield, we've got to be wary." He started to turn away.

"You lost your abilities?"

That made him pause. "Ten months ago."

"Then how did you know what would happen to Magnus?"

His body was rigid, fingers tightening on the door frame. "I don't know. But seeing your picture triggered it."

"Because it was my fault."

He shook his head. "You didn't slice Magnus's throat. It was Russell. Don't take the blame for that."

"But it happened because he was with me. I tried to call off the flirtation between us."

"Magnus could be persistent when he wanted

something. Or someone. He likes you. You weren't going to put him off easily."

Magnus liked her and this is what happened because of that. Guilt dragged her shoulders down. "Why did you lose your abilities? Pope lost his, too."

"Pope was court-martialed back in his dimension. They handcuffed his abilities, the deadly ones." He started to move away. "I'm surprised they didn't limit his ability to teletransport."

"Maybe he couldn't escape the place where they were holding him. And what about your ability?"

She saw pain in his expression and followed his gaze to a picture on the wall she hadn't noticed before, a family picture.

"When I astral-projected," he said, "it was like going into REM sleep. My body was paralyzed." His voice was low, each word pulled painfully from him. "I went back to the battle of Culloden, 1746. I acted out the battle along with the other Scots, fighting for Scottish freedom. I stabbed a Brit in the stomach. Someone tried to grab me, and I kept slashing until I . . . well, it was like waking straight out of a dream. The soldier I stabbed . . . it was my mum. I killed my mum."

She held in a gasp at those words. Only then did he meet her eyes, and she saw even more guilt than she'd just felt over Magnus.

"Overusing our abilities can make us go mad. My father spent the last many years of his life working on an antidote to prevent psychosis.

He felt responsible for those people getting that DNA, though he hadn't done it on purpose. Afterward . . . after I went crazy, I took the antidote, and it stripped my abilities. Magnus took it, too, in case you're worried. He was fine."

Was.

She wrapped her arms around herself. "I'm—"

"Don't say it. 'Sorry' means nothing. Believe me, I know."

"But what you did, it was an accident."

"My father warned me I was on the edge, to not astral-project anymore. But projecting was my escape, my entertainment. I became addicted to it. I am responsible." He nodded into the room. "Do you need anything?"

A hug. A touch. Her mouth parted, those words threatening to pop out. "A toothbrush. Soap."

He walked into the bathroom and looked through the cabinets. "Here's a new toothbrush." He set the package on the counter, along with a gnarled tube of toothpaste and a bottle. "Face soap. Nothing fancy."

"I don't do fancy." She couldn't afford fancy.

He set out a washcloth, too, and a small towel. "That should do you."

She nodded. "Thanks."

His footsteps echoed down the hall. She walked to the photo. It had been taken some years ago, when the boys were teenagers. Even then, Magnus was big and beefy; Lachlan was whip-lean, though still broad-shouldered. Their father had a shock of white hair and light eyes, their mother obviously the one they took their looks from.

She touched the glass, thinking of the one family photo she had, tucked away in a safe place. Why had he told her so much? It was obviously painful, and he didn't strike her as someone who shared his deepest feelings with anyone, much less a virtual stranger.

Because he wants you to know what he is.

Why hadn't he mentioned the ability that had obviously not gone away? She shivered. He was dangerous in his own right.

She stumbled to the shower. Maybe she'd wake up enough to drive home. Except that Russell was in town now, so staying here for one night, where it was safe, would be okay. She took a shower, losing herself in the feel of the hot water washing over her body. She ached, inside and out.

Afterward she wrapped herself in a towel and realized she had no clothes for tomorrow other than her dirty, bloodied ones.

Magnus's blood. Because of you.

She squeezed away the pain and eyed the dresser drawers. Maybe he'd left something behind.

Every drawer was empty. Fine, she'd sleep in the nude as she usually did and find something in the morning. Or not. What if she had a nightmare and Lachlan came running in? Which reminded her . . .

Wrapping the towel tight around her, she padded down the hall to the last door.

"Lachlan?"

She wanted to warn him she was coming, just in case, since it was open. She called out again as she approached the doorway and took in a room empty of anything but a bed, nightstand, and a small desk with a computer. No curtains or blinds on the French doors that looked out into the courtyard. No pictures, only a wall full of sticky notes. He walked out of the bathroom in his room, a black towel wrapped around his waist. He stopped at the sight of her.

She stared at him, his long hair dripping water down his bare chest, towel snug around his hips.

She pulled her gaze to his face, pausing at the bruises along his shoulder and arm. "Sorry, didn't mean to barge in. I called your name."

"Didn't hear you." His eyes were taking in her towel, all the way down to her bare legs. "You need something to sleep in, don't you?"

"Just something to put on tomorrow would be great, yeah."

He walked into a closet and came back with a bundle of clothes in his hand. "You obviously won't fit into any of my pants, but you could tie the string at the waistband of these sweats tight. The T-shirt's ancient. Haven't been shopping in a while and don't have much reason to." He tossed them to her.

She grabbed for them as they split apart in midair, and her towel came undone. It slid down her body as she held the shirt up against her. Which barely covered anything.

He turned around, hands out to his sides. "Sorry. Go ahead and put it on."

She could see the faint reflection of his face in the glass of the doors. "You're peeking."

He tilted his head back and slapped his hand over his eyes. "Happy now?"

She slid the shirt over her, the worn material soft as silk. "Delirious." Except she was looking at the indent of his back, the way his waist narrowed down to his hips, the way the terry cloth tightened over his ass. Doubly embarrassed, the words, "You threw this shirt at me on purpose. After a cheap thrill?" blurted out of her mouth.

He turned, his expression bland. "I have no use for cheap thrills. Or any kind of thrill, for that matter."

"Except when you're fighting a woman."

What was wrong with her mouth? Too tired, too much crammed into her fried brain?

His eyebrow arched. "What's that supposed to mean?"

"I felt . . . you were aroused when you were manhandling me at my apartment."

She figured he would deny it, but a puzzled expression painted his face. "I don't know what the hell that was about. I have no intention of putting my thoughts, or my hands, on you. Two reasons you don't have to worry about me." He held up two fingers.

He wasn't gay, or at least he sure didn't come off as gay, especially with the, uh, evidence.

"One, despite my errant cock, I've shut off those desires. And two, I would never put the moves on my brother's girl."

She flinched at *cock*, spoken so bluntly. "All righty then, good to know." The words about her being someone's girl, though, curled through her tummy. Should she correct Lachlan's assumption? No, better to leave it be, because him thinking that would keep a wall between them. Which was good because all this talk of cocks and desire tingled through her in a very strange way, and *that* was bad because she was looking at Lachlan as it happened. She would also leave the bigger question, of why he'd shut them off, alone. "Good night." She started to turn but paused. "I have nightmares sometimes, and it might sound like someone's killing me."

"I'll check on you anyway, just to make sure someone *isn't* killing you."

She nodded. "Hopefully I won't disturb you. Good night."

Unfortunately, *he* disturbed her. The awareness of him prickled through her body.

She paused at the sound of dogs barking in the distance. He stepped out of the room and cocked his ear.

"Not a wolf howl," she said.

"No, but I've never heard dogs barking out there before. It's odd, and I don't like odd right now." He flicked the switch in the hallway, dousing them in darkness. Only the dim lights from their rooms spilled into the hallway. He ducked into his room, killed that light, and returned seconds later wearing dark sweatpants. He carried the sword at his side, fingers gripping the handle. "Stay here."

"I don't think so."

"Do you have a weapon? You don't even have pants on. Stay here."

He opened the window that led outside and climbed out deftly, considering he carried a sword. She closed the window behind him before he could open his mouth to tell her to do so. He gave her an approving nod and disappeared into the night.

She prowled the hallway, going from window to window. Russell would blend right into the night if he Became. He'd tear Lachlan up before Lachlan even glimpsed his enemy. Her chest bloomed with fear.

Like hell I'm sitting here while you fight my uncle.

Jessie pulled on the pants and tied them as tight as she could, though they hung low on her hips. She climbed out the window, but before her foot had touched ground, a hand grabbed her arm from inside the house.

Inside!

"Where are you going?"

She yelped, falling the rest of the way out the window into a probably ungainly heap on the ground. Lachlan's voice. She lurched to her feet. "Going after you." She brushed leaves off her shirt. "How'd you get back in the house so quietly?"

"I have my ways. Here." He held out his hand, and gripped hers hard enough to pull her back in. She had a little more poise coming in, at least. Then again, his hands were on her hips to steady her, his fingers brushing against her bare skin. His gaze went down to his hands and he pulled away, a bit too fast, she thought.

He looked beyond her for a second, checking outside once more before he closed the window and pulled a leaf from her hair. "Get some sleep."

"No sign of any dogs?"

He shook his head. "Maybe some sod's hunting, thinking this is unoccupied land, and those were his dogs."

The words *Or maybe not* hung in the air.

He escorted her to her room, remaining by the doorway like a father watching his child. She couldn't see his face once he'd cut the light.

"Good night," she whispered, pulling the blanket up to her chin.

" 'Night." He closed the door.

She lay there, listening for any unusual sounds. Lachlan would be sleeping on the other side of this wall. It was comforting in a way. In other ways, not comforting at all.

Russell watched through his minions' eyes as the dogs roamed. He smiled, knowing that they would be the key to achieving his goal. He didn't use them in the fight with Jessie because he was injured, and thrown off. But now they would work for him.

They moved fast, too fast at times for him to see the surroundings. Images bombarded him, because he saw through all of their eyes at once. He could tell, though, that they were going south of Annapolis, over a bridge, and then into a rural area.

"Good doggies," he murmured.

They entered a large forest, hot on her trail. He couldn't see much here, only shadows and the trunks of the trees they passed. Suddenly, they stopped. He could feel their confusion. They'd lost the signal. They went in one direction, then turned and went in a completely different one.

Was she using Darkness as some kind of magnetic field? So far she didn't seem to know how to wield it as a weapon. She fought physically, and only Became when incited, having no definite form or weapon. She had managed to keep him at bay long enough to escape, but time was running out. Maybe he could ask for help. It would take a flight on a private chartered jet and some sweet talking. Begging even, if it came to that. Julian was the one person who could help him, and the one person who would least be willing to. But he would take that chance. If he didn't get Jessie soon, he would lose the most important thing in his life. And for him, that would be true darkness.

CHAPTER 6

There would be no nightmares tonight. That was the good news. The bad? Jessie couldn't sleep, at least not the deep kind. The bright moonlight wasn't helping, spilling in through the French doors and washing over her bed. She got up, and her gaze went to the courtyard. In the silvery, two-dimensional light, trees and statues seemed surreal. It looked cold, too, as though she'd woken in another world—another dimension. Like walking through the closet in the Narnia books.

Could she really believe that something in Lachlan, in her, came from a parallel dimension?

Which means you're not harboring a demon inside you.

So yes, she could believe. She would believe anything to put that horrible notion in its grave. But even Pope didn't know what Darkness was.

She unlocked the door and opened it. Cold air washed in, slapping her cheeks and frosting her nostrils. They were fortunate that the weather was on a warming trend, but it was probably around forty degrees out now. She'd been watching the temps all week because of the carnival. The hazards of having one in March, but that's when the vendors could afford to do it for charity.

She pulled on her pants and shoes but couldn't find where she'd tossed her shirt. Turning on the light would be too bright and harsh. Her coat was somewhere in the house. She went to the closet and found the coat she'd seen earlier, one of Magnus's, no doubt. The plaid, fleece-lined coat absolutely buried her, but in a comforting way. She stepped outside, closing the door behind her.

Someone had put little signs amidst the foliage, though she couldn't read the words. The moonlight felt good on her face, and she lifted her chin and soaked in the sun's distant reflection.

She continued walking along the flagstone path. In the corner, a large angel statue reached skyward. She wanted to believe in angels, in things that protected you, loved you. All she'd seen was death, Darkness. Maybe angels didn't protect and love aberrations like her. She turned away, but knew she could never turn away from what she was.

A few steps later another statue made her heart jump into her throat. A man, sitting in a meditative position on the flagstones, palms up, on his bare thighs. He couldn't be real, because no human would be sitting out in the cold wearing only shorts. Why was her heart still thrumming, then?

She tiptoed closer, saw that his eyes were closed. His long hair poured over his naked shoulders. Shoulders that trembled.

Lachlan.

He didn't open his eyes but said, "Go back inside. It's cold out here."

"Uh . . . *yeah*. Which begs the question, why are *you* sitting out here half naked on the cold flagstones?"

"It's just something I do. I have a routine. Now, go. Leave me alone."

Those last words dug into her, like the beak of a raven digging into the pulpy flesh of an orange. She turned and took several steps away. Her feet slowed with each step, as though there was a rubber band around her, him, and she could not walk any farther. He was watching her. She saw the effort it took him to turn and close his eyes.

Something about him sitting there pulled at her, tearing her own heart. *You see his loneliness, and it's a mirror of your own. The way he shuts you out, a mirror of the way you shut out others.*

Because I have to, she told the voice inside her that loved to point out what she held, and hid, deep inside. Her conscience, she guessed, always poking at her wounds.

She could figure herself out pretty well, at least the parts she knew. Magnus, she pegged as a flirt, daring, comfortable in his good looks and charm, living for the moment.

Lachlan wasn't easy to peg. Fierce, determined,

but driven not by rage. She thought of his bare room, the refrigerator lacking anything of real substance or pleasure. He'd shut off those desires. The realization struck her in the chest. He was punishing himself.

She walked back to him. He kept his eyes closed, though she could see them twitching beneath his lids, fighting to open. She sat down in front of him and mirrored his posture.

That got him to open his eyes. "What are you doing?"

"I want to know how it feels to sit out here."

"It's cold and uncomfortable."

Yeah, she got that, even with the coat on. "How long have you been out here?"

"Since four."

Almost an hour. He shivered from time to time, but his voice gave away no hint of how cold he was. Magnus had told her, back at the carnival grounds, that his brother was unbalanced. Breaking into her apartment proved he was on the edge of crazy. It also showed his devotion to his brother. In the end, Lachlan hadn't been so crazy after all. He'd seen a vision of the future, one that had come true.

He was beautiful in the moonlight, shifting beyond humanity to a silvered demigod. That stirred her in a place she'd never felt before, drawing her to him, to the dangerous edge of him.

An alarm beeped. He got stiffly to his feet and regarded her for a moment before holding out his hand to her. "Come on, go back to sleep."

As though he were beckoning her to his bed. A different kind of stirring now, lower, deeper.

She let him pull her to her feet. "Are you going back to bed?"

"No."

He walked in the other direction, to the back portion of the house. She remained there, watching him go into a door. Lights came on, revealing a long room with wooden floors and a mirrored wall at the rear, like a ballet studio. He walked into another room and out of sight. She took a few steps closer to the wall of windows, tucking herself behind a tree. A few minutes later he returned to the main room, wearing jersey pants but nothing else. He took a sword down from a wall that she could now see was covered with different types of weapons, mostly swords.

He'd tied his hair back and shaved his beard. He didn't look so rough or primitive with his face clean-shaven. His expression, though, was still fierce.

He moved with deliberate grace, like tai chi with a sword, stretching his body at angles that pushed his ribs against his skin. His movements quickened as he warmed up, lunging, slashing, moving as one with the sword. She saw none of that weird electricity she'd seen during his fight with Russell. He was quite skilled without it.

Oh, yes, he was beautiful in a fierce sort of way, and suddenly the coat seemed too heavy and warm. She started to pull it off but remembered she wore no shirt beneath it. She opened it down to the dip between her breasts, chilling the drops of perspiration gathered there.

"You might as well come in out of the cold."

She looked up to find Lachlan in the doorway. "How did you know I was out here?"

"I could feel you."

Whoa. She walked inside. "I can't sleep. You don't mind if I watch you . . . do whatever it is you're doing?"

"Practice, every day from five to six. Stay clear." He pointed with his sword to the far corner. "Over there."

"Don't worry about me. Pretend I'm not here."

He made a sound suspiciously like a grunt. "Then you'd better close your coat."

She jammed the edges together, her cheeks warming, and quickly changed the subject. "The bruises. Did I do those?" She walked up to him, taking a closer look at the ugly purple bruises on his shoulder.

He looked at them. "You fight like a hellcat."

She couldn't help herself, reaching out and gently touching the skin next to the bruised area.

He flinched but didn't move away. "Don't touch me."

She met his gaze at the soft order. "Does it hurt?"

"Yes."

Her fingers had barely grazed skin that had no

bruising. She let her hand drop and walked to the place he'd indicated before.

He faced an imaginary opponent, bringing his sword around. He pretended to meet his enemy's sword, his blade pointing downward. Then, rotating the sword above his head, he delivered a fatal, slashing blow.

The sword was black metal, with what looked like a playing card's spade at the base of the handle, and then a carved section of wood. The hand guards were angled toward the blade. The metal was pitted and seemed forever old. He was liquid motion, steel strength, and she could see how he maintained his lean but muscular physique. Her chest tightened as she watched, and that odd sensual heat curled through her like tendrils of fire.

He ran toward the far wall as though he intended to barrel right through it. At the last second he tucked his sword to his side and ran right up the wall, doing a complete flip until he landed on his feet again.

"Show off," she said with a smile.

"I'm pretending you're not here, remember?"

"Oh . . . right."

She'd put her hand to her chest, her fingers clutching the edges of the coat. If she watched him the whole hour he planned to be in here, she'd be a puddle on the floor. That every now and then he slid a glance her way made it even harder. She actually didn't get the sense he was showing off. Between those glances, he was focused, eyes as hard as the steel of his blade. He hated whoever he imagined as his opponent. Every thrust, every slash, carried the extra energy of that enmity.

"Who are you pretending to engage?" She followed his gaze to the mirror, seeing the recipient of that hatred.

He didn't answer, just gritted his teeth and kept fighting.

"You're fighting yourself, aren't you?"

He grunted, neither confirming nor denying.

He had gone beyond grief and self-recrimination, to punishing himself with meditating in the cold, these brutal workouts, and that bare room. Cutting off his desires, a psychic castration.

But she had made him respond.

It all stirred inside her, like a boiling witch's cauldron. She pushed herself to move away, walking to a collection of pictures, trophies, and plaques on the far wall. The plaques declared either Magnus or Lachlan a winner of some sort of competition or another, like the "2003 Kick Arse Highlander Warrior Award," given to Lachlan. Or the "2005 Shot in the Eye Archery Award," declaring Magnus the winner. The accompanying pictures showed the boys at various ages, their father or mother presenting the award. Interestingly, these were all competitions held at their home, with the brothers the only competitors.

She glanced back at Lachlan, unable to keep

She glanced back at Lachlan, unable to keep her gaze away for long. He was looking at her. She turned back to the wall, now shifting over to the pictures of the brothers in swordplay. Magnificence, especially the ones where they wore kilts. Never anyone else but the core family in the pictures.

She heard his heavy breathing as he came up from behind, and forced herself not to turn. The scent of clean sweat and male sent a spiral of heat right down the center of her body. He stepped up beside her, slick, tendrils of hair at the nape of his neck damp, chest rising and falling with his breaths.

Which reminded her of how good sex would be: sweaty, heavy breathing, and this hot, wet feeling flowing through her. She didn't even realize she'd begun running her finger along the edge of the coat collar, bumping over the ridges of her ribs.

"You'll see him soon enough," he said, nodding toward the picture.

"Who? Oh, Magnus. Yes, I'll have a lot to explain to him. I hope he won't hate me."

"He'll be angry at both of us, and confused, I'd imagine. But he'll come to see that it was the only decision we could make. Then he'll take you to bed and all will be well."

His gaze followed her finger and remained where her coat had fallen open enough to reveal the pale dip between her breasts. Her nipples had hardened, because of his standing there making her think of sex. But he was talking about sex with Magnus, which didn't feel the same.

"Stop talking about him taking me to bed."

"You're looking at his picture, obviously remembering how good it was. He's probably quite adept. We spent a lot of time . . . 'researching' sex as youths who had no way to experience it. Magazines, movies, chat rooms. There's a lot of information out there for hungry young men. But the most important thing we learned is that if the woman is enjoying herself, everything else will fall into place. You're thinking about how he made you feel, how much you want him again."

"You are completely, utterly rude and disgusting."

His mouth quirked. "Aye, that I am. Utterly. Completely." He leaned closer. "And I'm a sick bastard, too, wanting to hear how much you loved it, how he branded you with his tongue, his—"

She put her hand over his mouth. "Stop."

"Just tell me, and I'll shut up." His mouth moved against her palm, warm, moist breath pulsing against her skin.

She jerked it away, her throat going dry, heat pooling low in her stomach. Because she saw it now, his desire for her, the heaviness in his eyes before he caught himself and banked it. He wasn't being voyeuristic or even rude. He wanted to hear the words that would kill his desire, because wanting her was an unpardonable sin against his brother. *I would never put the moves on my brother's girl.*

"I hate to disappoint you, but I never slept with Magnus."

It wasn't relief that colored his face, but anger. "Why the hell not? He's charming, good-looking. What normal, hot-blooded woman could resist him?"

She gritted her teeth. "I'm not normal, in case you forgot." He spun around and stalked off. Before he could reach the interior door, she said, "I'm going to the carnival this morning. I've got to finish up a couple of things before it opens."

His shoulders tensed as he seemed to tamp down all that frustration and anger. He tilted his head up, still facing away from her. "No way."

"I can't just not show up. I've been too involved in this, and my absence will be suspicious. I have to tell Hayley not to go to my apartment. She's the girl the carnival benefits."

"The girl who got the anonymous bone marrow donation."

"Yes. There'll be people there, so it should be safe. And I need to go to my apartment, get my things."

"You'll have to tell them you can't stay long. You have a family emergency. It's not a lie. It's too dangerous to be out in the open."

"You think Russell would attack me in front of witnesses in broad daylight?"

"I would never underestimate what he might do. You shouldn't, either."

"All right, we'll make it short. I have to be there at seven."

She turned and walked out the door to the courtyard, into the cool early morning air. It was still dark, no hint of dawn yet. She shivered, but it had nothing to do with the cold. She knew what he meant when he'd said he could feel her out there watching him. She felt him watching her leave.

Nothing's changed. You're in no position to get involved with anyone. Not Magnus. And especially not Lachlan, for way too many reasons.

Still, she turned back and caught him standing at the wall of glass watching her.

CHAPTER 7

Lachlan hooked the half-lang sword he'd been working with that morning to his hip. He usually practiced with the replicas, but now he wanted the real thing. Made in the 1400s, this sword had been used in real combat all those years ago, no doubt responsible for many a death.

Back then, Highlanders were either on foot or horseback. Much easier to maneuver with a sword that way than to get in and out of vehicles with one. He donned a dirk, a smaller knife, on his other hip, hidden under his loose black sweater, then slid into his long black coat.

His hand remained on the hardwood handle of the dirk, fingers tightening. That strange energy flowed through him, and a flash of memory bombarded his mind: a hand clutching a similar dirk, swinging the blade down into the chest of a man in the coat and breeches of a British infantryman. Blood spurted out over his hand—not *his* hand, but the rough, blunt hands he'd seen earlier.

"Ready?"

He jerked out of the memory, of Culloden no doubt, and spun around to find Jessie standing in his open doorway.

"I need to go to my apartment first, get my clothes." She gestured to herself, wearing his black T-shirt.

She looked damned good in that T-shirt, even though it was large on her. There was something oddly intimate about her wearing his clothing. In his mind, he could see again that tantalizing hollow between the curves of her cleavage. He'd wanted to hear her say she'd made hot, sweaty love to Magnus. He needed that mental image, strange as it was. Not the details, but the idea that she was physically Magnus's. All the better if Jessie thought he was a weirdo. What he needed so bloody bad was to think, as he looked at her, that Magnus had nuzzled that hollow, slid his hands down between her legs. That would have dampened anything his crazy hormones were throwing at him. Maybe they hadn't had sex, but there was more to a relationship than that.

"Hello?" She waved her hand in front of his face, bringing him round again.

"Sorry. Let's go."

She pulled her black coat, trimmed in fake fur, from the back of the chair. "You were thinking about Magnus, weren't you?"

"Aye."

Lachlan punched in some buttons on the security system's panel.

"You called him Maggie."

He rolled his eyes. "Our childhood nicknames for each other. I hated when he called me Locky, so I called him Maggie. They stuck."

They walked out into the chill morning air.

She came to a dead stop, looking up. "Wow. Beautiful."

He glanced up. "What is?" He looked back at her, the way all her different lengths of shiny brown hair sprayed over her shoulders and made her look wild and windblown, even though there wasn't a hint of wind.

She gestured to the sky. "How can you not see that? Look at the colors, pinks, the most vivid orange I've ever seen." Her voice was saturated with awe, her eyes glittered, and her luscious mouth curved into a smile.

He now saw the splash of color against the steel gray sky. "Nice." He'd seen plenty of sunrises in the last year but never noticed the colors. "I'm going to put Magnus's car in the garage first. He ever give you a ride in this thing? He's a madman behind the wheel."

"We should check on him," she said as Lachlan opened the car door.

"Already did, first thing this morning. He's still sleeping restfully. His temperature's even, pulse is good."

Her smile returned, but not as bright. "Thank God."

"He'll forgive you. He's big on not holding onto anger or blame. And he'll need you as he comes to terms with his Darkness."

She nodded but didn't look especially convinced.

"I'll take responsibility for making the decision," he added. "Our relationship's already been through hell. But in the end, we're brothers. We're all we've got."

He got in and pulled the car up to the garage, pressing the remote to open one of the doors. Magnus made a game out of driving in as fast as he could, hitting the brakes at the last possible moment. Life was a game to him. How would he feel about life once he woke?

As Lachlan got out, Jessie walked in through the open bay to where he'd instructed her to park her vehicle. "I could pack my things," she said, "take care of the carnival, and go. You can put your energy into helping Magnus and not risk your life going after Russell. Magnus is safe, and if I go away, you will be, too."

"But you won't be safe." He had started closing the garage door behind Magnus's car.

"What? I couldn't hear you," she said when the doors had come to a stop.

He opened the door behind Jessie's vehicle and stopped in front of her. "*You* won't be safe."

"This is my problem, and besides, you'd be

doing me a favor. I already feel horrible about Magnus. If something happened to you . . ." Her chin trembled. "No, I won't let you do this."

He tilted his head at her. "If something happened to me, what?" It couldn't affect her worse than something happening to Magnus. "Never mind. I know guilt; he's a good friend of mine. But this isn't your choice. I need to get rid of this guy."

She shook her head, but the trepidation didn't leave her eyes. "Why do you need to?"

He studied the wall covered in tools and auto parts. "Because it's the one thing I can make right."

She remained for a moment, rubbing the keys in her fingers. "If something happens to you . . . I'll kill you. Understand?"

He couldn't help it; his mouth quirked in a smile. "Yes ma'am."

She drove, the two of them quiet at first during the twenty minute ride to her apartment. If her furrowed forehead were any indication, unpleasant thoughts roamed her mind. She turned on the radio. A pop song filled the car, and she tapped her fingers to the beat. Her nails were unpolished but neat.

At a traffic stop, she pulled out her phone and tapped on the screen. "Even though my security system is supposed to alert me if someone goes into my place, with Russell, I can't be sure." The light turned green, and she thrust the phone at him. "Watch the video, see if anything strange is going on."

"You didn't know I was in your place. Otherwise, you wouldn't have let me get the jump on you."

"I left the phone in the car when I ran in to get some papers I'd forgotten. I'd just been there so I wasn't worried."

"And then this brute grabs you. You put up a good fight, though." He rolled his shoulder.

"Sorry—"

"Don't even think about apologizing. I was the intruder. I should apologize to you."

She slid him a smile. "We both had good reasons for doing what we did. Let's leave it at that."

"Deal."

She pulled into her apartment complex. "I don't have that much stuff, so between us, we should be able to pack pretty quick." She nodded toward the back of the Yukon, jammed with boxes and bags. "I keep most of it here."

He hated that she had to live this way. It strengthened his resolve to wipe the son of a bitch off the face of the earth. "What about the furniture?"

"Came with the apartment. The first time Russell tracked me, I spotted him before he saw me. I grabbed the few things that meant something to me but had to leave furniture. Now I rent places furnished." She sighed, getting out of the vehicle and walking toward the bottom of the stairs. "And I lose my last month's rent and security deposit every time."

He remembered the coupons and the magazines with the addresses cut out. He'd seen that
before, at secondhand sales. She'd wanted a large
latte but got a small one, and wouldn't let Magnus
pay for it. She lived her life in fear, and yet even
now knelt and lifted the bloom of a pink rose to
her nose. Her eyes closed in pleasure.

He took off his coat and covered the sword.
"How can you do that?" he asked, coming up
beside her.

"Uh, I breathe in through my nose."

"Don't be cheeky. I meant, take the time to enjoy
something like that, with all the trouble you've got
on your shoulders."

She stroked the petals of the rose. "Because
there's so much beauty and goodness in life. I
need to live in those moments to balance out the
times when there's fear." The pleasure on her face
deepened when a butterfly landed on a nearby
rose.

"Look at the flutterby, for example." He heard
awe in her voice for something she probably saw
every day. "Appreciate the way she injects unex-
pected color and movement into this moment."

"Flutterby?"

"That's what they do, you know. They flutter
by. They're not butter that's flying. I think someone mistranslated the word somewhere along the
way." She looked at him. "I learned to appreciate
the little things from some of the kids in my foster
home. They were dying, day by day, or struggling

to live in bodies that wouldn't cooperate, but some of them saw the joy in life. They're my inspiration. My dad, too. He taught me to appreciate the beauty in all aspects of life, from a thunderstorm to a beetle zigzagging across the sidewalk. So stop, Lachlan, and smell the roses. Then you can scratch yourself with the thorns." She took the stairs two at a time.

"What's that supposed to mean?" He followed.

"You like punishing yourself." She unlocked the door and went inside, turning to him. "You think you're a bad person because of what you did to your mother. But you're not. You made a bad mistake, that's all."

He turned away, taking in her living room. "What do you need packed?"

"The fuzzy blanket on the couch, just about everything in the kitchen . . . but the kitchen sink," she added with a smile. "Definitely the pots and pans. Those were a huge splurge. I'm not leaving behind my food or spices either." She pulled out several soft bags from the closet. "There's a cooler under the table. Dump some ice in it and put everything from the fridge in there." She frowned. "I'll have to leave behind the B and J NYSFC in the freezer, though. No way to keep it that cold."

He pulled out the cooler. "What's the B and J and whatever-else-you-said?"

"Ben and Jerry's New York Super Fudge Chunk. Chocolate ice cream, nuts, and chunks of white and dark chocolate. It's sinful."

He didn't need to hear her say "sinful" when her ass was sticking out as she reached in to grab one last bag. He focused on opening the freezer and dumping all the ice from the bin into the cooler. One lone tub of B&J sat there. How much did she have to sacrifice?

She snapped open a large plastic bag. "Garbage goes in here. I don't want to leave a mess behind."

"What about your job? Magnus said you were good with the kids." He remembered how she'd poured on the praise to the young violinist.

Her frown deepened. "I'll have to quit. Again. The pay wasn't that great anyway. And some of those kids . . ." She grimaced. "The sound of off-tune guitars and pianos, some days I thought my eardrums would pop. Sometimes I wished they would."

Sour grapes. Well, he'd let her have them.

He turned back to the task. Interesting. The girl had food, all right. Not a lot of it, but she liked quality food, like buffalo meat, several varieties of cheese he couldn't even pronounce the names of, and fancy crackers to go with them. She had just about every spice and herb known to man. He jammed his arm into the cabinet and raked them all into a bag.

She came in and grabbed a heavy-duty quilted bag from the top shelf of one of the cabinets. "This is for the pots and pans. The towels go between them."

"Yes, ma'am." He couldn't help smiling.

She paused, then ducked away again.

She'd piled the bags and a couple of pull-along suitcases in front of the door. He supposed the bags were easier to handle and store than boxes, which had to be broken down and then taped together again. His smile dampened; she had to live with an escape plan. Even though they, too, had been in hiding, they'd stayed in one place for long periods of time.

"That's it," she said, returning to the kitchen.

She'd changed into a long-sleeved black top with a faded heart and the words LIVE IN YOUR HEART. She hadn't been wearing his shirt last night, only Magnus's coat. Watching her draw her fingers down the edge of the collar, her thoughts obviously on Magnus, had been painful in more than one way.

"How's it going in here?" she asked.

"Done." He picked up the notebook he'd seen earlier. "Don't want to forget this, I imagine."

She took it, flipping through the pages. "I do want to forget this. Now that I know what's in me, I don't need it anymore." She dropped it into one of the large plastic bags.

He handed her the container of B&J and a spoon. "You eat, I'll drive." She stared at the container. "Go on. You haven't had breakfast yet."

She took it, looking oddly touched. "Thanks."

They hoisted bags, and two trips down the stairs later, everything was packed into the back of her SUV. A rustle in the bushes caught his attention. A black dog backed away and ducked out of sight. Uneasiness settled over him.

"What?" she asked, catching his stare.

"Dog in the bushes. It's gone now." He scanned the parking lot, as he had the whole time they were packing. "Let's go."

He drove, and she ate, letting out pleasurable little moans punctuated by a crunch every now and then. Her head was tilted back, eyes closed, a smile on her face as she worked the ice cream in her mouth as though it were a fine wine. He took in the length of her pale neck. Hell, he could taste her skin, feel the soft texture of it.

Her eyes snapped open. "I was making noises, wasn't I?"

He cleared his throat. "A bit."

Her cheeks colored. "I love food."

He remembered the way she'd smelled the rose and marveled over the . . . flutterby. He, who had his whole life in front of him, had stopped living, while she, who lived in fear, savored every inch of it.

"You haven't eaten yet, have you?" she asked.

"I'll eat later."

She held out a spoonful of ice cream. "If you're not worried about germs."

It wasn't germs he feared; he leaned forward, and she slid the spoon into his mouth. Cold, creamy, with a chunk of dark chocolate.

"More?" she asked, digging into the container. *More. Much more.* "I'm fine, thanks."

Sharing a spoon felt too intimate, something lovers would do. Like her wearing his T-shirt.

He focused on the tangle of good luck charms hanging from her mirror. "Do you believe in luck?" he asked, nodding toward them.

"Not really, but I figure they can't hurt."

During the news segment on the radio, the DJ said another woman had gone missing, the fourth one in the last five months in the tristate area.

Jessie turned off the radio, shuddering. "I don't want to hear stuff like that."

He pulled into the carnival grounds' lot. Unlike the night before, the place was buzzing with activity. He backed into a spot where he could pull out in a hurry, if need be.

She took in everything with a glow in her eyes. "We did it. It's really going to happen. And it's not terribly cold, so we should get a good turnout."

"Uh . . ." He gestured to her mouth. "You've got chocolate there." He itched to rub it off with his thumb. *Admit it, you want to lick it off, you sod.* He held in a groan as she ran her tongue over her upper lip, dabbing away the chocolate.

"Did I get it?"

"Oh, yeah." He cleared his throat. "You're good. I mean, you got it."

She gave him a questioning arch of her eyebrow as she pulled on her coat and got out.

He maneuvered into his long coat and hooked the sword beneath it. She was already walking toward the entrance, hands clasped together in front of her, so excited about her carnival that she hadn't noticed he wasn't right behind her.

Something small and dark caught his eye. He turned toward the back of the SUV, then ducked to look beneath. Nothing. But the hairs on the back of his neck vibrated.

Nothing strange anywhere in eyeshot. Even so, the sooner they could leave, the better. He headed toward the entrance, where a couple of people stood talking to Jessie. She glanced back now, giving him a questioning look. He shrugged, then wiped the concern from his face. Let her enjoy this for a bit. He'd watch over her.

A woman bounded over, her body jiggling with her movements, pretty face aglow with excitement. He recognized her from the pictures in the paper.

"Jessie!" she said, wrapping her hands around Jessie's forearms. "It was you, wasn't it? The paper didn't give a last name, but I know you're Hayley's anonymous donor. I said to Gerry, that'd be just like her, to do that and keep it a secret."

Jessie's face fell, though she forced a smile. "I wish they wouldn't have put my name in there at all."

Then it clicked, that she'd given the needed blood marrow that had saved Hayley.

"You are an angel." The woman squeezed Jessie's hands.

"No, I'm not." Jessie meant it, too, her eyes darkening, mouth tensing at the corners. "It was just something I had to do."

Her gaze flicked to him, and in that moment he got it. She didn't know if Darkness could be transferred via blood. Saving Magnus wasn't the first time she'd had to make that terrible choice: let someone die or give them a life possibly tainted by Darkness. She had done something wonderful and brave, but she didn't see it that way.

A couple more cars drove into the parking area. He made a note to check the Yukon before they got in. Paranoid? Hell, yes.

Jessie interrupted whatever the lady was going to say. "We'd better get to work. We've only got a couple of hours before opening." She gestured to him. "This is Lachlan. He's here to help, too."

"Bob LaMott brought his RV for the volunteers to grab a break. A couple local delis donated sandwiches and water, and the bagel shop donated coffee and bagels. It's behind the Ferris wheel."

"That's great." Jessie headed to the right, all business now, going over a list of tasks. She glanced back at him from time to time, finding him following a few feet behind.

Over there. Had he seen something small and black? But Russell wasn't small. He caught up to Jessie, leaning close to her ear. She smelled good, like shampoo.

"We leave in half an hour," he whispered.

"An hour."

"Forty-five minutes."

"I feel like we're brokering a deal on *Pawn Stars*. Is there a reason you're extra paranoid?"

"Plenty." He glanced around again. "It should be fine, lots of people around, but the hairs on the back of my neck have been on end since we got here."

She pressed her lips together, seeming to take that seriously. "I need to stay until the carnival opens."

He released a breath. Aye, she was stubborn, all right. He knew, though, that this meant a lot to her. "Alright."

The decision weighed heavily in his chest.

CHAPTER 8

Lachlan helped Jessie set up one of the game booths. He hammered in the hooks and then hung up the prizes, stuffed animals and other toys, while she set up the heavy pins and instructed the volunteers who would man the booth. He'd made sure she didn't stray out of sight and even made her take his cell number. She'd accused him of being overprotective. So be it.

He hung the last teddy bear and stepped down, only to turn and find her standing next to the ladder surveying his work with a smile. "Nice job. I like how you staggered them."

Okay, it was just a little compliment, no need to feel all warm and fuzzy about it. He shrugged. "Have you told anyone that you're not staying long?"

"It hasn't come up yet. But I will."

"I don't like being out here, exposed." He swept the grounds again, but the area was too big, too cluttered with booths and rides to see much. It wasn't open to the public yet, but Russell could still manage to get in.

"Then don't expose yourself. It's against the law anyway." She gave him a wisecrack grin.

"It's no time to be joking around."

"It's a perfect time."

"Jessie!" The girl whose picture was on the front sign walked up.

Jessie's face lit up in genuine affection for the teen with the short pink haircut in a style like hers. Probably not a coincidence.

The two exchanged a bear hug. He saw *goodbye* in the way Jessie held on for a few extra seconds, her eyes squeezed shut. She backed up and fluffed Hayley's hair. "Big day's here."

"It's fantastic. Just knowing my parents will have some help with the bills . . . oh, Jessie, this is so wonderful of you."

"I had lots of help." She waved off Hayley's gratitude, not unlike what he'd done a few minutes earlier.

"Why don't you ever want to take credit for the things you do? None of this would have happened if you hadn't started it." Her expression took on a sheepish look. "They did keep your last name out of the article. I hope that's okay."

Jessie rearranged a stray lock of Hayley's hair. "It's fine."

People had been coming up all morning exclaiming over her good deed, and he knew it wasn't all right. Jessie clearly wanted no one to know she'd donated her marrow.

Now the girl's gaze swiveled to him. "Who's this?"

"Lachlan, meet Hayley. Lachlan is Magnus's brother."

"Saw you hanging up the animals. Thanks for helping." She looked around. "Where is Magnus?"

"He's tied up, can't make it," Lachlan answered. "She won't be staying long either, unfortunately. Family emergency."

Hayley's eyes widened. "Your uncle?"

Interesting and surprising that Jessie had told her so much.

Jessie nodded. "I'll have to go."

"Go as in . . . go? But you said it was fine."

"He found me anyway. I'll be all right."

"No, it's not fair. Can't we—"

Jessie wrapped her hand around Hayley's arm, halting her words. "I promise to drop you a note once in a while. I want to keep in touch." She forced a joking tone to her voice. "Never know what might come out of that blood I gave you."

Hayley's laugh was hollow. "Yeah, like I become a vampire or something." Someone called out Hayley's name. "I gotta go. Don't leave without saying goodbye." She ambled off.

His chest caved as he watched Jessie's face. "That's the hardest part, isn't it? Harder than leaving behind the last month's rent and security."

She bit her lower lip, avoiding his gaze. "Yes."

"Why don't we take a break?"

She led the way around the various booths to the far side of the grounds. The Ferris wheel spun in a lazy circle, happy music playing. Carousel horses pumped up and down, bright and colorful, their wild eyes looking behind them as though they were being chased. He smelled the grease on the gears as they passed the workers testing the equipment. It was a more interesting aroma than the sausages cooking in a nearby stand, reminding him of working on his cars.

"You're lucky you have your brother," she said.

"Aye, I am." Unimaginable, the thought of Magnus dying. All he had done so far to save him was allow him to be infected with some unknown energy. That wasn't good enough. He had to get rid of Russell.

"To have one person who's there, who you can always connect to. I can't do that."

She had to keep leaving people behind. His heart ached for her. "But you do connect, whether you want to or even whether you realize it or not."

"You're mistaken. I'm not even sure I can connect to someone anymore. What? Why are you giving me that 'I know better than you' look?"

"Because I do know better. You'll have Magnus, once he wakes up. Russell will be dead, and you won't have to run anymore."

"What if he's not dead?"

"Magnus will protect you. He's like that . . . as you know."

She paused on the metal step going up to the RV door. "So are you."

"I'm only doing it to make up for what I've taken away."

"Lachlan—"

"Wait. Let me check inside before you go in."

It didn't take long, as the place wasn't that big. A miniature home, with a small bedroom, couch, kitchen. "Okay, come in."

She walked to the little fridge, opened it and bent over to search the contents. Was he a complete jerk for noticing her fine arse in those jeans? It wasn't like there was much else to look at, and he *was* waiting to see what was in the fridge, and—yeah, he was an arse.

"Ham and cheese?" She held out a cellophane wrapped sandwich.

"Sure." He took it, and Jessie pulled another one out for herself.

She grabbed two bottles of water and stopped dead, staring past him at the floor. He spun around. A black Doberman pinscher sat by the door staring at them. Not a normal dog. Beneath its exterior, blackness churned like solid smoke. Lachlan pulled out his dirk.

The door opened and Russell stepped inside, two more dogs following him in. He locked the door behind him. "Finally, we're alone." He gave Lachlan a derisive look. "Well, almost. Dogs." He nodded toward Lachlan.

The beasts reared up and leaped at him, teeth

bared. Lachlan slashed, but the blade only seemed to nick them. Their teeth, however, tore into his flesh. He tried to move closer to Jessie, but they pushed him back.

"What are those things?" Jessie asked, hands poised, body in position to defend herself.

He smiled. "My minions. Jessie, I have no intention of hurting you. I know you'll find that hard to believe. If you come with me, I will explain everything."

"Like hell she will," Lachlan said, shrugging out of his coat while keeping his blade at the ready.

Russell flicked a cold look his way. "But I *will* hurt your friend if he continues to get in the way. You don't want him hurt, do you, Jessie?"

Lachlan shook his head. "I'm not going anywhere."

Russell moved like a dark blur—no, became a blur. Suddenly he stood behind Jessie, his arms clamped around her, man again. She twisted and tried to jam her foot down on top of his.

No, dammit! Lachlan kicked at the dogs with the heel of his shoe. They backed up, but only for a second.

"Fade!" she screamed, and disappeared.

Russell sent a shroud of dark fog over her, outlining her form. His hold didn't loosen. "That won't work anymore."

She appeared again, panic on her face. She pulled up the bottom edge of her shirt and slapped her hand over it. "Fade!"

Russell laughed and again threw his Darkness over her, revealing her.

Frustration tensed her face when she became fully visible again.

"You think that symbol makes you invisible? It means bird in some ancient culture. Your father studied the Mayans, and the Anasazis, the mysterious peoples he thought came from or consorted with beings from other dimensions."

The dogs kept pushing Lachlan farther away, down the hall toward the little bedroom. One tried to get around him, but he easily blocked it. He pulled his sword, so he held a weapon in each hand, and slashed at them. They yelped, tiny bits of their Darkness splintering off, but it didn't slow them down at all.

No good. How had he fought Russell before? He tried to summon the strange energy, imagining the lightning sparking down his dirk. Nothing. The astral projection, the strange energy, was it all a tease?

Jessie became a blur, then a dark mass, shimmering violently. Russell banged against the kitchen cabinet with her force, and she spun out of his reach. Russell stood between them now, keeping a wary eye on Jessie.

Someone tried opening the door, then knocked. "Jessie? It's Hayley. Peg saw you go this way. Why's the door locked?"

"Hayley, leave me alone right now." Jessie was

trying hard to modulate her quivering voice. "I'll find you in a bit."

"Are you all right?" the girl called out.

Of course she would be worried, and she might get others if she thought Jessie was ill.

"She's fine," Lachlan said, holding the dogs at bay. With Russell's attention at the door, the dogs settled. "We're, ah, busy. If you get my drift."

"Oh. *Oh.*" Silence as she obviously processed the oddity of Jessie doing the nasty there. Then, "Okay, come find me, after . . . well, you know."

A dog flew at Lachlan, catching his side and throwing him against the wall. The sword dropped to the floor. He reached for it and the dog bit his hand.

"All right, you guys, don't get too wild in there," Hayley called out again, her voice filled with her perplexity. Banging some guy in the break trailer wasn't in Jessie's character.

Russell Became, turning a larger, more vicious version of the Dobermans. With one paw he reached into his chest and pulled out a blob of Darkness. He flung it toward Lachlan, and the blob formed into another one of those devil dogs in mid-flight. He only had time to fling his hands up and throw the beast to the side. It bounced against the wall and fell to the floor. In a second it rolled to its feet, up and ready to attack.

Russell's voice was low and calm. "Kill him. Now."

"No!" Jessie whispered.

Lachlan jabbed the dirk toward the closest dog, slashing at its neck. It yelped and fell back, then started knitting itself back together. Dammit. He could injure them, but he couldn't kill them.

Jessie Became, launching herself at Russell's dark form. They bounced off each other, throwing them in opposite directions. She landed on the arm of the couch and rolled to the floor in front of the door, morphing back to her human self.

"Run!" Lachlan said, cutting the dogs and sending them into temporary retreat while they mended. Damned things moved like mercury.

"I'm not leaving you here," she said.

"Bloody hell, don't worry about me."

Another dog bounded his way. They were wearing him out, and he had no room to maneuver in the narrow hallway.

The dogs positioned themselves between Lachlan and his sword. One ducked beneath the dirk's blade and nipped at him. "Damn mutts." Pain seared his ankle, his arm, and his thigh, where they'd gotten him.

Jessie's cheeks flamed red in rage as she faced off with Russell. "What are you going to do, haul me out of here in front of everyone?"

"You'll come with me because you don't want me to hurt anyone who might help you." He nodded toward Lachlan. "This one is an adept fighter, but what about the others out there? The girl?"

She looked at Lachlan, agony on her face. "Please stop helping me."

Russell's mouth formed a cruel smile. "Oh, no, let me kill your boyfriend. I'm so looking forward to seeing him ripped to shreds. Then maybe you'll talk to me."

"I have nothing to say to you."

"Jessie," Russell growled. "You'll listen if you want to save your mother."

"Don't you dare talk about her. You killed her! You took everything from me. *You took my father's body.*" Overrun by emotions, she Became again, rushing at him.

Russell's instantly dark form grabbed her. Lachlan ran the final two steps into the back bedroom, leaped onto the bed and jumped over the dogs, aiming right for Russell's back. Lachlan plowed his feet into him, sending him to the ground. Jessie's form broke free.

Russell threw him back into the mass of dogs. Lachlan tried to keep his balance, to land on his feet, but momentum worked against him. The dogs jumped on him, a mob of claws and teeth. He struggled to get up but their weight pinned him down.

He wouldn't go down without a fight, raising his dirk and readying to slash it down. The foreign energy crackled through him. *Finally.* He slashed at one of the dogs; its head spun off and its body splattered into nothingness. The ghostly, blunt-fingered hand shimmered on the handle. Another dog bit the dust as Lachlan stabbed it and got to his feet. He lunged for the sword on the floor and held it out. Lightning flashed down both blades, sending two dogs flying backward and splintering into pieces.

Both in Darkness, Jessie and Russell maneuvered in the small space. She was quick, staying out of his grasp by seconds.

Wait. Was it his imagination that Russell looked less dense? And even better, that he seemed weaker?

The dogs. Maybe using his Darkness to make his minions drained his strength. Especially as each dog got obliterated.

Lachlan ran toward him, his power coursing through him as a jagged energy. He jumped on Russell's back, sending them both to the floor. Kneeling, Lachlan raised his sword and started to drive it downward. Russell bucked, still strong enough to throw him off. As Lachlan hit the wall, Russell opened the door with his paw and became a mist that disappeared.

Lachlan pulled the door closed before anyone could see in, then stumbled over to Jessie. "You all right?"

She got to her feet but wobbled. He put his arms around her to steady her.

"I let my emotions get the best of me." She looked at him, her eyes widening. "You're bleeding." She reached toward his cheek, her expression pained.

He turned away before she could touch him and went into the tiny bathroom to survey himself. He wiped away blood dripping from a cut on the cheek and pressed a clean tissue over it to stop the bleeding. He saw her in the reflection, taking him in from behind.

"God, Lachlan, those things really got you. Your arm, your ankle. You're bleeding all over, and your jeans are cut to shreds."

"I'm alright. Stop looking at me like you're going to faint. Or like I'm going to faint. But we need to get out of here." He grabbed the coat he'd discarded and pulled it on, closing it so it covered most of the tears and blood.

"You were right, I shouldn't have stayed as long as I did. This is my fault—"

He put two fingers over her mouth. "Stop." He pinned her with his eyes. "I'll be fine."

"This place is a mess," she said on a whisper. She started cleaning up, wiping away the blood on the wall and leather couch. He threw the sandwiches back into the fridge.

She ran her fingers through her hair to smooth it while he arranged the sword and dirk on his hips again. She reached up and finger-combed his hair, too. He stopped, completely stopped, as her fingers touched his temples.

She let her hand drop. "Let's go."

They stepped out to find several people standing nearby. Hayley came over from a nearby booth, a questioning look in her eyes. "Wow, you guys are wild. The whole trailer was rocking, and then this weird smoke came out." She sniffed the air. "You didn't set anything on fire, did you?"

Jessie started to cover her face in shame but halted and met Hayley's eyes. "I'm a person of bad judgment, poor timing, and questionable character. I'm sorry you had to see that side of me, but it's there, has been my whole life. I'm not someone you should be around." She squeezed the girl's arm and let go. "Tell Bob I'll make things right if anything's broken in the trailer." Jessie looked like a robot, stiff and expressionless as she stalked away, doing a good job of not meeting anyone else's eyes. Judgmental eyes, as far as he could see.

He couldn't keep from watching her, though, having tossed away her reputation to keep Hayley at a distance.

The girl's open mouth clamped shut as she gestured to his cheek, where he must be bleeding again. She stepped closer and whispered, "None of that was true, was it? What happened in there—"

He would not undermine the sacrifice Jessie had made, so he shook his head and caught up to Jessie before she got too far away. She was shaking, her arms wrapped around herself as she walked.

He pulled out her car keys. "I'll drive."

"No." She snatched them from his hand. "You're the injured one. And you're injured because of me."

"I'm injured because of Russell. Keep that straight."

"Semantics," she said, throwing his word back at him. "If you'd let me go, you'd be safe and cozy in your sanctuary."

"Aye, and that was working well for me."

She let out an exasperated sound as they reached the vehicle. "Well, at least you wouldn't be bleeding all over yourself. Should I take you to the hospital? We can say it was a dog attack. That's the truth."

"No, just get me back to the house. We've got medical supplies." He searched the vehicle before pulling himself onto the seat. Once inside, he inspected his ankle, the part of him that hurt most. Blood still oozed out and washed down his foot.

She opened the back and got in a few seconds later, a shirt in her hand. "Lift your ankle. We need to stop the bleeding."

"That looks like a nice shirt." She didn't have the money to buy a lot of clothing. "The blood will ruin it."

"Forget the shirt." She'd gone into some other mode, probably still fired up with adrenaline. She would not be argued with, he could see that.

She wrapped the shirt around his ankle, and he did his best not to hiss in pain. Fierce streaks of heat radiated up his leg. As though she'd read his mind, she opened the glove box and dug through several bottles. Her medicine chest. Poor girl lived out of her car for the most part. She opened a bottle of aspirin with trembling fingers, took out two, and handed them to him. Then she dug behind the seat and produced a bottle of water.

He dutifully took the two pills, then two more. Having her take care of him tightened and twisted in him. She pulled out of the lot, her mouth tightened into a thin line. Tremors rolled in waves over her.

He said, "I can drive—"

"You're staying right there and resting."

"Aye, ma'am."

He watched her for several minutes, but she kept her gaze straight ahead. He kept an eye on her, surreptitiously, though she maintained a grip on the emotions that had her squeezing the wheel.

He was so busy watching her, he didn't focus on his pain as much, nor did he notice that they'd driven the whole way until she turned down the gravel road that led to Sanctuary.

He said, "I'll open one of the bays for you. I want the car locked up." He got out and tried not to limp. The pain wasn't as bad, thanks to the aspirin, but the cuts burned. The door opened, and he waved for her to pull in.

"Let's get your things," he said as soon as she got out.

"No, we're cleaning your wounds first."

She hadn't lost any of that bossiness or the tension in her body during the drive. They walked down the pathway to the front gate and he unlocked it. He surveyed the area, though Cheveyo had put a shield over it. After all, even he had no idea how long it would hold against this new entity.

Lachlan led her into the house, dropping his ruined coat by the door. "Hold on, I'll get the medical kit." He returned a minute later with what was basically a tackle box.

She pointed to the sitting area. "Sit." She rooted through the contents and pulled out several things, including gauze. Then she went into the nearby kitchen, turned on the water, and grabbed the roll of paper towels from the silver holder. "Where do you keep big bowls?"

"Upper right cabinet."

A minute later she brought back a bowl and the roll of towels and sat down again. "Give me your foot."

He propped his foot up on the chair between them. She pushed back the frayed edges of the bottom of his pant leg. "You'll have to take them off."

"Forward lassie, aren't you?"

She didn't crack even a hint of a smile, nor did she meet his eyes. "Lachlan, this isn't funny." Her voice stretched tight over her words.

"I was only trying to lighten the mood."

"Just . . . don't."

He shucked off his jeans, kicking them away with his good foot. Her gaze slid up the length of his legs. She gasped. Good God, did he have a stiffy again?

"You're bleeding from somewhere up here." She leaned over and lifted his shirt.

Yep, he had several deep scratches where one

of the beasts had caught his side and thrown him against the wall. They had bled right down to soak the waistband of his skivvies.

She unbuttoned his shirt from the bottom up, so intent on her task she seemed surprised when, after reaching the top button, she was nearly face-to-face with him. Her breath hitched, and she blinked and shook her head before peeling off his shirt.

"Not too bad," he said, looking down at himself.

"They got you on the arm, too. And your hand." She shuddered. "They were awful. He sent them all after you."

"Has he made the beasties before?"

"Not that I've ever seen." She looked at him. "You slayed them with the arcs of energy you used against Russell the first time."

"Aye."

She was waiting for more of an explanation. Finally, she asked, "What is it?"

"Hell if I know."

"That wasn't something you could do before?"

He shook his head, his chest tightening. First the spontaneous astral projection, and into the future, yet. Then the wild energy. He didn't like either, but he needed them.

She took him in, and he felt her gaze sear across his skin. "Sit down, let me clean the wounds."

He sat facing her. She was trying hard to keep her focus, but he could see huge guilt when she unwrapped her quickie wrap job on his ankle.

She tore off a wad of paper towels, dipped them into the water and swabbed the cuts. She hissed for him, even as he banked his own expression of pain. That would make her feel even worse.

She chewed her bottom lip as she tended to him, rubbing salve in a thick layer. She opened the box and unwound the gauze, cutting it and winding it around his ankle.

He wanted to run his fingers through her hair, wanted to touch her. "I'm sorry you couldn't be there for the carnival's opening."

She sputtered what he thought was a laugh, though there was no humor on her face. "You're sorry . . . you're sorry. I almost got you killed. I should have listened to you in the first place."

She put the metal clip on the end of the gauze to keep it in place. "Give me your arm."

His hand was lacerated, but only superficially. She cleaned those scratches and put salve on them, then worked on his arm.

He wasn't feeling pain anymore. He felt her hands on his arm, fingers tight against his skin.

She scooted closer, her face only an inch in front of his as she brushed his hair away from his face. "I've never known a guy with hair as long as yours."

He lifted one shoulder in a half shrug. "Haven't had the gumption to get it cut."

"I'd love to have hair this shiny and thick."

He could feel her rolling a lock of hair between her fingers. She stopped, tore a fresh paper towel

from the roll, and washed the cut on his cheek.
Her eyes met his, for just a second, and she quickly
looked down.

It took every ounce of his willpower not to close
the gap and plaster his mouth against hers.

Hold yourself back. Do not go there.

"You have lovely hair," he said instead.

"Not really." She met his gaze, then dipped
down again. "Too fine."

Before he could think better of it, he'd reached
out and touched the strands that flipped up above
her shoulder. She stopped cold, as though he'd
touched her neck or maybe her ear. He let go.

"Seems perfectly nice to me," he said, training
his voice to be neutral.

She smelled good, the clean scent of her sweat
and the sweetness of shampoo. She hadn't almost
gotten him killed, but she was killing him now.
He kept the agony from his expression.

Her breath fanned his cheek in rapid puffs. He
wanted to taste her so badly, his mouth watered.

Her hand was resting on his shoulder as she
leaned over. She treated the slashes on his thigh,
then his side, and then her hand slid down over
his chest. He closed his eyes at the sweetness of
that touch, and oh, aye, torture. He'd get attacked
by supernatural beasties anytime to feel her hands
on him.

Ah, so you are mad.

She braced her hand on his side while the other

hand cleaned those slashes. "When I touched you before, you said it hurt. But I wasn't touching the bruised part of you."

It bothered her, and puzzled her. He could see it in her eyes.

She finished with the bandage and placed her hand on his chest. "Does this hurt?"

He closed his eyes for a second. "Aye."

She looked again at the place where she touched, seeing nothing that should cause pain.

"But—"

He took her hand in his, squeezing it a bit too hard before releasing it, and got to his feet. "Thank you for nursing me."

She blinked, her body stiffening. "It was the least I could do."

He felt his own body straining toward her and pulled back. "You said you didn't take a distinct form like Russell does, but could you if you tried? Could you create minions?"

"I don't know. I don't want to know." She turned and walked toward the door, grabbing up the coat she'd discarded when she'd come in.

"Where are you going?"

"I'm not doing this with you."

His eyebrows raised. "Doing what, exactly?" His mind supplied flashes of what they'd just done, with all the excruciating feel effects.

"Putting you in danger. Involving you in this. I have to go."

He stepped up beside her. Her quick glance down his body reminded him he was nearly naked. *Don't make me touch you, lass.* "I made a promise to Magnus that I'd keep you safe. Doesn't matter whether he was awake to hear it or not. I won't let you go out that door to fight this alone." He knew where to dig, the tender parts of her soul. "You've been alone for a long time, Jess. Long enough. You don't have to do this alone anymore."

Jackpot. Her eyes glittered with tears, though none fell.

Yeah, nice guy, making her cry.

"I do have to do it alone. You heard him. He wants to kill you."

"And you would have gone with him to save me and everyone else there."

"Of course I would." She pointed to herself. "One life for many; that's no real choice. Russell wants me. Supposedly to talk to me, though I doubt it's only that. Bastard, bringing my mother into this, trying to use her to trick me. Why should you die because of me?" She gestured to his body. "Why should you suffer?"

"Like you said, there's no real choice."

"You would risk your life to save me." It wasn't a question, but she added, "For Magnus?"

"Yes. For you as well."

She crossed her arms over her chest, regarding him. "Would that make you feel better? Would losing your life trying to protect me make up for your mistake?"

"Yes." Now she was digging into his tender spots, too.

She let out a groan of frustration and pushed at his chest. He didn't budge. "I'm not Magnus's girl. You're putting a lot of weight into that idea. We flirted, had lunch once. That's it."

"He likes you. He thought you were special."

"Yeah, I'm special all right. He'll drop down to his knee and propose when he finds out what I've put in him. And he'll love me to pieces if I get his brother killed."

"Let him decide that. You saved his life, at whatever price. You have a bond because of that and the Darkness. Let him work it out."

"We never kissed."

"You must have." He'd tortured himself with the image, all the while reminding himself that she was not his to want.

"Sorry to disappoint you. If it makes you feel better, we almost kissed, but I turned so that he kissed my cheek. I daydreamed about him. He's got a nice mouth, full, lush, with an intriguing cupid's bow." She flicked a glance at his mouth. "Runs in the family, I see."

Did he imagine a spark in her eyes? "You wanted to kiss him."

She shrugged. "Sure, but not in an I'll-die-if-I-don't way. I think about kissing any attractive guy who flirts with me. But there's no point in that kind of activity."

"That kind of 'activity'?"

"Kissing. Touching." She met his gaze, licking her lips in an involuntary way that tightened his groin. "Making love. For me, anyway."

He mirrored her action, chastising himself for focusing on the way her mouth had wrapped around the words *making love* and drawn them out. "Why not?"

"The Darkness, of course." That came out a whisper laced with fear. Her gaze speared past him. "Intense emotions triggers it. I Became when Russell attacked me. And when you broke into my apartment. I've heard having sex is intense, at least when it's done right." Now she met his gaze again. "When it's right, it's supposed to be like fireworks. I'd be terrified of Becoming in the middle of a mind-bending orgasm."

What she was saying punched him in the chest. "You never . . ."

She went on, her eyes taking on a heavy, sleepy look. "I've heard you can lose your mind. Lose yourself in each other. The slide of bodies against each other, the way I'd feel when the right man filled me." Her gaze slid down his chest, and he felt it tingle across the breadth of his shoulders. She fixed it there and seemed to pull herself from the vision she was talking about. "I can't lose my head. Ever. Because if I Become Darkness, I could kill you." She drew her gaze back to his. "I mean, 'you' in a general way, of course."

"Of course." The words came out gritty. He'd

felt her words, and their bodies gliding against each other, his cock filling her. It was growing even now, and would be damned obvious in his skivvies.

"And if it's not fiery and wonderful, what's the point of doing it?" She shook her head. "I can't take that chance. Besides, I could never think of getting involved with a man, or anybody, really, with Russell on my ass."

A noise escaped his throat, like the throaty whine of a hungry dog.

"What? Are you laughing at me because I'm a virgin?"

"No, not at all." He scraped his finger in an X shape on his chest. "Cross my heart."

She softened from the edge of anger to soft and vulnerable, backlit by something else. Something that sent an answering call to his body. It twisted inside him, her confession, her loneliness, churning and pulling until his hands tightened and his fingers clenched. She had never made love to a man, never been intimately touched by anyone, including Magnus. Her eyes went soft and heavy again as she looked at his mouth. "I don't want to kiss Magnus anymore."

He could hardly breathe. "No?"

"I want to kiss you."

The words flashed in him like the bright red of a marine emergency flare against a black, endless sky. Only it didn't go out. She wanted to kiss him.

He fought the pull to fulfill her wish. His wish. "That would be a betrayal—my betrayal—of my brother."

She laughed, even though her cheeks flushed pink. "I only said I wanted to. You can take off that heavy mantle of brotherly honor. Didn't you hear what I said? I would never let myself give in, at least not to more than a kiss."

"You'd be okay with a kiss then?" *Hell.* "Forget I said that." He swiped her keys from the table. "You're not going anywhere. I'm part of this now. I know you don't want me hurt, but you've no choice. I'm making that decision. My life, my choice. As much as you hate that, I see in your eyes that part of you wants it."

"You're wrong. Not one tiny part of me wants you involved."

He put his hands on her shoulders. "You're not alone anymore, Jess. See, when I said that, your eyes gave you away. They went mushy. You've been alone a long time. Fighting, lying, hiding all by yourself. No one should have to endure that. I'm not letting you fight alone. I may be a lot of things, and I'm sure you have a few choice words in mind right now, but I'm not a man who can let a woman go off and face a man/beast by herself. I've got more expletives for myself than you do, guaranteed. If it makes you feel good, go ahead and let some loose."

He saw the moment she gave in. Her shoulders sagged and she released a soft if agonized breath.

"You didn't see me get mushy. I like being alone."

"Of course."

"I'm only staying because you're a pushy brute."

"Right. Now, let's go into the studio and work on your Darkness. You need to master it, and I'm the one person you can practice with. I can handle it." He gestured toward himself, then remembered his state of dress. Or undress, as it were. "When I get clothes on, that is."

Her expression fell. "No."

"You don't want me to get dressed? It's only proper—"

"Lachlan, you make me crazy." She pressed her palms to her temple. "You want me to Become? On purpose?"

"How are you going to learn to do what Russell can if you're afraid of it? You have an incredible power inside you. Use it."

That power sparked in her eyes, tightened her mouth in a determined line. She turned all of that on him. "Only if you tell me what you are."

She was agreeing. He grabbed onto that, and only a second later realized the price. "What do you mean?"

She crossed her arms over her chest. "What makes the magic, the arc of electricity?

CHAPTER 9

Russell hated knocking on the door of a place where he was unwelcome, especially when he'd chartered a flight all the way out to Arizona. His efforts wouldn't be appreciated. He hoped to wear the boy down. Well, "boy" wasn't accurate. Julian was twenty-seven, not the twelve-year-old he left behind when he'd "died."

Julian yanked the door open, obviously having seen him through the peephole. His dark blue eyes were narrowed, the shadowy expression reminding him of the sulky boy he'd been so many years ago.

"You're here," Russell said, hearing relief saturate his voice.

Julian had been his first stop when he got out of prison, even before beginning to search for Jessie. His son. He'd ascertained that the men he asked to take care of him had done a good job.

"What do you want?" Julian's hard gaze raked over him, obviously still not used to the way he looked now.

"Your help. Can I come in?"

He didn't budge from the door opening. "Speak your piece."

At least he hadn't shut the door in his face, though it was clear by the tension around Julian's mouth that he wanted to.

"Do you really want me to talk out here where others can hear?"

Julian glanced around, seeing the open window of the apartment next door. After a second's pause, he stepped aside. "You have one minute."

Russell looked around the space: built-in bookcases crammed with books, drapes drawn against the midday sun, splashing a bloodred hue over the room. Julian was still corded with muscle, oddly enough, bringing back the image of the boy again. Julian had started building his strength, whipping through his homework so he could lift weights, running for hours, as though he could tame Darkness with physical strength. Obviously he was still playing at that game, but now he saw only resignation in his son's eyes, the color of a chip of a frozen blue sea.

"Your anger, it's over your mother still?" Julian had shut him out that first time he came to see him. Now Russell needed to resolve this issue, needed to reunite with his son.

Julian leaned against the back of the kitchen counter, his arms crossed over his chest like a shield. He didn't need it. The anger set in his features, and the bulging muscles of his arms were shield enough. "Her murder didn't just go away."

"I have explained all that to you. It was an accident. The courts even said so. She tripped and fell off the cliff."

"But you and I know different."

It was unfortunate that the boy witnessed it. Russell kept his voice gentle, conciliatory. "She cheated on me. It was a harsh way for you to learn about Darkness and how it reacts to such violations. Perhaps now I could control it, but not then. Not when I was young and in love."

"Yeah, thanks for passing that on to me."

He had seen his son's Darkness. He had incited it himself, having this very discussion. "Surely you can't blame me for that. I didn't know it could be inherited."

Julian laughed, or what could possibly pass as a laugh, without a smile or light in his eyes. "I don't blame you. I merely hate you."

"But Darkness is not a bad thing, Julian."

"Not a 'bad thing'? That I can't ever be with a woman for fear of Becoming a monster and tossing her off a cliff or worse? That I've got a temper that overcomes me?" He pointed to a gash in the wall.

"You just have to learn to control it. That will come with time. I can help." He put his hand on Julian's shoulder, but his son flinched away. "Think about it. You and I, working together. A team."

"Like hell. You're too busy chasing down some woman to be a member of a team."

Russell gritted his teeth. "You have never loved,

or you would understand. When we love, it consumes us. Like a fire within. Once I have my love by my side, I will be stronger, more stable. Until then I'm no good to you or anyone. I am distracted. I know what it is to have a goal, to put everything on the line for the greater good. My brother and I did that, but we failed. You think me dark, vile, and weak. I am none of those things. Let me show you. Torus has done a good job raising you, but you haven't had a real father in your life since you were twelve. Let me in. I'll never abandon you, Julian. Never again."

Julian's eyes softened at that. A boy needs a father, he thought, even a boy of twenty-seven. He had lost so much, first his mother in a violent way, and then his innocence, and then his father. He had gone through much before Torus and his men had taken him in. Russell knew the Callorians. They suppressed their emotions, their passions. They would have taken care of Julian, but had he known a connection?

He pressed on. "I need your help. This is where we work together, just you and me. There is a woman, a very troublesome woman, and a man. They are in the way of my accomplishing my heart's desire. Other than reuniting with my son, this goal is the most important thing to me."

Julian's eyebrows knitted together. "I don't understand this obsession you have for a woman."

"Someday you will, Julian. I promise you will, and you'll—"

"No, I won't. I will never let a woman push me to mindless violence, or to this weakness I see in you. I don't see the purpose in emotions."

Torus had trained him well. The boy was hardened, but was he beyond hope? "They have tricked you into thinking that way about emotions. They can be incredible, exhilarating. Let me teach you to master your abilities. Let me be your father."

"I'll think about it."

Not an outright rejection at least. Russell let out a breath of disappointment. He'd hoped to snag him now. "Think about us, working together. Harnessing your power. And think about changing the world, Julian. Inside you is a beast, and it can do amazing things."

He walked away, trying not to look back and see if his son was watching him. It would only be another disappointment. He got into the rental car and pulled up the newspaper article on his phone, staring at the girl who kept him from achieving his goal.

"Jessie." The word had come out as a growl.

He spotted another link on the page of the carnival story and clicked on it. He read the related story about the girl who was benefiting from the carnival. Jessie's name was only mentioned once. But it was a very interesting mention indeed.

CHAPTER 10

Lachlan had brushed off his part of the bargain, but Jessie wasn't letting him off the hook. He went to get dressed, and she went to her car to sort through the clothes she'd packed, consolidating what she'd need for her enforced stay. Lord, him standing in his briefs telling her she wasn't alone anymore, seeing her need. She could have melted into a puddle. Okay, she'd liked the sound of being Magnus's girl when Lachlan first assumed it, the idea of belonging to someone like that Jackson Brown song of years ago, "Somebody's Baby."

I can't believe I told him I wanted to kiss him. That was brilliant. Never gonna happen.

No, Lachlan would never let a kiss, or anything else, happen. He already hated himself, and no matter that she wasn't Magnus's girl, he would only see her as that.

She grabbed up three bags and turned, letting out a scream. "Ohmigod, you startled me."

"Sorry." Lachlan held out one hand to take her

load. "Didn't want you out here by yourself."

She nodded toward the sword he held in his other hand. "You're doing an admirable job of protecting me."

He grunted. "I'm not looking for a pat on the head. Like you said about donating bone marrow, it's just the right thing to do."

He waited for her to walk in front of him, then stepped up beside her. His jersey pants rode low on his hips, and the white T-shirt clung to his shoulders.

"It wasn't the right thing to do, though. I'm scared to death I'm going to get a call from her someday telling me she turned into a horrible creature."

"Like with Magnus, you saved her life at a cost."

"Yeah, but neither of them got to make that choice. It's not like I could tell her. Besides, I was her last hope. She probably would have said yes anyway. As you know, when you're desperate, you'll take any lifeline. I only hope she doesn't get it."

"The Darkness seems to be a form in itself, not attached to your blood or body. You used Darkness to heal Magnus, but not Hayley. I think she'll be okay."

The irony of Lachlan was, he thought he was a terrible person, but he showed his heart, his goodness.

Once inside the house, they turned left and went into the room she'd be using.

"I'll bring in the cooler," he said, setting the bags inside the door.

"I'm going to change into something I can work out in. Meet you there."

Her penguin. Penny looked as bedraggled as Jessie felt. She tucked the stuffed animal into her bag where she could see it, then dug through another bag and found black yoga pants and a Spandex workout top. She threw on the matching jacket, tucked her feet into sneakers, and found Lachlan waiting by the door. They made another trip to the garage, this time bringing everything to the kitchen. It felt oddly domestic, unpacking bags of food, putting things away together . . . too much like she was moving in.

You'll be packing up here, too, before long.

She changed her dark thoughts. "This kitchen rocks. I love the red glossy tiles and black cabinets."

The countertops were gray slate, and all the appliances were stainless steel. It was shaped around the corner of the house.

" 'Rocks'?"

"Yeah. It's cool."

"Ah. Groovy."

"You don't really keep up with the outside world much, do you? I'll bet you don't Tweet or Facebook or anything."

"There was a time I lived on the computer. I socialized there." He left it at that, and she quelled her inclination to probe as to exactly how he was socializing. "Not anymore. I pick up a magazine once in a while, but I let the satellite dish subscription go a while back, and no, I've never been on Facebook."

Not that she had a page herself. No one to keep up with, no one to friend. She unpacked her cooler. "I'm making lunch from my food. You haven't descended to bread and water, but it's not far from it."

"I wasn't exactly expecting guests. Speaking of food, you never did get to eat this morning."

She tugged grapes off a bunch before putting them in the fridge. "I'm not hungry now." Thinking about why they'd missed their snack, and what he wanted her to do next, shriveled her appetite.

"How about a coffee?"

"Mm, you tempt me." She turned and met his eyes at that. *Oh, boy.* A spark of electricity seemed to arc between them, not unlike that weird magic of his.

"I can make you a latte, if I remember how Mum did it. She was the coffee fiend in the family." He pressed a button on a square machine that was tucked into a corner of the kitchen and it whirred to life.

She felt her body move toward it automatically. "Is that a—"

"Espresso machine. That's what she called it anyway. Mm, she had the same look on your face as you do when Dad gave it to her for Christmas."

She was probably doing everything but drooling, and wiped her mouth just in case. "Lucky. You can have a latte every day, whenever you want, without paying five dollars and eighty-two cents." The thought of it brought moisture to her eyes.

He held up a jug of milk. "I'll take that as a yes."

She put her hand to her chest. "I would ohmigod *love* a latte."

He got out a mondo mug from the upper cabinet and then the little pot and pitcher, grinning the whole time. Amused by her, yes, but damn if she cared. It transformed his face and created smile lines at the corners of his eyes and mouth.

"Mum put a spoonful of sugar in the milk and five drops of French vanilla."

"Perfect."

As he went through the steaming process, she imagined him wearing only one of those barista aprons and briefs, which unfortunately wasn't a big stretch of her imagination.

"Mm, Heaven." He turned around, and she added, "The aroma of fresh-brewed coffee. Nothing like it."

A minute later he handed her a steaming mug.

She wrapped her hands around it and inhaled. "How'd you know I like lattes?"

"Maybe I'm a mind reader."

She took a sip. "This is so good I could faint."

He pulled out a knife from the butcher block, flipped it handle out, and handed it to her.

She blinked, staring at it. "You want me to stab you?"

"Cut my hair."

"Why? It's beautiful."

"Reason one. I don't want 'beautiful' hair. I've let it go, like everything else in my life, these last months. It didn't matter before."

She hid her smile as she took another sip. "But now you want to impress me."

"Why would I need to do anything more? I swept you off your feet at our first meeting."

"As I recall, I swept *you* off your feet."

He nodded. "Knocked me on my arse, you did."

Their eyes locked for a moment, making her stomach jump.

He pulled his hair back. "Reason two: it gets in the way when I'm fighting. And gives the enemy something to grab onto."

"Okay, first of all, you don't cut hair with a knife." She waved it away. "Scissors are better."

He reached into a drawer and produced a pair of silver scissors.

She didn't take them. "You know, the salon near the music store was having a 'Locks of Love' promotion last week. That's the organization that provides wigs for kids who have conditions where they lose their hair. You get a free cut and style when you donate the hair. Good cut, good cause, good price."

He set the scissors down. "But I'm not after some fancy cut."

"No, you wouldn't be." She tilted her head, studying him. He was rough, but not unkempt.

"You've lived out in the boonies your whole life. I don't imagine you had reason to impress anyone."

He crossed his arms in front of him as he leaned back against the counter. "My mum cut my hair when it got to be too much, at least in her opinion. I didn't really care one way or the other. Magnus either, until he got his freedom." He laughed. "Then he cared a lot. He was so pretty, with those curls. Still is, though he hates when I say it. When we'd go into town for supplies or a movie, women would make a fuss. Later, it was girls who'd come over and say something about his curls. Once he was a teenager, he didn't mind that at all. He'd take any excuse to chat up the girls. That wasn't my thing."

"Girls weren't your thing?" She didn't know why she wanted to poke at him a bit, but she loved his facial expressions. He did this thing with his eyebrows that accented the intriguing slant to his eyes.

"Thinking I'm a winky wanky wonder boy?"

"A what? Is that some Scottish word for gay?"

"Heard this homophobic bloke say it on a BBC show once." He ran his finger around the inside of the steam pitcher, then stuck the foam in his mouth. "I go for girls, thank you very much. They're soft and curvy and everything wonderful in the world."

She couldn't help smiling at that, especially the glitter in his eyes. Given his isolated existence, a spike of curiosity pricked at her. "I don't imagine you got to meet many girls living the way you did."

"Not much. As soon as the man who'd been hunting us was dead, Magnus raced out into the world like a dog unleashed at last. Hooked up with a band, started hitting bars, socializing."

"Hooking up with women, you mean." Hm, was that the kind of socializing Lachlan had done on the computer?

"He was making up for lost time, aye, but he used protection, so no worries there. At least he'll know what to do when you . . . well, you know."

She raised an eyebrow, a wry smile on her lips. "What about you?"

He looked surprised, obviously not expecting her to turn the questioning to him. "What about me?"

Now that the thought was planted in her mind, she had to explore it. "When you got the freedom, did you run to town, too?"

"I was never comfortable meeting new people like Magnus was. I stayed round here, helping my dad with his research. Magnus, though, kept trying to tempt me into going out, telling me about all the wickedness in the world." He gave her a wicked smile to go along with that. "I was going to give in, but then"—that smile faded—"after my psychosis, none of that mattered."

She wasn't sure if he was being cagey or obtuse. "So, before that, you didn't . . . socialize? In person, I mean."

He got that cute expression again, his mouth

turning up slightly in a smile. "Are you asking if I'm a virgin? Getting a wee bit personal, aren't you?"

A laugh burst out of her. "Oh, do not pretend modesty with me now. You blew that card when you were standing there in your skivvies and not the least bit bothered."

He shrugged. "Magnus and I spent a lot of time running around in our skivvies in the heat of summer. But I do make a point to get dressed when I go out in public."

"Smart of you. Nice as you look in your skivvies, the public in general takes a dislike to nudity." Oops. Had she actually said that?

"Why, thank you."

She liked this more relaxed side of him. "So? Are you a virgin?" Now that she'd introduced the question, in her mind at least, she wanted to know. Really badly.

"Aye." He said it without shame or even a hint of chagrin.

The thought of it tickled through her like fingers skittering across her stomach. She took another sip of her coffee, focusing on the light brown liquid in her mug and not on him, because she loved the idea of this gorgeous man being a virgin like she was. She realized that when he'd made the snorting sound at her confession that she was a virgin, he hadn't been making fun of her. He probably couldn't believe the coincidence. "I don't want to be a virgin anymore."

He was taking a drink of water and nearly choked on it.

"I wasn't making a request," she added. At least, she didn't think she was.

He pounded on his chest and shook his head. "Nothing to do with what you just said."

Yeah, right.

He grabbed up his sword from where it leaned against the corner of the kitchen with a graceful swipe. "Let's get to work."

"Sure, go and ruin my coffee."

She followed, knowing he was right, hating that he was right. He had a slight limp, from his ankle wound, no doubt. Still, his butt had a nice sway as she followed him down the hallway. Even in those old jersey pants and T-shirt, with his loose mess of waves hanging down his back he looked as yummy as the latte. She remembered seeing him at the music store, stopping at the sight of him with his rock-and-roll looks.

"I'm not some innocent, prim and proper flower," she said.

He spun around. "Did I say you were?"

"No. But people have this misconception about women who haven't . . . you know. I like the idea of sex. I have a vibrator."

He slapped his hand over his forehead.

"What? Is that an improper thing to say? According to *Cosmopolitan*, self-pleasure is no big deal. Recommended even, for a single gal."

"You're asking *me* about propriety, the guy who

was standing in his skivvies and not bothered?"
He dropped his hand and pinned her with a look.
"Stop talking about your sex. I mean, about sex.
You know, if you and Magnus marry, you'll be
my sister. So when I watch you walking down the
aisle, I don't want to be thinking about you diddling yourself with a vibrator."

Oh, the idea of that! First the diddling part, and
then . . . she punched his upper arm, her fist connecting with hard flesh. "Stop marrying me off."
God, the thought, having Lachlan as a brother-in-
law when she'd had lustful thoughts about him.

They entered the studio and he snapped on the
lights. He hung the sword on hooks designed for
that purpose, walked over to an elaborate stereo
rack and cranked Bon Jovi's "Living on a Prayer."
He grabbed the bottom of his shirt and pulled it
over his head, tossing it to the floor.

She hated that he had injuries because of her.
She'd dragged two men into her danger. But Lachlan was dangerous, too. And not only because he'd
tangled in her heart like a vine, with his loneliness
and honor.

She slipped off her jacket, set it on the floor,
and took one of the swords down. The weight of
it made her bend over, but she stood straighter.
"Teach me how to fight with a sword."

"Uh-uh, you're not getting out of working with
Darkness."

She approached him, sword held up and out
to the side, sort of threatening, but probably not

threatening at all considering *she* was holding it. "After you tell me about your ability."

"I don't have an ability anymore, other than the one time I astral-projected by accident and saw the future. I couldn't do it again." Those last words came out hard and brittle.

She shook her head, trying to look intimidating. "Both times you fought Russell, I saw a blurry form, like a ghostly imprint all around you."

Surprise transformed his expression. "You saw it, too?"

Okay, he was admitting it. Sort of. "Wait, I'll show you."

She gently set the sword down, dashed back to her room and grabbed her phone out of her bag. A smart phone was a big expense, but it was cheaper and more portable than a computer. She came back, touching the screen to go to her security link as she walked.

She stepped up beside him, holding out the phone so he could see the screen, too. "My security system records whenever someone trips the alarm. So I have us on video."

"Kinky."

She shot him a look. "Shush. Here it is."

It was odd watching this with Lachlan now that she knew him. "Right there." She pointed to his image. "It's hard to see on this tiny screen. I watched it on a computer at work."

He squinted as he watched. "I can't really see it." He held out his hand and stared at the back of it. His expression darkened. "It's only happened since that spontaneous projection. I see hands on my sword handle. Not my hands, but big burly ones. Like you said, a ghostly imprint. Only when I've fought, when I feel anger and adrenaline. When I want to kill."

"Did you want to kill me?"

He met her gaze, heaviness in his eyes. "I didn't want to kill you, but I would have, to save Magnus. Now I'll kill to save you."

Her throat tightened at that. He meant both. "So what is it, Lachlan?"

"Whatever it is, when I feel the energy, it's something bigger and darker than me. I mean to find out. My anger is his rage."

"You said 'his.'"

"I did, didn't I? But what is he?"

She looked around the empty room. "Come out, come out, whoever you are."

Lachlan looked at his hands. "Maybe I have to be pissed off before he'll come."

"Then be pissed off."

He took his sword from the hooks and got into a fighting stance. "That's easy. All I have to do is think about that bastard with his hands on you. Trying to use your mother and my safety to get you to go with him. What does he think you are, stupid?"

He slashed with each sentence, his jaw rigid, eyes blazing. He was fierce, his moves efficient and smooth, his muscles flexing, hair flowing.

Her chest tightened. There, a shadow moving a millisecond behind him! She picked up the sword she'd set on the floor, fingers tensed on the handle.

"Come on, you bastard! I can see your hands," Lachlan said through gritted teeth.

The form took shape, a man as big as Magnus, in a kilt, black hair in a ponytail, with a full beard. Like a special effect, he appeared as a transparent overlay on top of Lachlan. Her mouth dropped open and she pointed to him, unable to say a word.

That wasn't necessary. Lachlan stared at his reflection in the mirror, chest heaving but eyes wide.

"Dinna call me a bastard," the form said. " 'Tis disrespectful to your kin."

The form's brogue was far heavier than Lachlan's.

"Who the hell are you?" Lachlan said, his voice a low growl.

"Olaf. I'd shake your hand, but . . ." He lifted his arms, then let them drop.

She held onto her sword as she walked closer. "You're a ghost?"

"I'm no' a spook. Don't know what to call me, exactly. Olaf will do."

Lachlan tried to step sideways, but the form followed, attached to him. "But you're dead."

"Aye, though I don't like that word either." He shrugged. "But I am. Dead."

Lachlan furrowed his eyebrows. "Did you say you're my kin?"

"Aye. I'm sure that's why I could attach myself to ye. At first I thought ye were a ghost standing there on the battlefield. I were lyin' there wi' my life blood draining out of me body, and you jus' appeared out of the mist. Ye weren't an angel, not carrying your half-lang sword."

He fisted a beefy hand at his chest. "I could feel ye, and knew ye to be kin. Come to pull me to the great beyond, I thought. Not that I deserved that. My soul lifted and went right to ye, drawn like a horse to oats. Not jus' because of our relation; I felt your fighting nature, your want to kill the British and fight for freedom. I went into ye and been here ever since."

Lachlan's body twitched. "You *possessed* me?"

"Nae, nothin' like that. I—" He looked up, scratching a mangy beard. "—attached myself to ye."

Lachlan's eyes narrowed and his jaw tightened. "You were the reason I went mad and slashed at my family."

Olaf lowered his head. "Bad bit of business, that. Once I joined with ye, we were a frenzy of energy and rage, and ye got lost in it. My soul kept fighting, and it wasna until the big lad knocked you out that I seen we weren't at Culloden anymore."

Lachlan jerked his sword toward his neck. "Get out of me."

"Och, ye would cut off your own head to be rid of me?"

Jessie ran forward, gripping his hands with her free one. "Don't. Stay in control."

"Listen to your lassie. Ye held on when ye were fighting the man who became the beast. I don't mean to take over. The first time our energies collided, it threw us off. That willna happen again. Besides, how else did ye think ye could do that strange kind of traveling when ye saw your brother dying? And the magic that helped ye fight the beast?"

"You did that?" Lachlan was looking at his reflection, his expression taut. He hadn't lowered the sword yet, and Jessie hadn't loosened her grip.

"Not so eager to get rid of me now, are ye?"

Jessie moved her hands away, comfortable that Lachlan wasn't going to slash himself. She could see him processing all this.

"I don't trust you," Lachlan said. "You made me kill my own mum."

"I couldna know what would happen. She knew ye dinna do it on purpose. I saw her soul leave her body."

Lachlan took a quick breath and turned to Jessie. "You do see him, right? I've not gone round the bend?"

"I see him."

"What do I do with him?" This time he was asking himself, his voice barely audible.

"Use me, lad. Ye got a big problem and a pretty lass to protect. I can help."

Lachlan still hadn't let go of the sword, but he'd pointed it downward. "You won't take over?"

"Nae."

"I can send you off anytime I want?"

"Aye. Except when you're fighting. Then ye draw me to ye. We both have the MacLeod blood running through our veins. The need to fight for what's right. The need to kill what stands in the way." He looked at Jessie. "And the need to protect what's ours."

Even while those words tightened her chest, she said, "Oh, I'm not—"

"Be gone!" Lachlan said, startling the rest of her words right out of her.

The apparition disappeared.

Lachlan patted his body, wincing as he hit his injury on his side. "He's gone. It worked."

She shivered. "That was crazy real."

He ran his fingers through his hair, pacing. "What do I do with him?" he asked again.

"Well, he probably saved your life when you were fighting Russell and those dogs. His magic did, anyway. You're damned good with a sword, but without the magic, I don't think you could have destroyed those dogs."

He came to a stop in front of her. "Then I keep him around. And hope he doesn't take over."

CHAPTER 11

Lachlan stood in front of the MacLeod family tree he'd put together on his bedroom wall. At the top, next to the clan flag, was a plaque with the family crest and motto.

"I was wondering what this was," she said, standing beside him. "It didn't look like To Do stickies."

"I was sitting here one night and just started writing down what I knew on the Post-its. Before I knew it, I'd used the whole pad." He pointed to one. "My mum came here from Scotland when she was fifteen. She missed her homeland, talked about it all the time. She probably would have gone back if she hadn't met my father. She would have been alive if she had."

"You don't know that. I think when it's our time to go, it doesn't matter where we are." At least she hoped that was the case.

"I think one decision can change your life, or screw up someone else's. Sometimes it's just taking one way to work instead of another. In my case, it was to sneak around projecting even after my father told me to cut back. You heard Olaf. The rage, the need for conflict, it's in me. I went back to witness battles, wanting so badly to participate."

"Could you?"

"I couldn't move anything at the target location, but I could be seen. My soul projects, so anyone at the location will see what they think is a ghost. We weren't supposed to reveal ourselves. Sometimes I did."

He could feel her, the heat of her body, her energy, and her total focus on what he was saying. "How?"

"I saw ugly things, like men raping women. All's fair in love and war? That's what they thought. My father was such a purist when it came to time, to affecting the past. If we saw something like that, he would make us leave. 'It's already happened a long time ago. We can't change it,' he'd tell me while I was going crazy not being able to help."

He glanced at her. "But when he wasn't around, I could do as I pleased. And what man wants to force himself on a woman when he's seen a ghost? Kind of spoils the mood."

Her smile, full of pride and warmth, tightened his chest. "So you went back to help people," she said.

You don't deserve that warmth. "Mostly I went back for bloodlust. Don't make it into something altruistic. I was cocky and rebellious. I disobeyed and I killed my mum."

She touched his arm. "It was the fusion of you and Olaf. Don't you see? It was an accident."

"But that fusion would never have happened if I had shown restraint."

"You're exasperating."

He looked at her, tilting his head. "That's all you've got? Come, you can think of worse things than that."

She laughed, a full-out beautiful sound that lit her hazel eyes. Even though he didn't deserve to bask in it, he let it unfurl in his chest and open his heart just a little anyway.

As their gazes met, though, her laughter quieted. "Yeah, I could think of other words, but you wouldn't want me to say them. They're not the awful things you want to hear."

He turned away, facing the notes stuck to the wall. He could fall for her so easily. It surprised him that he hadn't killed that part of himself after all. Not only had his body awakened, his heart had, too—amazing, because he'd never felt like this with anyone.

To fall would shatter any shred of self-respect he might have left. "After my mum's death, I wanted to connect to her somehow. She had a folder full of notes on her family, but I made my own. It's not pretty, but it gave me something to focus on."

He searched through the notes. "Olaf said he died at Culloden, so he would have been born around here." He pointed to one of the branches of the clan. "There he is, born 1720. He was twenty-six when he was killed, no wife or children." His father would have calculated the exact age, down to the day.

She pointed to a group of notes connected by a line that separated them from the tree and then continued down. "Here, the spelling of the name changes from MacLeod to McLeod."

"It had something to do with them running to Ireland. They came here in the next generation."

She followed the progression with her finger all the way down to the piece of paper that held his and Magnus's names. She stood so close in front of him that he could smell her scent, could reach out and touch her with the slightest move. He breathed her in, filling his lungs, fighting not to lean forward and touch his mouth to her hair.

As though she sensed what he felt, she turned to face him, her eyes searching his. "I changed my mind. I want to do more than just want you to kiss me." She gave her head a quick shake. "I mean . . . kiss me, Lachlan. I know you want it, too."

Her words shivered through his body. "Aye, sod that I am. But there was a time you wanted to kiss Magnus, remember? You daydreamed about it. I saw those romance novels at your apartment. Were they your research? Tell me, did you use your vibrator while you fantasized about him? What kinds of things did you do in those fantasies?"

Go ahead, slap me. Tell me again how utterly rude I am. She'd be right, too, but he needed to jam those images into his brain to remind him how wrong wanting her was.

She didn't slap him or look horrified or even angry. In fact, she looked speculative. "You were right. I was getting a bit hot in the studio. You want to know what I fantasized?" She put her hand on his chest. "Doing this." She slid it slowly, agonizingly, down his stomach, her fingertips brushing the waistband of his pants. He should move away. Run like hell.

"And this." She stepped so close, her body pressed against his. He tried bloody hard to make himself step back. That wasn't happening. Or at least not to react. Too late for that.

She slid her fingers into his hair. "This." She pressed her mouth against his, moving it back and forth over his. "But I wasn't thinking about Magnus. I was hot from watching you."

His lips softened, and in a blink he yanked her fully against him, dipping his tongue into her mouth, tasting her. He let his mouth move instinctively, fitting hers, imprinting every sensation into his cells. It was like what he'd seen in the movies he'd watched over the years, and it was different, too. It was real, the feel of her hot, moist mouth, her tongue dancing with his.

His hands slid up and down her backside, itching to slide inside the waistband of her pants, to cup her arse.

What the bloody hell do you think you're doing? Proving that you're crap?

They both stepped back simultaneously, breathing hard.

"I don't know what got into me," she said, putting the tips of her fingers against her mouth. "Maybe I have a dead prostitute's energy clinging to me." She gave him a wry smile.

He couldn't help smiling at that, but it quickly fled. "And I am an idiot."

"You're only an idiot because you're fighting a lost cause."

"The last time I gave in to something I wanted that I shouldn't have, I killed my mum."

She grasped his hands in hers. "Kissing me isn't going to get anyone killed."

"It would kill me if, when Magnus wakes, I had to say, 'Glad you're back, and oh, by the way, I stole the first girl you ever said was special. Sorry 'bout that.'" He realized he was stroking her fingers and released her hands. "Until you came along, I had no hope of ever regaining my honor. But protecting you, making this situation right, and not giving in to my feelings for you, I get the sense of it again."

He pointed to the clan battle cry, on a plaque along with the clan badge: a bull's head between two flags. "Hold fast. That's what I have to do. You tempt me, aye, you do." He brushed aside her bangs. "And not just because you're beautiful. You're brave and strong and you've got a fire for life. I see why Magnus was drawn to you, and that's all I can think about: Magnus was drawn to you. I *need* to keep this last scrap of honor, Jess."

Her chin trembled. "I don't want to be a source of angst for you. Maybe what I feel for you is because you're helping me."

"What do you feel for me? No, don't answer that."

"I'm not sure I've got it figured out myself. Why I want to kiss you, that's easy. Why I want to go into your shadows and turn on the light, not so much. Maybe we're drawn to each other because we're lost souls. We are drawn to each other; we can't deny that. But getting involved would cost too much. Your honor, maybe even your relationship with Magnus. And me, I can't dream of having a boyfriend or husband. I'd be afraid of losing my temper and Becoming Darkness every day of my life. I can't have children because I'd pass it on to them. There are many pleasures in life besides falling in love and having a family. Those will have to do."

God but he wanted to pull her against him. To pick up where they'd left off, to hell with honor. He couldn't bear to think of her living out her life without children, not the way she'd interacted with them at the music store. Not without love. No, she'd find it with Magnus. They'd work it out. And he would have to see her and know the taste of her and how she felt against his body. He would get plenty of torture then.

"I want to find out more about Darkness," he said. "I'm going to project back to the day your mother was killed. Maybe I'll see something that will give us a clue. Before I took the antidote, I could travel at will, just pick a date and place or event and go. Past or present, but not future." He hadn't been able to travel back to the carnival, though. "How long ago did it happen?"

Her expression darkened. "Fifteen years ago."

He flopped down on the bed, settled his hands on his stomach and closed his eyes. He waited for the familiar spinning sensation. Nothing. He sat up, rolled his eyes upward. "Olaf!"

The Highlander's energy buzzed through him, and Lachlan could see the imprint of him on his own body.

"Ye called upon me? I am honored. Or are ye gonna tell me to be gone again, and rudely at that?"

Lachlan felt his mouth quirk in a smile he tried to bank. "Ask the lass here. I can be mighty rude. Not as rude as, say, someone latching onto a person without asking permission, I might add."

"Is that what ye summoned me for, to take me to task?"

"No, I need your help with the astral travel. Seems I can't do it without you."

The ghostly man crossed his arms over his—well, Lachlan's—chest. "Told ye."

"I mean to go back and solve a mystery for the lass here."

"Are ye asking? I haven't heard ye ask yet."

Another roll of his eyes. "Please help me astral travel."

"Be happy to."

Lachlan dropped back, his body going limp. He felt the weightlessness, the spinning. He was in a dark space and heard soft whimpers and stuttered breathing. A door opened, sending enough light in for him to see a little girl: Jessie, with long brown hair and eyes filled with fear and tears. The sight of her grabbed his chest like a fist.

She nudged the door open and inched out of a closet, pulling herself by her fingers until she could see down the hall into the kitchen.

Blood. Lots of it, slowly spreading across the white tile floor, and a woman lying in it. Jessie whimpered, her body trembling. He wanted to go to the kitchen, but a stronger need kept him there, with her. She was so focused on the scene, she didn't see his ghostly image there. He wouldn't leave her alone, though.

He couldn't see either man, but he heard them. One wanted to heal the woman with Darkness. The other man didn't want that to happen. They stepped into view, Russell squaring off with the other man. Except the man who looked like Russell was really her father. They talked about Jessie, and Russell wanted her contained, trained. Was that what he was after now?

The men Became wolves, fighting, tearing up the kitchen. Lachlan started to go to the kitchen, but her whimpers kept him there. He was torn. He compromised, moving out a few feet when the black smoke surrounded the gray smoke.

"I banish you to the Void, Henry!" Out of the smoke, the man appeared, the one he knew as Russell. A thin trail of gray smoke drifted upward, following Russell's pointing hand. "Go and be no more."

Jessie got to her feet, stumbling.

No! He wanted to warn her, to stop her, which was ridiculous because she was obviously all right.

Curiously, the man knelt by her mother and sent the Darkness into her body, as Jessie had done with Magnus. But it wouldn't penetrate, and he shot to his feet and turned around. Jessie was running toward him now, holding the penguin he'd seen in her bedroom.

He knew the instant she realized he wasn't her daddy. She came to a stop, and he grabbed for her. She yelled, "Fade!" and disappeared. Russell swiped at her, but Lachlan saw a door at the end of the hallway move as someone passed by. Russell kept searching for her, heading toward the room. Lachlan grabbed his sword and followed the man.

He felt hands gripping his wrists, and his eyes snapped open. He stood now, hands on his sword handle, Jessie standing in front of him with her hands on his wrists.

He'd done it again, acted it out. "What the hell are you doing? I could have cut you."

"I knew what was happening, and I wasn't going to let you hurt yourself."

He dropped the sword on the bed, rubbing his forehead. The fatigue he usually felt after projecting weighed heavily on him. He could see Olaf's ghostly image, could feel his fighting energy. Or was it his own?

"That's what happened with my mum," he said. "Remember when I said it was like being in REM sleep, where my body was paralyzed? With Olaf, it's like the sleep disorder where you're not paralyzed. People drive, walk, even run through glass windows. I could have hurt you."

She stood right there in front of him. "I'm not afraid of you and your sword, Lachlan."

The words stirred him. "Then you're a fool."

"Look, if anyone can handle your . . . situation, I can. I've dealt with worse." Her mouth tightened. "As you know."

He touched her cheek, because he couldn't stop himself. If he could go back and change what had happened, prevent her father from being killed. Except . . . he wasn't dead.

She leaned into his hand, probably an involuntary movement. "You look . . . haunted. What did you see?"

Focus on that, not on her. "Did your father ever mention someplace called the Void?"

She shook her head.

"Russell sent your father's soul there. I could see it go."

"You mean he could still be . . . alive? Or here, like Olaf?"

"I'm no' alive," Olaf said mournfully, head drooping. "Dead I am, ne'er to come back. My own kin sends me off like a bad dog what's peed on the rug."

Lachlan said, "For pity's sake, I was testing your word."

"Is that an apology?"

"You can take it that way."

Olaf patted his chest. "Ye need me. Let my men down at Culloden, I did. Should have been ready for the enemy to come up on our flank at Culchunaig. Left us wide open to the loyalist Highlanders who betrayed us. Our own clansmen fought for the British. 'Twas shameful, it was."

Lachlan realized that for Olaf, that had happened mere months ago. This cousin many times removed had died at roughly his age, fighting for what he believed in. Maybe it was as much their sense of failure as their hunger for battle that united them.

Still, it was the getting rid of him that worried Lachlan.

"Olaf, snap out of it," Lachlan said. "You can't do anything about that. You *can* help us now. Have you—"

"I had a lass, too. As bonnie as Jessie, she was, and a spitfire, too."

Lachlan reined in his impatience. "Olaf, I'm sorry for your loss."

"Sorry, that ye are. I get to live longer through ye, and ye hardly live at all. Not till she came along."

Lachlan rolled his eyes again. "Can we focus? Have you heard of the Void?"

Olaf paused. "Dinna know what it's called, but there's a place, a dead area, if you will. Scary. I've felt it around the bloke what turns to the wolf. Like if the area got too close, I'd be sucked in."

Jessie stepped closer. "You think my father is there?"

"Sounds like it. Olaf, how do we get there?"

"Dinna know. I can have a look." He didn't sound very enthusiastic about it.

"Please." She said the word on a breath.

After a pause, Olaf said, "I'll try my best, lass." His energy left Lachlan in a soft *whoosh*.

"Don't get your hopes up too much, Jess. That was a long time ago."

"I know. But if there's a chance of bringing my father back to his body, I have to take it."

"Of course you do." He expected nothing less of her.

CHAPTER 12

Lachlan and Jessie waited for fifteen minutes for Olaf to return.

She spun her fingers in her hair, the movement growing faster as time ticked by. "He was worried about getting sucked in. What if he does?"

"Then we carry on. Instead of sitting round here worrying, let's go into town so I can get that haircut." He grabbed his black coat, tattered and bloody at the bottom edge, and paused. "My favorite one, too."

"Sorry."

He looked at her. "It's just a piece of material. I've got others."

She followed him through the kitchen and a dining room to another room. It was crammed with pictures, and too much furniture. He walked to the closet, and she looked at some of the pictures stacked on the floor. Family pictures, some posed, some candid. A folded blanket that looked so soft she *had* to touch it. Two televisions, a stereo system pushed off to the side. The stuff he'd taken out of his room.

He walked out of the closet holding a coat a lot like the ruined one. "Ready?"

"When are you going to stop punishing yourself?"

He looked at the coat. "It's not that bad."

"This is all your stuff, isn't it? You took it out of your room so you could live like a monk. When does your self-imposed sentence end?"

"When I can get something right, for you and for Magnus."

"When you sit out there meditating, what are you thinking about? I've tried meditation, and it's damned hard to clear your mind completely for more than a second or three."

"I ask God for forgiveness."

"He's pretty easy about that, you know. You ask, He forgives. You're the hard-ass."

"I know it's not right asking someone's forgiveness when I can't forgive myself."

Lachlan walked past her, leaving her to follow again. Fine, she'd follow. He punched in a code on the alarm pad, and they walked out to the garage. He entered a code for a bay that did not hold her vehicle. His vintage red truck was revealed inch by inch as the door rose.

He opened his door and carefully set the sword in the back. It had been scary when he'd grabbed the sword, an agonized ferocity in eyes that were clearly seeing something that wasn't there. Her first instinct had been to run, but she was tired of running all the time. Running from Russell. From affection. From wanting Lachlan. So she'd taken hold of his wrists and stopped him. She felt stronger for it.

"Why swords?" she asked. "Because of your Scottish history?"

"That and I like the primitive feel of them. Broadswords were considered the darling weapon of the Scots. Their style was to rush onto the enemy. I don't trust guns as a rule. They misfire, jam up. Dad trained us to shoot from early on. I held my first gun at age five."

"Five? That's ridiculous. And probably illegal."

"We didn't live by the rules of society. But to be clear, I'm talking BB guns. At least until we were ten. He wanted us to be able to protect ourselves. Not only from the man who was hunting him, but we did live way out in the woods. Bears, cats, crazy people . . . best to be prepared."

She knew prepared. "My dad must have lived the same way, always looking over his shoulder. He didn't teach me to shoot, but he gave me this symbol." She ran her fingers over the cross in her skin under her shirt. "But Russell threw Darkness over me so I couldn't hide." It left her bereft, knowing that this symbol wasn't protection. She'd had it carved into her skin for nothing.

"Don't you see? It's Darkness that lets you Fade.

Your dad wasn't ready to tell you that yet, so he came up with the symbol. That was easier for a kid to understand."

She walked around to the passenger side and stopped at the sight of a car's carcass and an array of parts all over the concrete floor in the last bay. "It looks like a car exploded."

"A 1969 Camaro. That's what I do."

"Tear apart cars?"

He chuckled. "Aye, actually. Then put them back together. I buy old cars, rusting masses of metal, and make them pretty again. People pay a lot of money for a vintage car. Word got out and now they come to me with cars they want restored."

She looked at all the pieces and realized there was a method to the chaos. "This truck is one of your projects, too?"

She saw a hint of pride as he patted the roof. "Just finished it."

She turned back to the shell of the car. "So what got you into doing this? It must take a lot of time, and it's probably a lot of work."

"Aye, and that's a good thing. I can lose myself in the process, and I get the satisfaction of seeing it through to a finished state. I take rusty, broken cars and make them shiny and whole again."

She tilted her head, seeing his passion but also a yearning. "You do see the profundity of that, don't you? That you take something broken and make it whole? That you're drawn to that, feeling so broken yourself."

He looked right at her. "No, dinna see it at all."
Then he got in.

She took one last look at the car and got into the
truck. "You're starting to sound like Olaf. Did you
hear yourself just now?"

"I said 'dinna.'" He shuddered. "Hope he's
not planning to take over my body. Russell used
Darkness to do so with your dad. Don't know if
ghosts can do that as well."

"Olaf lost his life, and sees you not living yours
to the fullest. It bothers him."

"Hopefully not enough to justify him taking
me over." He started the engine and looked at her.
"I have something to live for at the moment."

She shivered at those words. She had given him
purpose. Well, her situation had, anyway.

She rolled his words around in her mind as he
drove down the long gravel road. "You have a bit
of brogue anyway. Magnus said he got his from
your mom. Your 'mum.'"

"Aye. She had a thick brogue, and being that
we weren't around other people, Magnus and I
picked it up. Even Dad would sometimes slip into
it when he was in a playful mood. Didn't even
know I had an accent until ladies commented on
it when I went to town for supplies. 'Ooh, I love
your accent. Are you from Scotland?'"

She had to laugh at his impersonation of these
"ladies" and the way he tilted his head, batting his
eyelashes and fluttering his fingers. He seemed
surprised at her laughter. He had a way of raising

one eyebrow and giving her this adorable puzzled look with a hint of a smile.

"Mm, is that what they did?" she asked. "And you loved every second of it, too."

He shrugged, his smile reserved. "It was alright. Magnus sucked it up more than I did."

"Magnus is a flirt of the highest order. How did you and he end up being so different?"

"Curious, isn't it, being we only had each other growing up? We were close, but different from the beginning. He craved connecting with other people. When we'd go to town for supplies or the occasional movie, he'd migrate to other kids and within minutes be playing with them like he'd known them for years."

She flicked a piece of tartan material that was hanging on a chain from the rearview mirror. "You're really okay with having no connections to people, to being alone?"

She remembered making a similar statement, and him refuting it. He nodded, and she thought maybe, just maybe, he meant it. Or believed it, in any case. "Aren't you lonely?" Because she was. "I don't understand how you can not be so lonely that sometimes you want to just shrivel up and die from it."

"Like you?"

"Nah, I meant it in a general way."

He'd obviously heard the emotion in her voice; he slowed to a stop. "You have us now."

Those words caved in her chest, stole away

her breath. *No, you can't hold onto them.* "What if Magnus doesn't want me anymore? What if he hates me?"

"I know my brother. He won't hate you."

"You don't know him with Darkness. And if he blames us for making that decision, you'll both hate me. There are too many variables. You can't make that kind of sweeping statement."

"I just did, though."

She wanted to smack him on the arm; she wanted to crawl in his lap and hold on. What worried her most was that he would risk his life to save hers because he didn't think his life was worthy. Because it would redeem him.

She threw herself back against the seat, arms crossed over her chest and eyes closed. "Just go."

"You want me to leave?"

"No, I mean, keep driving."

He was probably giving her a curious look now, and she fought not to look at him. The truck pulled out onto the road, and the smooth rumble of the engine lulled her into a doze. She got those dreams that weren't really dreams but snippets of scenes or memories floating through. In one, Lachlan said, *You have us now,* and then kissed her like he had earlier. Her eyes snapped open and she saw he was watching her.

"You were making noises," he said, "Like a cat purring."

Enough of that. She reached into her bag and pulled out her cell phone. "I'm going to check in with Hayley, see how the carnival's going."

"It's going great," Hayley said a minute later, excitement in her voice. "I wish you could be here to see it, tons of people having fun. But there's a lot of buzz and concern about what happened to the trailer and to you."

They'd left it a mess, possibly with blood. *Cringe.* Lachlan's blood. *Double cringe.*

"What did you tell them?"

She didn't like either of the stories, that she and Lachlan were having wild sex or that her uncle was stalking her.

"I didn't know what to say." The strain was evident in the poor girl's voice.

Damn Russell. He'd spoiled it. Now all those people who thought she was so great would think she was so awful. "Tell them Lachlan and I went a little crazy. If they mention blood, I accidentally cut him."

"But that's not what happened, is it?" Hayley asked.

"I don't want you involved, okay? Let's leave it at a lapse in judgment, my wild side exploding. I'll be in touch."

"Please do, Jessie. No matter what you said . . . I don't want to lose you in my life."

The words tore at her. "I'll talk to you soon. 'Bye." Unless . . . dare she hope that they could kill Russell?

He took in her sad expression. "You alright?"

She always put on her everything's fine facade,

but she didn't have to with Lachlan. "It's so hard." Except it felt strange, opening herself up that way. "I've done it before, I'll do it again. Saying good-bye is part of life."

He saw right through it but said nothing as he continued to head down to where she worked. Used to work, anyway. Another lie to make up, another goodbye to say. He parked along the side-walk. She got out, letting the sun warm her as the cool air embraced her. He started to reach in back for the sword but paused. "That's not going to work, having the sword when I'm getting my hair cut. I'll attach the dirk to the inside of the coat and hand it to you to hold."

"Sure." She looked at the sign: MUSIC TRIPP. Sighed. "I'd better get it over with. I feel terrible quitting without giving them notice. Can you give me a couple of minutes?"

"I'll stay here." He looked like a warrior, wide-legged stance, ready for anything.

She went in and found Glen Tripp talking to someone by the guitars. She waited, catching his surprised look.

He excused himself and walked over. "Hey, why aren't you at the carnival? Toni and the girls are there now, probably looking for you."

"I have to leave town. I'm so sorry, but I won't be in next week."

"Is everything all right?"

"It's complicated. I don't know when I'll be back, and I don't expect you to hold the job for me. But

I've enjoyed working with you and the family."

"Can I help?"

She sighed again. That's what she liked about them; they were do-anything-for-you people, her dream family. She shook her head. "Just don't be mad."

"Of course not." He put his hand on her shoulder. "But I'm worried about you. You're the most conscientious worker we've ever had. Whatever is making you quit like this must be serious."

Great, now she wanted to cry. She cleared her throat. "Tell Toni and the girls I said goodbye and that I'll miss them."

Lachlan took her in as she walked out. "That must have been hard."

"Not really. The pay was pretty low. With my erratic work history, I can't score a high-paying job. The Tripps are nice, but it was just another job."

He totally surprised her by pulling her close and kissing the top of her head. "Go on, have a cry."

Damn, could she not cover any of her emotions? She closed her eyes and savored the feel of his comfort. For just a moment. Then she stepped back. "I never cry."

"Never? Not even when—"

"Not even then. Let's get your hair cut."

They walked five storefronts down to DORIS JEAN'S HAIR SALON AND GENERALLY COOL PLACE TO HANG OUT. He regarded the sign.

"It is," she said. "Doris cut my hair during the Locks of Love thing, which was the only way I could afford a real haircut. I started coming down on my breaks, having a cup of coffee, and . . . well, hanging out. They like to give me hair and makeup tips." Doris was probably fifteen years older than her but seemed to take a motherly role with her. Jessie liked it.

She reached for the door, but he beat her to the handle and pulled it open. "I forget gentlemen are supposed to do this sort of thing. I've been remiss."

"Yes. Yes, you have."

He gave her a sheepish look, no doubt thinking of all the ways he'd been remiss.

Doris, a bundle of energy who seemed bigger than her five-foot-two frame, squealed and came running over in her four-inch heels. "Jessie!" She started to give her a hug but stopped at the sight of Lachlan behind her. Her smile morphed to a predatory one. "Well, well, who's this?"

"Lachlan," Jessie said before he could.

He took in the gazes of every female in the place, including the clients who were getting treatments. "Uh, hello."

Doris thrust her chest out and took several mini-steps over to shake his hand. "Pleased to meet you." She reached out and took hold of a lock of his hair with her other hand. "What gorgeous hair you've got. Please tell me you're here for a service."

Her forwardness threw him even more. He

opened his mouth, paused, and then asked, "Service?"

"Haircut, style. We also offer chest and back hair removal."

His hand involuntarily went to his chest. "No, that's quite alright." Jessie liked the way he ran *all right* together, and she loved the expressions on his face. He said, "Jessie said you cut long hair for wigs. Can you throw me in to that?"

Doris reached for his hair again. "I could throw you into a lot of things." She waggled her eyebrow, the unabashed flirt.

His smile was stilted. Poor guy. She had thrown *him* into a den of single women. Two other stylists had moved in, too, both closer to Jessie's age. While a part of her enjoyed Lachlan's reaction, another part felt like a cat dunked into a tub of water, growling and with claws flying.

Macy said, "I'll do him. I'm open for the next hour."

"I can do it. My specialty is long hair," Cammie said.

Doris pointed to the plaque on the wall: DORIS JEAN'S HAIR SALON. YOU GROW IT, WE'LL STYLE IT. "See whose name is on that sign? That's who's doing him."

Jessie leaned toward Lachlan. "They don't get a lot of good-looking guys in here." She'd heard the laments before. Doris had been trying to advertise at men, even changing the color on the sign from pink to blue. Wasn't working.

Doris grabbed Lachlan's hand and dragged him off to the sinks in back. "I give the best scalp massages."

He glanced back, giving her that adorable worried look.

You're safe, she mouthed. Maybe. The cat growled again, a low, long one. *Come on, what's wrong with you? He's not yours, and he's not even flirting back.*

Macy and Cammie closed in on her and talked at once. "Who's that?"

"And what happened to the big hunk with curls?"

Jessie had referred Magnus to the salon. Doris had cut his hair, too, raving about all his curls, just as Lachlan had said women did. Now, she watched as Doris settled Lachlan in the chair. He'd obviously never been to a proper salon before. He jerked up when the chair tilted backward.

"That's Lachlan, Magnus's brother," she said.

"His brother? Ooh, you bad girl, you, cheating on one brother with the other!" Cammie said.

"Or is it something kinky?" Macy said, nearly salivating at the prospect. As Jessie and Macy exchanged romance novels, Jessie knew her taste ran toward erotica. "Do you have them put on kilts and—"

"Lalalalala." Jessie covered her ears until she saw Macy's mouth stop moving. "Do not put those images in my mind. We're just friends." Except for that kiss.

"Friends. Yeah, sure." Macy glanced to where Lachlan was getting to his feet and holding a towel turban over his wet hair. "The way you were looking at him . . ."

"And the way he was looking at you," Cammie added.

Macy held out a lock of her hair. "I might be blond, but remember, it's a dye job. You're not fooling me."

Was she . . . was he . . .

He was now within earshot, and Doris was asking, "Was that the most wonderful hair wash ever?"

"It was quite nice," he said, and dammit, he meant it.

You are not feeling jealous because she got to run her fingers through his hair, got to make him feel good. Right?

Right.

Doris pulled a wide-tooth comb through his hair. "How short do you want to go, honey?"

"Not too short," Jessie found her mouth saying. "Uh, it might be a shock, after having long hair for so long."

Macy gave her a *See, I knew you liked him that way* look, accentuating it with a nod.

"Whatever you think is best," he said to Doris. "I trust you."

Doris gave Jessie a sugar-sweet smile. "He trusts me." She turned him to face the big mirror and pulled the mass of long wet hair up to give him an idea of what shoulder-length hair would look like. "How about this?"

"Aye, that's fine."

"*Aye.*" Doris wilted, looking at the three of them. "I *love* his accent."

Jessie met Lachlan's eyes and burst out laughing. He shrugged, giving her a crooked smile. But he was laughing, too, and she felt a jolt shoot right through her as their gazes locked.

"What's so funny?" Doris asked, her gaze going from her to him. "Oh, some kind of private joke."

"'Private.'" Macy gave an exaggerated nod of her head.

Oh, boy. Jessie could feel herself slipping. The trill of excitement zipping through her, the smile she couldn't get off her face . . . all bad signs. The more he relaxed and opened up around her, the more appealing he was. Knowing his shadows, his fears, well, that made it worse.

The jealous cat growled as Doris's fingers moved through his hair, the worse sign yet. The more Doris touched him, the more Jessie wanted to go all wild on her. Which was plain crazy.

Doris put his hair into three ponytails and cut each one. She held them up. "Say goodbye."

Lachlan waved that off. "It's only hair."

Doris prattled on about everything and nothing. Every few minutes his gaze would slide to Jessie's. There was the jolt again.

Macy got a walk-in, and Cammie finally drifted off to straighten her station. Doris dried Lachlan's hair, turning her wrist expertly and leaving his hair fluffy and shiny. When she was finished, she spun the chair so he faced her directly. "Well? Is he gorgeous or what?"

Well, he'd *been* gorgeous in a rough, Highlander sort of way. Now his dark hair tapered back to the base of his neck. He looked . . . civilized, but not completely.

"I like it."

Doris unclipped the cape and released him. "Do you need any product?"

"Product?" he asked.

"Shampoo, hair spray."

"No, I'm good." He followed her to the register.

Doris gave him a twinkle-eyed smile. "You sure are, sugar."

He gave her a big fat tip, the kind Jessie wanted to give her but couldn't. Jessie slid her arm around his. "I'd better get you out of here. Thanks, Doris."

Every woman in the place called out farewells with their fluttering fingers. *Sheesh.*

Lachlan took his coat back as soon as they walked outside, checking their surroundings. Satisfied that things were clear, he ran his fingers through his hair. "Feels strange."

He didn't even get that he'd created a stir, that most of those women would have thrown themselves at him if she hadn't been there looking so obviously . . . with him.

"How long have you had long hair?"

"Dunno, probably since I was fifteen. Not as

long as it was, though." He looked around again. "You want to go by the store, get food or anything else?"

"Yeah. I want to make dinner." It was late afternoon now, and her tummy was beginning to growl. "You're not having boiled chicken and brown rice either. Do you like things spicy?"

He lifted his eyebrow, with a decidedly devilish gleam in his eyes. "Are we talking about food here?"

She pointed at his chest, her finger poking hard muscle. "Do not flirt with me, Lachlan McLeod. It's wrong and unfair and . . . frustrating."

"Was that flirting?"

On anyone else, she'd suspect that guileless expression was an act. "Yes. You do this *thing* with your eyebrow, asking if we're talking about *food*, and it makes me all crazy inside because you can't go there and I can't go there. So stop."

"I was flirting, eh? Mm, interesting. It just sort of came out, the spicy thing, and I didn't know I was doing a 'thing' with my eyebrow." He released a huff of breath. "It's so damned easy with you, Jess. I was being honest when I said I'd shut that part of myself off and you turned it back on again. Just goes to show you what a sod I am, flirting with you and not even realizing it."

He did not need to add anything else to his things-to-hate-himself-for list, as he'd said. She would be strong, too, and not add anything more to her list of awful things she was responsible for.

She put her hand on his cheek. "Don't beat yourself up either. We're only human."

The strong sense of being watched spiked through her. She turned and found four faces watching them with the kind of expressions they might have over a juicy scene from a soap opera. Just like those scenes, she would leave them hanging.

CHAPTER 13

The kitchen hadn't been such a mess, and hadn't smelled so good, since Lachlan's father's death nine months ago. Lachlan usually threw a chicken breast into the microwave, cooked some rice, heated some canned green beans, and that was about it. All he needed was sustenance. The way his mouth watered at the aroma of tomatoes, garlic, and chicken cooking in the pan . . . well, she'd awakened his hunger for good food, too.

She tasted some of the sauce, rolling her eyes in pleasure. "Mm, perfect."

She'd set him to chopping lettuce and carrots for a salad, having already whipped up a dressing from scratch. She flitted from thing to thing, humming, a smile on her face.

"You do love to cook, don't you?" he asked.

"My dad and I used to cook together. It was special. I felt all grown up, like I was helping. My mom was sick a lot, and Dad ended up doing a lot of the household chores." The smile on her face showed him how much those times meant to her.

"What was wrong with your mum?"

"The doctors couldn't find anything, but she'd been sickly her whole life. Failure to thrive, she said they called it. I took care of her, played mommy. She started getting better in those last couple of months."

She moved with grace, whisking a bowl of homemade salad dressing filled with herbs and a touch of balsamic vinegar; she liked to tell him every ingredient, like one of those cooking show hosts. She had a lovely glow on her face, putting a flush on her apple cheeks and a sparkle in her hazel eyes. He had to stop watching her or else he'd chop his fingers off.

"Here, try this," she said, suddenly beside him with a spoon of the tomato sauce.

He obliged and leaned down, so used to his hair falling forward he almost made to push it back.

He had the same reaction she had, rolling his eyes and letting out a soft *Mmmm*. "Incredible." Except he was looking at her. He shifted his gaze to the now empty spoon. "You said it was chicken cacciatore?"

"Yep. I got it from this old Italian cookbook I picked up at a thrift store. You know it's good when there are food stains and notations on the pages."

A large pan nestled with chicken thighs, onions, and mushrooms, bubbled gently. His mouth actually watered. Of course, he was looking at her again, so he couldn't be sure which had done it.

He heard a groan come out of him, and yet he hadn't made the sound. Olaf's energy suffused him. Bloody hell, he *could* come uninvited.

"I can smell it through ye," Olaf said, making a long, snuffly sound. "Food. Like nothin' I've ever laid me eyes on, but heavenly all the same."

She walked closer, looking at him, but not at him. "Did you find out anything about the Void?"

"I seen it. Scary thing, scarier than the Light."

Jessie's face was filled with both fear and hope. "The Light? You mean the light people see when they die?"

"That's the one. I didna want to go to the Light when I was dyin'. Go and be judged for my sins? Och, no way. I committed plenty."

Lachlan tapped the knife's handle on the counter. "So you're a coward, then? Afraid to go to the Void?"

Rage exploded through him. "Ye'll not call me a coward! I faced a hundred swords in my life, gave my life for Scottish freedom."

The same darkness he'd felt the first time Olaf came into him now inundated Lachlan. He held on, his fingers tightening on the edge of the counter. *Focus on the cold stone, on being here, now. Don't let him take over again.* Because in his other hand he held a knife.

Lachlan lost his vision for a few seconds, but he came back to find Jessie shaking his shoulders, a fearful look on her face. "Come back, Lachlan!"

The knife was jammed one inch into the cutting board. He had no memory of doing it.

"Olaf, back off!" he commanded.

The rage ceased, but Olaf remained. "Ye know the MacLeod temper."

"Is that supposed to be an apology?"

"More like a warning, I'd say. Dinna disrespect your kin."

"And clinging to me isn't disrespecting *me*?"

"I'm no' ready to go yet, Lachlan. Ye've given me a second chance. I'll no' be giving it up soon."

Lachlan knew the spirit would definitely be trouble. He would only tolerate him because he needed him. "Olaf, we'll be with you after dinner. Be gone."

Olaf didn't go. Lachlan's chest tightened.

"Ye would deny me a chance to taste of the living, just once? I been trapped here, denied the chance to live, to eat, to feel anything. Suffering so."

He might have been denying himself, and thus Olaf, but at least he didn't whine about it. "It's not like you can eat with us."

"Nae, but I can watch you eat, can smell through you."

"I don't want you groaning and sniffing while I eat."

"I'll be quiet. Won't even know I'm there. Go on, then."

Lachlan tightened his lips on words that wanted to come out.

"All right, I'll go, leave ye to your dinner. Dinna worry, lass, I'll come back to tell ye more about the Void. I think I can help. But there'll be a price to pay."

Lachlan felt the whoosh, almost a vacuum, as Olaf left. "I dinna—do not like that he can come and go as he pleases. We don't know if we can trust him. Look what your uncle did to stay alive."

She had her arms wrapped around herself, her earlier glow gone. "I know. But I need him to find my father. Whatever price he wants, I'll pay it. Daddy . . . he's my kin. My only kin. I'll do whatever it takes to get him back."

"Don't let Olaf hear you say that." He didn't know if Olaf could hear or see what transpired when he wasn't present. The thought pricked at Lachlan. He hoped not.

"Let's eat," she said, pulling the plates close to the pan.

He lit a candle that sat in a red glass bowl on the table after blowing off the dust. They shared a bottle of wine with dinner, but he only poured himself a token amount. She wouldn't let him open the bottle unless he was going to share it with her, so he'd said he would. He wasn't much of a wine drinker, though, so after swigging the splash, he brought back a can of Guinness and a glass.

"Not really in a wine mood tonight." He poured the beer into the glass.

"Look at the way the foam kind of moves down,

instead of up, like rainfall." She leaned forward to watch. "It's all creamy, and the contrast between the dark and the light is pretty." She grinned. "Who would have thought beer could be pretty? Especially *black* beer?"

He'd been watching the foam, too, as she'd described it. He'd never noticed it before.

She gave him such a sweet smile, it made his throat go dry. "Silly, huh, getting all excited about beer foam?"

He lifted the glass to her. "I'll never look at it the same again. Cheers."

They drank then, sharing a smile. Their gazes held for a few moments, moments that felt like hours. He pulled his away and took another gulp of his beer, hardly tasting it. They grew quiet as they tucked into their meal. Salads he could take or leave, but the main dish was as incredible as its creator.

She made these intriguing sounds as she ate, closing her eyes and sinking into it. Everything she did, she savored. While cooking, she'd inhaled the garlic on her fingers as though it were the scent of the gods, commented on how the spices swirled in the oil and vinegar. Life was a sensual pleasure to her, and watching her was a sensual pleasure to him.

One he shouldn't be partaking in for many reasons.

The candle cast a warm glow over her face, flickering as though it were alive. Could Olaf move currents, make breezes? Weren't ghosts supposed to be cold?

She took another sip of wine. "Mm, I love the sweet-but-not-too-sweet flavor of this one, with just a hint of cherry." She looked at the label on the bottle and laughed.

"What is it?"

"Ménage à Trois."

Weirdly appropriate and inappropriate. He decided not to comment on that. "I know nothing about wines, but my parents liked this brand. I hadn't even noticed what it was called."

"I'm no expert either. I don't buy much of it."

Probably couldn't afford it. He'd had to fight her on who would pay for the groceries. He'd taken her hand, wrapped around her wallet, and told her in no uncertain terms that he had plenty of money and would pay. She threatened to pay the next time.

Right.

Even in hiding, his father continued to work, getting grants and writing papers under a pseudonym. He made money, and he played the stock market. Lachlan and Magnus were set financially. Now Lachlan was making his own money with the car restoration business. No way would he let her pay a dime when she clipped coupons and bought cookbooks at thrift stores. Nor would she be paying for the damage to the trailer.

"You're giving me a fierce look," she said, peering at him from beneath her lashes.

"Sorry, just thinking about that price Olaf

wants. Never mind that." He took another drink. "Why haven't you gotten jobs at restaurants? You're amazing."

She smiled, and he could see a hint of a buzz in her eyes. "I love to cook, but if I had to do it for a living, I'm afraid I'd lose that passion. Maybe if I opened my own place someday . . ." Her expression dimmed. "But that would entail a lot of paperwork. Possibly a liquor license. I don't think so."

"Who's Jessie Bellandre?"

She blinked at the question. "Uh, me."

"Jessie Bellandre died eleven years ago from a fatal form of muscular dystrophy. A disease that touches your heart. So who's Jessie? Or more importantly, who are you really?"

She ran her finger along the top rim of her wineglass, deciding what to tell him. "You found that out when you thought I was some homicidal freak out to get your brother, I suppose."

"That made me even more suspicious. Now it just makes me curious."

She took a sip of wine, still buying time. "You're going to hand me over to your brother when this is all over. Why does it matter to you?"

Her words spiked through him. "We are friends, aren't we? If things go well with you and Magnus, we'll be in-laws."

"And how will he feel, you knowing my secrets before he does?"

He wanted to kiss that little smirk off her face. Something else he'd done before Magnus, but he would cut out his tongue before saying a word about that.

"Point made, you cheeky girl."

"Cheeky? What does that mean exactly?"

"You know, because you're being it."

She tried to hide her grin by taking another sip, finishing off her glass. "Time to clean up."

"You sit. I'll take care of it." He stood and picked up their plates.

"Really?" She had a lazy smile on her face as she took him in. "Mm, what a prince you are."

"No, no prince. Just a guy grateful for a good meal."

She helped anyway. "It'll make it go faster. I want to get it done so we can talk to Olaf."

"And find out what price he intends to exact."

Jessie and Lachlan went into the family room a half hour later. Though it was open to the courtyard, it was the darkest room of the house, having no exterior windows. His father had designed it that way to cut the glare on the huge television mounted on the wall. The furniture was earth tones, but the accent lighting and décor pieces, like the kitchen and sitting area, were bright colors and contemporary styles.

He remained standing, hands at his sides, tense expression on his face. "Time to find out what he wants. Olaf!"

"Ye've no need to yell, laddie. I'm ne'er verra far away."

That's what worries me. Lachlan held out his hands and saw the ghostly imprint of Olaf's hands, even the dark, coarse hairs on the backs. "What did you find out about the Void?"

Olaf breathed in noisily. "Still smells delicious. Ah now, ye want to get right down to business, eh? I saw a great round ball, black as a stormy sky, it was, a place that felt like nothin'. Nae, less than nothin'. It could be the Void ye were talkin' about."

Jessie stepped closer, her face tightening. "Could you see inside?"

"It was solid, like the beast that man becomes. There was an opening, like if ye made a shallow cut into a melon. I could see in, but not verra far. I stayed away from it, and don't ye dare call me a coward for it. I'll no' be trapped in some place for eternity, no' even for a bonnie lass."

Her expression fell. "But you said you could help."

"I was afraid ye were gonna give me that look, like I let you down." Olaf released a low sigh. "I think I could bring ye with me. If ye dare, ye could go in. I'll hold onto ye, use the same magic that helped Lachlan with the hell doggies."

She said, "I'll do it," at the same time Lachlan said, "No way."

A ferocity blazed in her hazel eyes. "It's my dad. I have to see if he's there."

"And get trapped there?" Lachlan's heart squeezed at the thought of it.

"I'm sure you did everything you could to save

your father when the house was burning down. But what if there had been one more thing to try, one last chance? You'd have done it, wouldn't you?"

"That's harsh, using my pain to convince me." He ran his fingers through his hair. "But you're right. I would have done."

"Think back on those moments when Magnus was lying there dying. When I gave you that terrible choice. How did you feel?"

Desperate. In agony.

She nodded even though he hadn't spoken the words aloud. "And if you could take the Darkness for him, you would have."

"Aye."

"That's how I feel right now, about my father."

She had him there. He would do anything for the people he loved. He couldn't expect any less of her.

"I couldn't live with myself if I didn't at least try. Olaf, is that the price? The risk that I might get trapped?"

"Nae, lassie. I dinna want to go back to that place. I'll protect ye as well as I can, but I'm taking a risk myself. I'll be asking for a taste of something pleasurable before I go."

She smiled. "I'll cook for you, anything you want. I'll learn how to make a traditional Scottish dish."

"Nae, that's no' the pleasure I mean. I want to feel a woman's body one last time, feel everything that's soft and warm and curvy about it."

Was it a coincidence that he'd used words similar to what he himself had used earlier? Lachlan wondered. Probably not. Bastard, what was he on to?

Her face flushed, and she braced herself against the back of the couch. "But you can't feel."

"I can through the laddie, here."

Lachlan's hands fisted at his sides. If he could punch Olaf without punching himself, he would. "That's disgusting. I won't do it."

"Och, I'm not asking ye to fondle her girly parts. Her shoulders, her stomach, her neck, and a kiss. It's no' much to ask, considering what I'm doing for her. Dinna tell me it's something ye've not done with her yourself."

"I cannot touch her like that. She's my brother's girl. You, a clansman, should understand and respect the code of honor between brothers."

Olaf's laugh was brusque. "Have ye read about the clan wars, how brother killed brother to steal his wife or to become head of the clan? I understand honor, but I feel what ye feel for the lass, how ye want to—"

"But we can't always have what we want." Lachlan didn't want to hear what the spirit picked up.

Olaf's essence blurred as he looked around. "Where is this brother, then? Why has he left his lassie alone?"

"He's been injured," Lachlan said. "He's recuperating elsewhere, and I would be the lowest of the low to move in on her while he's down."

"I ne'er went off to battle without a kiss from a fair lassie. Still won't." Olaf crossed his ephemeral arms over his chest, as stubborn as any Scot.

"I'll do it." Jessie laid that soulful gaze on him that made his heart bleed.

Hell, he was only a man, and as it turned out, not a very strong one. Even worse, he couldn't tell if the feeling of exultation was his or Olaf's.

"Dinna worry, laddie, it's not on ye. It was forced on ye, and ye wouldna let this lass down."

They didn't even know if Olaf could take her there. He might be making it up. Lachlan could see, though, that doubt didn't matter. If there was a chance, a wee one, it was all that mattered to her.

"I'm going with you, then."

"'Tis honorable, but it'll be enough to keep her from floating off. Dinna worry, I'll do my best to keep her safe."

"For my dad," she whispered, stepping closer. "It won't mean anything. It's just a touch between friends." She gave him a hesitant smile, knowing he wasn't buying that.

"And ye touch him, too, lassie. I want to feel a woman's touch on me."

"Olaf, you're killing me." Lachlan tilted his head back and squeezed his eyes shut for a second.

"Let's get to it," she said, all business. She squared her shoulders and held her breath, which raised her knockers and made them swell. The black lace around the edge of her dark green top contrasted with her creamy skin.

"Put ye hand right at her neck—"

"One condition," Lachlan said between gritted teeth. "No directing. I can manage on my own."

Olaf didn't say anything for a moment. "All right. Suppose ye dinna want me making groaning noises either."

"Definitely not."

Lachlan waited for a moment, making sure Olaf was in the background. Silence. He touched Jessie's face, running his thumb along her cheek and down to her jaw. Her eyes fluttered shut in pleasure but she forced them open. His thumb ran over her mouth, the mouth he would kiss. He ran the back of his fingers down the length of her neck and over the curve of her shoulder. Then he reached the fabric of her shirt. There wasn't much skin showing. The top with faded words about rock and roll had long sleeves. As though she, too, realized that limitation, she grabbed the bottom of her shirt and pulled it over her head.

He could hardly breathe at the sight of her. The delicate pink bra left her cleavage a shelf of tempting flesh. The spray of freckles over her collarbone and shoulders and the mole at the curve of her neck were all now seared into his mind.

She started unbuttoning his shirt, all of her attention on the task. Her nails grazed his skin as she worked the buttons. He could see down into her bra, the intriguing crevice that begged for his tongue to dip into. When she got to the bottom buttons, she'd no doubt see his cock straining against his jeans.

He didn't want to think about that. He ran his fingers through her hair, down her neck in the kind of stroking motion that—

He stopped the thought. *Keep it together. No matter how hard it is, no pun intended, you've got to get through this with your honor intact.*

He trailed his fingers down her back instead as she worked the last buttons. She might be afraid, but she was fearless. She'd stood in front of him while he'd been out of it and wielding a sword, for God's sake. Jessie would do what needed to be done, because she was amazing, strong, brave . . . and incredibly soft. Her skin felt like silk beneath his fingers.

She pushed his shirt back, and he shrugged out of it and let it drop to the floor. She touched his pecs, first with her fingertips, then the whole of her hands. She drew her hands down him, avoiding the bandage and the bruised area. He forced himself to breathe. The heat from her touch sank into his body, as though he were a block of butter and her hands were made of fire. He melted around her, felt all of him melt. He shut his eyes against it, all the while his body yearning for more.

No, he couldn't lose himself in her. *Not mine. Never mine.*

"Am I hurting you?" she asked, her voice barely a whisper.

He was grimacing, he realized. "Aye, it hurts."

She tilted her head. "You don't mean on the outside, do you?"

"No."

"When you said that before, I couldn't figure it out. But now I know." She nodded toward his hand on her back, her eyes closing as she seemed to sink into his touch. "I know exactly what you mean."

It was no less painful to touch her. He hoped Olaf was feeling that part, too, the bastard.

She'd left her hand flattened against his stomach, her fingertips tensing against his skin. He fanned his fingers across her collarbone, tracing the edge of the bra and fighting his desire to dip down into that crevice. He touched her stomach, making it tremble and her breath hitch. Just looking at her, head tilted back, mouth curved into a soft smile of pleasure . . . bloody hell, he could fall into a different kind of void right there.

He took a deep breath, tracing the etching of the cross. Her pants rode low on her hips, and he traced the hip bones that jutted out slightly, following the top edge of her waistband. He wrapped his hands around her waist, and his fingers could almost touch. He yanked her toward him, holding back at the last second before grinding her into his erection.

He lowered his head, whispering against the

top of her head, "Can't do this anymore. Too much." He could hardly talk.

She nodded, bumping her head into his chin. "But we have to kiss."

She faced him, her mouth relaxed and parted. Her fingers were pulsing against his back, kneading him. Her other hand was on his hip, clutching at the denim.

"A kiss." The word came out on an agonized breath.

"Just one. He didn't say kiss*es*."

"One simple kiss. Then we step back."

She nodded again, her pupils dilated, lids heavy. She slid her other hand around to his back and stepped up against him again.

He braced his hands on her face, the safest place for them to be, and moved in. Their mouths connected, moved back and forth. He remembered her quip about having a dead prostitute's energy clinging to her. He could believe it. Other than being so completely entranced when she'd put her hands on him, she didn't lack a sense of sensuality or ease with her body.

One kiss. They'd done that properly. So back away now.

She sucked on his upper lip, softly, pulling him closer just as he was about to move back. The graze of her teeth twisted him up inside, coiling, spiraling. Somehow his hand had slid down her back, fingers tracing the indent of her spine, flaring at the base of it. She let out a soft groan and shifted against him. For a dreadful second he thought he'd go off right there, but he held on. He hadn't done so in more than a year. If she moved against him again—

She opened her mouth, just a little, and it was the most natural thing to slide his tongue inside. The agonized groan that came out now, that was him, pulled from deep within. She tasted of wine, sweet with a hint of cherry. His fingers dipped down beneath her waistband, middle finger nudged in the top of the crack of her fine arse. She raked her nails up and down his back. Killing him. Time to close it down. Shut it off.

She wiggled, just one wiggle, and then a *grind*, and his body jerked. He set her away from him, feeling the sticky release. He tilted his head back and slapped one hand over his eyes.

"Och, that was even better than I thought 'twould be," Olaf said.

"All right, you voyeuristic perv, you've had your fun," Lachlan growled.

"Aye, and ye had your fun, too."

She was still standing there, looking delicious and flushed and a bit piqued. "You got off?"

Well, he could hardly hide it. "I didn't mean to. A man can only take so much." He was wet, uncomfortable, embarrassed, and still hard.

"That's so unfair." She crossed her arms over her chest, pushing those knockers into luscious mounds.

He raised his eyebrow, now wondering if that

was the eyebrow *thing* she'd mentioned. "Unfair? Don't you mean disgusting and wrong?"

"No, I'm going with unfair. I felt every bit of what you felt, and *I* didn't get off."

He did not like where she was going with this. "My going off was your fault."

"*My* fault! How?"

"First you sucked on my lip."

She snatched up her shirt. "And you stuck your tongue in my mouth."

"One begged for the other. What happened to the nice simple kiss?"

She jammed the shirt down over her head, catching her nose for a second. Her hair was adorably messed when she yanked her head free. "Still, a kiss is just a kiss. It shouldn't do . . . that to you." She gestured to the region of his pelvis.

"It wasn't just the kiss. That revved me, sure, and then you did a . . . *wiggle* thing."

"I didn't 'wiggle.'"

"Aye, you did. Like this." He imitated it as best as he could. "Then you did a *grind*." Just the word conjured it up again. "And that did it."

"You're arguin'? After that bit of business, the two of ye are arguin'?" Olaf said.

"Oh, shut up," They both said in unison.

"Fine, I'll be leaving, then. We'll go on the morrow when I'm ready."

Arguing was much better than what they'd been doing. Lachlan didn't want to think about her getting off, or not getting off. Except she still looked quite stung about it, and yeah, it *was* unfair when he thought about it.

Which made him want to do something about it.

Which was an even worse idea than this kissing for Olaf business.

He lifted his arms. "Look, I'm sorry guys get off easier and faster than girls do. God got pretty mad about that whole apple thing, I guess. Eve was the one who tempted Adam, if you'll remember. That's what women do, tempt the innocence right out of us."

She pursed her lips in irritation. "You are . . . are . . ."

He curled his fingers, beckoning. "Bring it on. Throw any word you want at me." He deserved all of them.

"I can't even think of a word suitable for you right now. I'm going to bed."

"Good night," he called after her, watching her depart with an irritated sway to her arse. "Oh, and I won't think less of you if I hear the wee motor going in the night."

She flipped him off and stormed down the hallway.

CHAPTER 14

on't think any less of you . . .'" Jessie mimicked, staring at the ceiling in her room, arms crossed over her chest.

She was so pissed at him she'd lost all desire to get off.

She wasn't pissed because he'd gotten off and she hadn't. Well, maybe she was. Heck, she didn't know.

Yes, you do. Seeing him like that brought out all that sexual stuff you've been trying to stifle. Knowing you'd done that to him. And totally giving away that you wanted it, too.

Luckily, exhaustion claimed her before she could delve too deeply into any of it. Unluckily, she dreamed of the kiss, of his hands on her bare skin and the way he felt beneath her hands.

Then things got ugly. The nightmare. Always the same. Terror. Fear. And afterward, carnage, screaming, and she at the center of it.

She never felt the screams leave her mouth,

only heard them echo off the walls and pierce her eardrums. *Stop. Pull them back. Stop.* She couldn't stop once it had begun. Like a wind-up toy, the screams had to run their course. Her eyes strained in the dark, everything so dark, to find reality.

Her door burst open and light flooded the room. Lachlan's wild eyes found her first, sitting up in bed obviously unscathed. Then he searched the room for the horror that had made her scream.

"Night . . . nightmare," she managed after the last gasps of screams. Spasms that had wracked her body, the last of the dream memories pulsing at the edge of her mind. " 'Member, I warned you."

He came to her bed and wrapped his arms around her. He wore just shorts and was cold, so cold. It was after four. He'd been outside, sitting on the stones. "Bloody hell, it did sound like someone was killing you." He squeezed her tight, pushing the last of the nightmare away. "You alright?"

She sank into the feel of him, cold comfort in a literal way. "F-Fine now."

"What are they about? You said you'd been having them since you were a child."

"I d-didn't know what it was at the time, but now I do: Darkness. Coming out in a classroom full of children, killing them." She shuddered. "All dead."

She hadn't realized her arms had gone around his shoulders. Her cheek rested against his chest, and his heartbeat thudded in her ear. She felt safe, far from the nightmare now.

He squeezed her tighter. "And you? Does the monster kill you?"

"I'm the monster," she whispered. "It's me, my Darkness that kills."

"It was only a nightmare."

"Children. They were only children. I never see what sets me off, only when it begins. When I went into the first foster home, they couldn't handle the nightmares. I don't blame them. It disturbed the other children, scared them. I ran away, afraid I'd hurt them. After that I got labeled a problem child. They already thought I had emotional problems. I told them what I'd seen the day my mom died, the Darkness, and how my uncle was in my father's body. Of course, they thought it was the trauma and my imagination."

He was rocking her now, slowly back and forth. "It must have been awful."

"It worked out all right, though. Mrs. Marsh— the lady who took in special needs kids—could handle the nightmares. She was up through the night anyway with some of the other kids."

"You hear how awful foster homes can be."

"The Marshes were good people. They didn't do it for the money. They had lost a child many years before from a degenerative disease. They wanted to help other kids."

He was stroking her arm with his finger, an absentminded motion probably. "You push everyone out of your life to protect them. But who has ever protected you?"

She turned to look at him, his face so close to hers. "You. You've protected me."

He turned away from her, from the raw emotion he'd heard in her voice. "I haven't killed the bastard yet."

He would give himself no credit. She ran her hands down his arms. Still chilled. "Stop, Lachlan. Stop sitting out there in the cold punishing yourself."

"I haven't done anything to redeem myself. Hell, I'm backsliding."

"What will you have to do to redeem yourself? Kill Russell? Get Magnus and me married with kids? Or die? Will that do it?"

"If I die . . . if I give up everything, that will make it all right."

"No, it won't." She was shaking her head. "It won't."

He backed off the bed and got to his feet. "You'll be okay. Go back to sleep."

A few minutes later he took his place on the flagstones. Yeah, like she could go back to sleep now. She got dressed and slid out the door that led directly to the courtyard. The cold air nipped at her.

Stupid man.

He tried to ignore her as she stood next to him, but she knew he was aware of her. He'd know even if she'd slithered out stealthy as a snake.

"Let's talk to Olaf," she said. "I want to go to the Void."

He cracked an eye. "What happened to going back to sleep? It's a god-awful early hour of the morning."

"Interesting that you'd notice. But I can't sleep now, not with you out here and monsters roaming in my head."

He got to his feet. "Remember the last time I thought something was a bad idea?"

"Going to the fair," she said in a low voice. At least he hadn't said, *I told you so.*

"I think this is, too."

"It's my daddy. I can't leave him there."

"We don't know if he's still there."

"I have to find out." She saw him give in, resignation tightening his mouth. "Besides," she added, "we already paid the price." She punched his arm.

He pulled back with a hiss. "What was that for?"

"That smart-assed remark you made earlier. You deserved it."

"Aye, I did. And more. Told you I was an arrogant arse."

She walked back to the house, leaving him to follow. They passed through her room and out into the hall.

"You really trust Olaf?" He ducked into his room, coming out with a long-sleeved shirt.

"I have to. He's my only way to the Void."

"You don't know what this place is, but it scared a big galoot like Olaf. And he's dead." His eyes darkened. "Aren't you afraid of anything?"

"Everything. All the time. But I don't let it stop me."

"I know," he muttered.

As she passed the living room, she tried to forget what had happened there that night. Fat chance. She stopped in the kitchen. "We'll do it here. I like this space."

"Good idea." He pulled the shirt on. "In case something happens, it won't be far from the front door."

"What's that supposed to mean?"

"One of the Offspring astral-projected and got her soul snagged. If Eric hadn't gotten her body to where her soul was being kept, she would have died. But I can't go to this Void with your body, so I'll have to take you somewhere. Haven't got a clue where."

"You're trying to scare me."

"Is it working? Even a wee bit?" He held his finger and thumb an inch apart.

"Nope."

He looked up. "Olaf."

The ghostly image appeared, overlaying Lachlan. "Ye've changed your mind, 'aven't ye? Can't say as I blame ye, lassie. It's a scary bit of business. What if I can't hold onto ye?"

"I haven't changed my mind."

"Not for lack of my trying," Lachlan added, leaning back against the counter. He hadn't buttoned his shirt, and she could see his nipples, hard from the cold, and the goose bumps across his chilled skin.

Olaf let out a resigned sigh. "All right, then. I live up to my promises."

She stood in front of Lachlan and Olaf, her body stiff. "Let's go." A tremble rippled through her.

Nothing happened.

Olaf said, "I need a connection to ye, I think."

Lachlan's eyes narrowed. "If you're going to say I have to kiss her—"

"Nae, I'm not saying a kiss. If I'm being honest, it was a bit much. Felt like an electrical storm, but I enjoyed it verra much."

"Glad to oblige you," Lachlan growled.

"Just hold hands."

That should be safe enough. No way was she commenting on the storm. She linked hands with Lachlan. His were still cool. She blinked at the feel of Olaf's energy, like touching something alive with a mild electrical current. Maybe this would work after all.

"Ready, lassie?" Olaf asked.

"Take care of her." Lachlan's voice was a bit louder than necessary. "I'll hold you responsible if something happens to her."

"What are ye gonna do, kill me?"

"Boys." She cleared her throat. "Can we just do this? No one but me is responsible if . . . if I don't come back."

The room disappeared. Her *body* disappeared.

She felt nausea and the tickling sensation of spinning too fast. She could see nothing, feel nothing outside of herself, like flying through thick fog. She couldn't even see Olaf. Panic! Had she lost him already? Was she floating in the ethers? Suddenly, she felt his hands on hers, thick hands holding hers tight. Olaf's hands.

In the distance, to the right, it looked like the sun was trying to shine through the fog. She felt a pull toward it, and then a counterpull away from it. Olaf. Was that the Light he was so afraid of?

They veered to the left. There, up ahead, was the opposite of the Light. A shape that pulsed with darkness. She felt like she was in one of those outer space movies where they close in on the evil starship. It was a sphere, perfectly round, with the texture of roiling black clouds. Like Darkness. She could feel it, the dark pulse thrumming through her being. That's why Olaf was unnerved by it. Though they had no bodies, they could still feel the thing, like a living creature. She could also feel the emptiness of it, the vacuum that lent it its name.

"That's it," Olaf said, though she hadn't actually heard his voice. Was he in her head?

Fear pulsed through her. And excitement.

"There's the doorway I told ye about."

She spotted it, a narrow opening in the curtain of black. "How will this work?"

He spun his hand and out rolled a golden rope. "It's what I use to stay with Lachlan. Hold onto it.

Give it a tug, and I'll pull ye. Don't tarry, lassie."

"I won't."

She saw him clearly now that he wasn't over-laying Lachlan. He looked a bit like Lachlan, the longish dark hair, brown eyes, but bigger. His handsome face creased in worry.

She grabbed onto the rope and floated toward the opening. It pulled her, too, but gently, with a soft throbbing motion. Her hand went out as she reached the slit, grabbing onto the edge. Her soul shuddered as she looked inside. It wasn't an open space like she'd imagined, but filled with gray masses of . . . she didn't know. Flesh, maybe.

She reached out, her hand the same ghostly quality Olaf possessed, and touched the clos-est part of it. *Ewwww.* It felt mushy but solid and warm, and was throbbing in that same rhythm. . . . like the inside of a body. As though the Void were a living, breathing organism. That made her want to head straight back to Olaf, who watched from a distance.

No, you can't give up now. Remember what Lachlan said: you're not afraid of anything. And he's proud of that, even though he wouldn't admit it.

She wound the rope through her fingers, around her wrist, and then held it in her hand. The gray masses left little space between them. When it breathed, or whatever it was doing, the gaps opened a bit. The rhythm matched the speed of a heartbeat, steady, even. She waited for the out breath, when the gaps relaxed, and pushed her way in. A second later the gaps closed, squeezing her between the layers.

Stay calm.

She could still see the opening on the left. To the right . . . nothing but more of this stuff. Two more breaths had passed. On the third she moved, inch by inch. Two moves in and she couldn't see the opening anymore. Panic squeezed at her, even stronger than the organs.

You have the rope. That's your guide out of here.

Another breath, another step. She had taken twenty of them, counting each one, when she felt it. She couldn't quite name it, other than a sense of familiarity. Comfort.

"Daddy?"

Not spoken aloud, yet she heard the word echo through the "flesh."

Nothing.

"Daddy!"

Louder this time.

"Allybean?" Disbelief saturated the word.

She didn't have a heart here, strictly speaking, but it constricted anyway. "Daddy!"

She moved now with more purpose, sliding through the gaps, waiting through compression, another step. Following the feeling. Ahead, she saw a chamber, between the gaps. She didn't wait for the out breath anymore; she pushed through, grunting with the effort.

Breaking through, she stumbled on the uneven floor. The space was no bigger than Lachlan's living room, the walls that same sluglike material. The bumps in the floor reminded her of the roof of a mouth. She searched, expecting to find him right away. Where was he?

"Oh, God." Her gaze had skipped over him the first time. What she saw, it was too bizarre, too terrible to comprehend. "Daddy?"

"Allybean, what are you doing here? Please tell me you're a hallucination. I've had them before, but not so real and vivid and beautiful."

Her nickname, again. It sent a warm wash of emotion through her. As she took him in, though, it was followed by nausea. Her knees went to gelatin. All she could see was the front of his face and the tips of his fingers and toes. He was embedded in the wall. *Embedded*.

She took a tentative step toward him. "I'm real. I came here for you." Then she ran the last few steps, stopping in front of him, still not believing she'd found him. "You're alive."

"My soul is here, but I'm not alive. You have to get out of here. This place will swallow you."

Everything warm fled. "That's what's happening? It's swallowing you?"

He couldn't even nod, though he tried. "How did you get here?"

She raised her hand. The rope wasn't wound through her fingers anymore, but she still had a grip on it. "A dead Scotsman, if you can believe it. I just found out Russell put you here. He's using your body. Now I'm going to get you out."

She reached for his fingers but they slipped out of her grasp. Not enough of them sticking out to get a hold on. She dug into the "flesh," and though it felt slimy, it was solid. "What *is* this place?"

"Russell created it. It's supposed to be a jail, but like everything Darkness, it has a life of its own. He hung me up here, but the walls started absorbing me, little by little."

"That's horrible." The thought of him being here, slowly devoured . . . She shuddered. "You've been suffering for so long, Daddy." Tears washed over her voice.

"Time here, outside our bodies, feels different. How many years have I been gone? Quite a few. You're a grown woman now."

She saw pride in his eyes, and it warmed her. "Fifteen."

"Years. I seem to remember they felt like a long time, but then not long at all." He let out a ragged sigh. "I should have told you more, but you were so young."

"About Darkness, you mean?"

"Yes. I knew you had it, but I hoped . . . prayed it wouldn't manifest."

She searched for something to use as a shovel. There were small stones, and she grabbed the flattest one. "Tell me now."

His fingers flexed. "This is going to sound unbelievable."

She kept digging around his hands, grunting

with the effort. "You're from another dimension."

His eyes widened. "How . . ."

Tiny dig marks. Dammit, that's all she was getting. Everything here felt physical to her. Even she did. But she couldn't put enough strength into it. "I've met others who have DNA from . . . I can't remember the name of the place."

"Surfacia. These others, are they hunting you?"

"No, helping me. They don't have Darkness, don't even know what it is. One of them is from there. He was sent by their government to hunt you and Russell down, but they wouldn't tell him what it was. He sensed it in me. Russell *is* hunting me down. He went to prison for killing Mom. They thought you did it."

His eyes darkened. "I'm so sorry, Allybean."

"It's okay now. I'm going to get you out of here."

"You can't. I'll tell you about Darkness, and then you must go."

"I'm not leaving without you." She chipped harder, her arms aching.

"In Surfacia, we had to suppress our emotions. Emotions are energy. All of those negative emotions accumulated and became a huge, dark mass hovering in a subdimension. Darkness." His fingers flexed again. "Can you scratch my nose? That's the worst, I think. I don't need food or water, but sometimes I have an itch."

She obliged. "So Darkness is a mass of negative energy?"

"Yes. Russell and I found a way to tap into it. We needed power, and it seemed that Darkness would give us that power."

"Power to do what?"

"Obliterate the Collaborate. The government. They'd killed our father. Justice is different there. There is no jury of peers. If they suspect you're lying, they SCANE you. It's a mind probe, and usually means either death or a vegetative state. Our father was arrested and underwent a SCANE. He was lucky; he died.

"Revenge united Russell and me for the first time since he'd been born. You see, I blamed him for our mother's death. His birth caused a fatal hemorrhage. He craved my attention, approval, but I . . . I couldn't give it to him.

"There were rumors about Darkness, about sorcerers who could tap into it, manipulate it. With that kind of power, we could destroy the government, destroy the SCANE machine. We found a way, feeling it pour into our bodies as though we'd freed the devil. We worked with it, forming it into destructive power. We had good intentions, but things went wrong and we failed. We managed to wreak havoc, but that was all. So we escaped here through a crack between the dimensions."

"Why did Russell want to hurt you?"

"Stop, Allybean. You're hurting yourself."

The tips of her fingers were raw, bleeding. "No."

"We both fell in love with the same woman once we settled here. Your mother. I managed to charm her away, and we married, had you. I worried about passing on Darkness, but I convinced myself it wasn't genetic. I could feel it in you the day you were born. Not as strong, and I hoped not as dangerous. Darkness makes us like animals—territorial, vicious. Russell felt that I stole his mate, and he would do nothing less than take my life to get her back. I can't blame him, because I felt the same way."

Jessie paused, covering her mouth. She'd felt the cat, hissing and growling inside her when Doris and the girls were flirting with Lachlan. "Russell can turn into a wolf. Can you?"

"That's what we focused on becoming. They're cunning, smart, and strong. You can become what you want."

"He can make dogs from his Darkness. They're separate from him, and he sends them after us."

Even without much of his face showing, she could see the puzzlement in his expression. "I didn't know it could work that way. I left you in a mess, didn't I? But I'm not putting you in any more danger. You have to go. You'll be trapped here."

"I have a rope to lead me out." She looked down and gasped. "It's gone!" She'd been so busy trying to free her father, she hadn't noticed it fall from her hand. She spun, searching for it on the ridged floor. It was moving away, as though someone, or something, was pulling it into the fleshy organs with every breath. Only two inches were left. She dove for the end. Another inch slipped away.

She grabbed at the final inch. It slipped in her bloody fingers. She clutched it as the next breath tried to pull it completely in.

"No, you don't, you disgusting beast." She jerked it when the breath expanded the crevice. An inch. One more.

"Go!" her father yelled. "Get out of here now."

When she had several inches wound around her fingers, she turned back to him, tears welling in her eyes. "I don't want to lose you again."

"When it swallows me . . . I'll go on. Don't worry about me. Leave, now, while you can."

There was still a tug on the rope, the Void trying to pull it from her. A sound snagged her attention. Other than the breathing, she'd heard nothing until now.

Then, someone calling from a distance: "Hello? Is someone there?"

"There are others trapped in here?" she asked.

"Go!" her father said. "And never come back."

She waited for the gap to open and slipped in. She turned and saw her father one last time before moving inward. Clutching the rope, she pulled herself along as though climbing up a mountainside. It felt like a year before she emerged through the slit and into the open. She sucked in air that her body didn't need. Openness, thank God for openness.

"Och, did the thing swallow ye?" Olaf's face was scrunched up in disgust.

She looked down at herself. She'd been slimed. "Get us out of here."

She lurched, eyes snapping open, gasping for breath. A face loomed over her. It slowly came into focus: Lachlan. She blinked, tried to orient herself. He was sitting on the kitchen floor holding her. No Olaf.

"You collapsed the moment you left," he said. He was studying her. "Then you went deadly still. It was eerie, like you were . . . well, you're back now." He'd been worried. She saw the creases in his forehead where he'd been frowning. "Did you find him?"

She opened her mouth to answer and a great big sob came out. She wrapped her arms around his neck and buried her face in his chest.

He stroked her back. "Cry, Jess. You're going to hurt yourself holding it in. I can feel you heaving with it."

She shook her head.

"What are you afraid of?"

"That I'll never stop." Her voice sounded muffled against his shirt.

"As far as I know, it's never happened, someone crying till they died. Go on, then. You're safe."

Those last words did it. She let the sobs come out, waves of tears and awful sounds that reminded her of a dying animal. But with all of that, with the shirt she'd soaked, she felt a release of grief. Through it all, he held her and stroked her back, saying nothing until she'd finally spent her tears.

"You're right. I didn't die from it," she said, grabbing a napkin from the table. She wiped her face and blew her nose.

He took her in, tilting his head in sympathy. "I'm sorry. You knew he might not be there."

"No, it was worse. Better but worse. He *was* there." The whole thing poured out of her. What was in her. The horror of her father being buried in the wall. Leaving him. She looked up at Lachlan, wiping away fresh tears. "I know how you felt now, having to leave your dad there to die. It ripped my heart out."

He nodded. "Aye. It's the hardest thing you'll ever have to do."

She shook her head. "No. Getting him back will be the hardest thing I have to do."

CHAPTER 15

Jessie finally fell into an exhausted sleep. She knew that much, felt her body being lifted, shifting with his movements, but she couldn't rouse herself. Then he laid her on the bed and pulled the blankets up around her.

She tried to thank him but words failed to come out cohesively. He brushed her hair from her forehead and left. Thank God her sleep was dreamless, or at least, she remembered nothing as she climbed to consciousness. She'd been asleep four hours. The chair near the bed indicated that he'd sat there for a while, watching over her.

That tightened her heart in a bear hug. He'd left a note for her on the seat: *In the garage. Come out when you wake.*

She looked down at her fingers. Undamaged, no trace of blood. Whatever happened to her sort-of physical body wasn't real. Not slimed, but still, she got into the shower and washed away the feeling of it. If only she could wash away Darkness.

Knowing what it was . . . did it make it better?
She'd always sensed she was dangerous to others.
Now she knew she was, especially to a man who
loved her. After putting on one of her dark, ruffled
shirts and black pants, she went to the kitchen. Her
stomach growled, and poking through the fridge,
she popped grapes in her mouth while toasting
bread for peanut butter and banana sandwiches.

She inhaled the sandwiches, but not quite ready
to face Lachlan, or anyone, just yet, wandered to
the room where he had gotten his second coat.
She wasn't sure why she was going there until she
picked up the stack of framed pictures and sat on
the bed. Happier times. Seeing Magnus was painful, all the more so knowing exactly what she'd
infected him with. Seeing Lachlan also was painful, for different reasons. He was never as jovial
as Magnus, but he'd been happy then. His eyes
crinkled into the most amazing brightness, his
smile low-key and sexy.

This room was on the other side of the formal
dining room, so it didn't have doors leading to
the courtyard. Instead, it had a window that over-
looked the woods. Soft light pooled in through
the open drapes, sparkling on the dust she'd sent
spinning into the air.

She turned to the pile of belongings that had
to be Lachlan's. There were stacks of DVDs, some
typical guy movies, others decidedly more interesting: *Basic Instinct, Chloe, Blue Velvet, Eyes Wide
Shut*. Sexy movies. She remembered him talking

about research. Yeah, she supposed she had used romance novels as a learning tool, too.

Books were stacked on top of the dresser. Nothing happy or uplifting here, only a lot of dark drama, as far as she could tell: *The Girl with the Dragon Tattoo*, *The Corrections*, *The Road*, *The Heart Is a Lonely Hunter*. He had also read the classics, like *The Pillars of the Earth* and the *Sound and the Fury*.

She pulled the incredibly soft blanket up over her lap and reached for a stack of music CDs. Some Scottish music: Ashley MacIsaac, Loreena McKennitt, one with bagpipes. The rest were more contemporary, though nothing recent. U2, no surprise. Alternative rock, classic rock, and several mixes he'd burned. She pulled one of those out and set it in the stereo system, which she had to plug in. She wasn't familiar with the groups on the mix: Staind, Limp Bizkit, Live, or Fuel. Her tastes ran to pop, happy music, like Natasha Bedingfield and Jason Mraz. Or soulful songs that spoke to her, like Sia and Sarah McLachlan.

She started the CD. The first song was "It's Been a While." Not screaming rock, like she'd expected, but soulful in its own way. She listened to the words, feeling them tug at her. It had been a while since he'd been able to hold his head high. Consequences. A man who'd messed up his life. She pulled the blanket to her chest, clutching it in her hands, felt the singer's pain and Lachlan's pain. Then the singer sang about how long it had been since he'd seen the way candles lit her face, but he could remember just the way she tasted.

She shuddered, because she wasn't thinking of the taste of her lips, but of other places on her body, erotic places where no man had ever put his mouth.

Another song, by the same group featuring Fred Durst, singing about being outside looking in. She had been a freak, something dark, all her life, the only aberration she'd ever known. Now she'd found someone else who, in a different way, was like her.

Jessie was totally sucked into the words, into Lachlan, his pain, and the erotic interpretation of the lyrics, when he stepped into the doorway. He wore a black shirt, half buttoned, smelling of car oil, a smear of it on his neck, rubbing his hands with a towel. His jeans were tight, hugging his lower body, in contrast to the loose shirt that hung over his waistband.

"You had me worried, when I couldn't find you." He took her in. "What are you doing?" His question wasn't interrogative but merely curious. His gaze fell on the CD she held and then went to the pictures on the bed next to her.

"Seeing who you were. Before." She got to her feet and walked closer to him. The oil smelled good, masculine and capable. "You still are that man, you know."

The curiosity in his eyes changed to something

liquid, like the ruffled surface of a lake during a windy day. "You can't say that."

"But I can. I know what you've done, unless you have other skeletons hiding in your closet. Making illegal copies of music, maybe. Running a red light. Parking tickets, I bet." She took the cloth from his hands and rubbed at the oil on his neck. His body stiffened at her touch. She showed him the grease stain, then handed the cloth back.

"I figured out a way," he said. "The whole time I'm working on the carburetor, I'm thinking about how to make it fair for you."

She blinked. "Fair?"

"Without touching you."

It hit her, what he was talking about. Her cheeks flushed and she gave an embarrassed laugh. "I was being silly. Really. Nothing is fair when it comes to men and women. Don't worry about it." She waved it off but stopped in mid-motion. "What was the way?"

He gave her the most sinful smile. "If you're game."

Her heart spiraled, spinning her stomach right along with it. She felt her pulse pounding at her throat. "You said it earlier. I'm not afraid of anything." Lord, she sounded all breathy.

"You're terrified, but you'll do it anyway."

She half expected him to produce a vibrator, having dug through *her* things. But no, she could see both his hands, now tucked into the front pockets of his jeans. "What do you have in mind?"

"You do as I say. Your hands, my command. I keep my honor, and you . . . well, you get off."

Now the spiraling sensation went right down to between her legs. "You're going to watch me?"

"No way. I don't have that kind of willpower. Clearly. We'll be back-to-back. No touching or seeing each other."

Okay, breathe. Excitement coiled through her, throbbing with the mere thought of it.

He raised his eyebrow. "I assume you've gotten yourself off before, given our earlier conversation."

"Well, *yeah.* I'd be all shriveled up down there if I hadn't. I've just never done it . . . with anyone around."

"And you've never had a guy do you?"

"No. One guy tried to ram his hand down my pants while he squeezed my breast with the other, and that was after the first kiss. I mean, *minutes* after the first kiss. So no, I never let him go any further. Or anyone else."

"You're too sweet." His gaze swept down her, heating her skin. "But not some innocent, prim and proper flower."

Oh, gawd, he'd remembered her exact words. She was in trouble. Big trouble. "I'll go find my . . . you know, my thing."

"Your vibrator? You weren't shy about saying the word before."

"That was different."

"No vibrator. Use your fingers."

Her eyebrows rose. "I've never done it that way before." At least a vibe looked like a man.

"First time for everything."

"Fine. But I'm not doing this alone."

Again, that inquisitive rise of his eyebrow. "Meaning?"

"I've never touched a man, but I want to direct you, too."

He groaned. "You're not going to make this easy on me, are you?"

"I'll be less self-conscious. It'll make it easier on me." She gave him a big smile. "You do know how to get yourself off that way, I assume. You're a guy, and I've heard guys . . . well, you know."

"If I didn't, I'd be all shriveled up down there."

They laughed, but it didn't last long.

"You're serious?" he asked.

"Very."

Resigned, he walked to the window and closed the drapes, making the room nearly dark. The glow of the stereo lights, red and green, gave enough light that she could see him unbuttoning his shirt. He flung it to the side and started on his jeans.

She pulled her top over her head, then unclasped her bra and dropped it to the floor. They slid out of their pants at the same time.

She let out an inaudible sigh at the sight of the colored lights washing over his chest and averted her gaze. "So how are we doing this?"

"We sit on the bed, back-to-back." He climbed

to the center and sat, facing the headboard. "Lean against me."

His back felt warm and smooth and incredibly sexy because it was bare and hers was bare. *Breathe. This is going to be fantastic. And wild. And embarrassing.*

"Take off your panties," he said.

She shimmied out of them and realized it was the first time she'd been naked around a man. "You, too."

"I'm not wearing panties."

She rolled her eyes. "Your skivvies." Damn, her throat felt like she'd swallowed a wad of tissue.

He pulled them off and resettled against her. "Spread your legs and—"

"Start somewhere safe. Ease me in."

"Safe. Alright. Run your hand down your collarbone."

The song that was playing now, so appropriate, the male lead singing, "Come my lady, come come, my lady." Something about butterflies.

"I don't feel any movement," he said, a teasing lilt in his voice.

"Lachlan . . . I don't know about this."

"You wanted to get off."

"No, I was mad because you got off."

"So now it's your turn. We don't have to do this if you're scared—I mean uncomfortable."

Oh, he had to throw the word scared out there, didn't he? Because he was drawn by her fearlessness. How brave was she when she could face Russell but not touch herself?

"I'm moving, I'm moving." She slid her hand down the center of her chest.

"Too fast. Take your time, draw the tips of your fingers around the curve of your breasts, and then circle your nipples."

She opened her mouth to protest but closed it and did as he said. Touching herself was far different than using a device. Was it cheating to imagine his callused hands on her?

His voice softened to a low, almost hypnotic tone. "Put your hands on both breasts, feel their weight, their softness."

It hit her then. *This is what he'd be doing if he could allow himself to.* She closed her eyes. *Him touching me. His hands on me.*

"Your turn," she said. "I want you to wet your fingers and run them around your nipples." She'd seen that in a movie once. "And then blow softly."

She felt the circulator motion of his arm, heard him blow out a long breath. She imagined his nipples-puckering. "Now do the other one."

After he had done so, he said, "Move your hands lower, across your stomach. Feel your fingers on your skin, how soft it is. Skim the upper edge of your pubic hair, and then cup your hands over it."

She felt the warm pulse of the pressure against her pubic bone.

"Slowly, up and down, round and round," he said, his voice low and soft and persuasive.

She was already hot and throbbing. She'd never gone from zero to eighty so fast before. It was hard to focus on what she wanted him to do, with her own distracting sensations. What did the women in the novels do? "Move your hand down that hard, ridged stomach. Down through your hair, next to your . . . shaft. Just brushing by it."

She could feel the movement of his arm, following her directions, his body twitching as he, no doubt, brushed past his penis. Being in control, telling him what to do, heady stuff.

"Slide your fingers to your inner thigh," he said, "Tracing circles, moving closer, closer with each circle. So close that your finger brushes that delicate ridge between your thigh and your vagina."

How did he know so much? Did those erotic movies teach him that this felt good, an innocent touch that grazed the part of her that wanted lust, that felt wet and hot?

"Wrap your hands around your cock." His word for it. It sounded raw and slightly dirty as it came off her tongue. "Keep the touch light and stroke up and down." She imagined his body, what she'd do to him, though she hadn't seen him completely naked. She saw herself being creative, confident, and sexy. She felt his body move in accordance with her orders.

"Bring your fingers to your cleft, slowly," he said. "Don't touch your . . . I'm not sure what you call it. The nub. Put your fingers on either side of it, sliding back and forth. Are you wet?"

"Mmm hmm." She could barely talk. Just the slightest brush of her fingers had her toes curling. *Not ready to go off yet.* "Grab your cock firmly, and rub your thumb over the tip. Are *you* wet?" Did men get wet, too?

"Aye." He shuddered.

Guess so.

"Did you—"

"No." The word was strained. "Try different kinds of movements. Experiment and find what feels good to you. Guys like a quick, firm stroke; I'm not sure what gets a girl off."

It felt different using her fingers, more intimate. Real. She was so ready. But it wasn't her touch alone. It was him, the feel of him against her, directing her and pushing her envelope.

She felt his movements, slow and languid. Lord but she wanted to touch him, to wrap her fingers around him and know she was causing him to make those soft gasps. She sucked in a breath, feeling the storm moving closer, thunder vibrating through her.

Hold on. What was the MacLeod battle cry? Hold fast!

He said, "God, you don't know how hard it is—"

"Very hard, I imagine."

"No, how . . . difficult it is not to reach around and do what I'm imagining you doing."

She leaned her head back against him. "Yes, I do."

"I did not need to know that."

"Sorry."

"Tell me what you feel like, Jess."

Because he'd never touched a woman. Couldn't learn that from a movie or magazine. "Slickery. Hot and swollen." *Touch me, Lachlan. Feel for yourself.* She held the words in. *If you do that, he'll give in and touch you, oh my, touch you and slide into you and*—she blinked—*and hate himself afterward.* "I'm about to go over the edge," she said on a gasp.

"Me, too."

"Can we go together?"

Their backs moved against each other, hot and moist.

"On the count of three," he said, breathless. "One . . . two . . ."

Lightning struck, making her body go rigid as spark after spark of pleasure rolled over her. She let out a series of quick gasps, trying to hear him over her own noise. His body had stiffened, too, and he leaned harder against her.

They both shifted and fell backward, next to each other, chests rising and falling, the musky scent of sex faint in the air. Her head was next to his knee, but she could lift her head slightly and see him.

He flopped one arm over his head. "Haven't gone off in almost a year, and now I've come twice in a day's time."

She lifted her head more. "You haven't even . . ."

"No. Nothing. Not even thoughts of it, until you came along. Damn ye."

He'd twisted the end with the Scots accent, and a smile. She could hear it in his voice, see it from her side view.

"So, are we still considered virgins?" she asked.

"We can swear in a court of law."

She dropped her head back onto the bed. "It sure doesn't feel that way." If this was what having sex with a man was like, she was going to like it. A lot. The only problem was, she couldn't imagine it with anyone but Lachlan.

CHAPTER 16

Jessie was *here*? But . . . how? How could she have possibly come here? You're sure?" Russell looked at the wall inside the pulsing mass the Void had become, at the soul embedded there. There was only half a face left in the wall.

"I could feel her. She came for Henry. I heard them talking, though not what they were saying. There's too much noise, the breathing, the muffling of everything."

He sensed the frustration, heard the underlying fear. He had created this prison for Henry, and it had taken on a life of its own, filling in the once empty space with itself like a tumor . . . drawing its life source from the Darkness he'd created it out of. He didn't know all the secrets of Darkness. There had been no one to ask, no manual, only a desperate need for vengeance and two brothers who didn't bother to wonder about the consequences.

He was still that same man.

Every time he visited the Void, it consumed more and more rapidly. Desperation consumed him the same way.

It stunned him that Jessie had somehow managed to come here. How had she even known about it?

"You haven't talked with her yet, I take it?" the face said.

"She won't believe anything I say. Now she has the man with magic protecting her. He's put some kind of block around wherever they are. It throws the dogs off, like sending a compass spinning. They think they've got the scent and then they run off in another direction."

"Julian wouldn't help?"

He shook his head, heaviness at the thought of him. "He still hates me."

"I'm sorry."

"No, it's okay. I wasn't counting on his help. If only I'd known Jessie was here. Everything would have been solved." But they couldn't communicate unless he was here.

"It's not like I could tell you. But she'll come back."

His heart lifted. "How can you be sure?"

"I felt her agony over leaving Henry behind. She's stubborn and loyal, and, as we've seen, strong. When she returns, I'll get her attention. She won't leave him here to be swallowed up. I'll use that loyalty and tell her the truth. She'll give us what we want then."

Hope bloomed in his chest. "I have to go." The breathing, the ever-encroaching wall of flesh . . . how could one stay here without going insane?

He left that chamber, and as eager as he was to get out of there, slid through the layers and stepped into Henry's presence. He took pleasure in seeing him there.

"You come here often, and yet you rarely visit me," Henry said. "Is it guilt that keeps you away?"

Russell stepped closer. "Guilt? You think I should feel guilt for putting you here? Did you ever suffer guilt for how you treated me? For hating me only because I was born? For outright blaming me for our mother's death? When you stole my lover, did you feel a twinge then? No, I doubt you ever did. You took her only because somehow it made us even, didn't it?"

"I did, yes. In life, I would never have admitted it. Blaming God for taking our mother seemed too dangerous. Blaming you, a defenseless boy, was much easier and safer. You took away so much, what little we had after her death, what little of our overworked father's time. Then we met Calista, and she filled me as I hadn't been filled in years. But there you were, as always, horning in on our time, being the pesky younger brother. She pitied you, Russell. That was her biggest feeling toward you. I saw how you were trying to manipulate her emotions, and that's when I pushed ahead on my plans to marry her and leave you behind."

Russell felt exactly how he'd felt then, despair, anger. "She loved me."

"Like a brother. But then you snuck back into her life and manipulated her again."

Russell smiled, feeling smug about those last months when he and Calista were meeting furtively, when she told him that he brought her to life again. That was before he'd begun to heal her. Then he became her savior. "I gave her the one thing you couldn't: healing."

"By using Darkness, without knowing what it would do to her. Hadn't you learned yet what playing with this . . . this dark substance can do?"

He would not address his recklessness. If Henry knew what he was planning, what he'd done, the lecture would really kick in. "Your daughter was here."

That stilled Henry's words, putting shock into what little Russell could see of his expression. "Leave her out of this."

"She is to play a very important role in my life, Henry."

"No! You've destroyed enough. She's innocent."

Russell smiled, backing toward the door. "I have no intention of hurting her. Indeed, she and I will be close. Very close indeed."

After an early lunch, or a late breakfast, depending on how you saw it, Lachlan dragged Jessie back to the studio to work on her Darkness. The air in the courtyard felt only moderately warmer than it had in the dark of morning.

"Lachlan, I'm going back to the Void."

"What?" He didn't stop, his hand on her wrist— yes, literally dragging her.

"If I can get my dad out of that wall, maybe I can bring him back to his body. His soul is still here. Well, *there*, technically. It's still around, and so is his body. I can bring them together like you were talking about earlier. I have to go back and get him out."

"You're not going back."

"Uh, somehow you missed the part where I wasn't asking permission."

He paused and faced her. "When you left, and you collapsed in my arms, do you know how it felt to watch you and wonder if you were coming back?"

"No, how did it feel?" She wanted to know, to hear what she saw in his eyes now as he thought about it.

"It scared the hell out of me."

Okay, maybe she didn't want to know. "I'm sorry about that, but I'm going."

He tunneled his hands through his hair, obviously still used to having his longer locks as his fingers kept going past the ends. "If you never come back, and your body dies, I'll bury you in the plot near my mum."

Trying to intimidate her, was he? "The plot will be fine. You'd have no believable explanation of my condition if you took me to a hospital, and you could get into trouble. I don't want that. I'm sorry you'll have to dig a big hole, though. But no one will report me missing. No one will be looking for me. And no one will miss me."

His mouth tightened into a line. "*I'll* miss you."

Her heart caved on those words. Was he just manipulating her? "No, you'll be glad to get rid of a troublemaker."

"Troublemaker?"

"Yeah, you know, the one who almost got you killed twice, screwed up Magnus's life."

"Don't be so hard on yourself. You gave me something to live for, for the first time in almost a year. Maybe ever." His fingers tightened on her wrist. "Your father said Darkness could be controlled. You're going to learn to control it, especially if you're going back there."

She'd given him something to live for. Those words twined inside her. "And what if *I* kill *you*? Maybe you'd better show me where the plot is, and the shovel."

"You are the most exasperating person I've ever known."

"Ditto."

"You make me all knotted up inside."

"Ditto."

"And you're bent on driving me absolutely crazy."

"Ditto. We're not talking about just going to the Void anymore, are we?"

He grunted, pulling her along again.

Just as she suspected. "What's that?" She pointed to a portion of the house next to the studio, which had only one small window and a solid door.

"My dad's lab. He kept specimens in there, and Blue Moon, the Callorian's DNA. It's where he worked on the antidote."

She looked down, now near the place where Lachlan meditated. "So these weird things all over, they're fungus?"

"Aye, his beloved fungus and slime molds. He was obsessed with them, always had been, he said. The only way to get his attention, really, was to talk fungus with him, or go on meteor chases."

"Sounds like you had to compete with fungus, you and Magnus."

"We did, but he loved us, we had no doubt of that. In his way. He protected us, made a nice life for us."

She knelt down and studied what looked like a cluster of purple balloons. The sign next to it read: METATRICHIA VESPARIUM. "Wild stuff."

"You're stalling."

"Yeah, pretty much." She stood and allowed him to lead her to the studio door. He was right, of course. She'd been hiding from her Darkness just like she'd been hiding from Russell.

She walked beside him, and he loosened his grip. She liked the feel of his hand on her, though. After their . . . well, she wasn't sure what to call it.

Afterward, they got dressed in the dark and went on as though it hadn't happened. But something had changed between them, at least on her end. She was ultra aware of him now, of his physicality, masculinity. He had done all of that for her, guided her, and touched himself. Even though they hadn't touched each other, it had been an erotic encounter. She felt an odd mix of embarrassment, though not shame, and hunger. She wanted more.

He'd changed into the jersey pants that molded his ass so nicely, and the white T-shirt that was tight on his chest but hung loose over his stomach. They faced each other, standing in the center of the room like two gunslingers with their hands at their sides.

She closed her eyes and willed it. Fear dried her mouth, parched her throat.

Nothing happened. She opened her eyes, staring right into Lachlan's. "I can't seem to do it without a trigger."

He rushed her, pushing her until her back pressed against the wall. His hands pinned hers up by her head. "When I broke into your apartment and we fought, you Became. Go back to that time. Fight me."

She played the video in her mind, him waiting for her, grabbing her and pinning her like this. She remembered that part well enough. That's when she'd felt his erection and was scared to death he was there to rape her.

Her mouth twisted into a smile. "It's not going to work. I'm not scared of you anymore."

He huffed a breath and stepped back. "Put yourself back in the moment. Feel what you felt then. When your mind experiences an event in the past, or even something imagined, your body responds as though it's happening now."

"Yeah, but the problem is, what I'm feeling as you're pinning me there is not fear because I know you now." *And I want you now.* No need to complicate things by saying it aloud. The truth was, she'd been intrigued by him even before she knew him. She remembered watching the video, eyes focused on his body, on the way they interacted.

"How about imagining Russell, then?" he said.

She closed her eyes again and remembered that night at the carnival, watching him slash at Magnus. Forcing her to make that terrible choice to heal him.

She felt the energy moving, shifting. She felt fear of it, too, but pushed past it. And she focused on becoming a tiger, like the cat she'd felt at the salon. More vicious than a wolf. Bigger fangs, sharper claws. Russell had done this to her, made her infect Magnus, made her Become on purpose. *Bastard.* He had killed her mother and taken her father's body. *Son of a bitch.* She could kill him.

The roar rose in her throat, like a bubble of air. She flexed her fingers, imagining claws extending out. She would kill him.

What if she killed Lachlan instead? The energy vanished. He stood there with wide eyes.

"Did I change at all?"

"Before you became a blur. This time you had more shape. Paws. I definitely saw claws extending from your hands."

"Did it look anything like a tiger?"

He rubbed his chin. "Aye, a bit. Do it again."

"I'm afraid to hurt you."

"You weren't afraid of me when I was wielding my sword."

She raised her eyebrow and gave him a naughty look. "Well, I couldn't actually see you wielding your sword. We were back-to-back, after all."

For a moment he looked puzzled, and then he got it and barked a laugh. "Cheeky girl. I'm talking about the time you had your hands on my sword."

Oh, just the thought of that swiped the smile from her face. "Mm, that time. Well, we both have something that could kill the other. We need to be afraid or at least wary."

"Wary, aye. I can handle myself, as can you."

She warmed under his confidence. Then something occurred to her. "If we kill Russell, we'll kill my dad's body, the only chance he has of coming back. We can't hurt him physically." She glanced at the swords hanging on the wall. Yes, hope *was* a double-edged sword.

"Well, that's going to make defeating him a bit difficult, don't you think?"

She paced, biting the end of her fingernail. "What will happen if I can free my dad's soul? Will he go back to his body or be like Olaf? Either way, it's better than where he is now. I have to free him. How do I do that?"

"I wish I had an answer. Other than to use Darkness, if you can while you're in the Void."

"I don't know. I couldn't feel it there, that heaviness that's always inside me." She paused in front of him. "You're right, I do need to control Darkness."

He cupped his hand behind his ear. "Wait a minute. I was right? Did I hear that correctly?"

She smirked. "Yes."

"Could I be right about not going back to that wretched place as well?"

"Not at all." She brought up the anger at Russell again, walking, wringing her hands. She could feel Darkness growing in her. Like before, when she'd thrown Lachlan across the room, everything blurred. *Tiger.* Through the blur, she saw Lachlan standing in front of her. *Mine.*

The possessive thought threw her right out again.

"What happened?" he asked.

"It's hard to focus." *Not mine.* Not when she had this inside her, not now that she knew what had driven Russell to kill. She took a deep breath. "Okay. Russell. Bastard."

She used the memory of her father in the wall to dredge up everything she felt for the man who put him there. The dark blur enveloped her body, as slippery as oil to hold onto.

"Let me try something else." She held out her hands, palms up, and imagined breaking off pieces of herself. Tried so hard her head hurt.

The black fog swirled in her palms. She pushed harder. Yes, they were forming into round balls. Russell could direct his dogs. He'd used them to track her, probably. They were part of his Darkness. She could do it, too.

With sheer force of will, she directed them to a place on the far wall. They shivered and trembled, their fog tightening into form.

Yes! Go splat.

They both launched off her hands . . . and fell to the floor, where they splintered apart. She let out a sigh of frustration. "Russell's had a lot longer to work on this stuff. He probably did it in his cell during lights out. And he's Callorian, and the one who tapped directly into Darkness. I inherited a weaker version of it."

Lachlan was still staring at the floor where they'd hit. He finally looked at her. "But you did it. Which means you can learn to master it."

At least someone was excited about it. And he hadn't rubbed it in that she'd also had plenty of time to work with it. Instead, she'd taught herself karate and kept in shape to be defensive. Now she had to go on the offensive.

She closed her eyes, held out her hands and concentrated.

Two grueling hours later she was lobbing black blobs toward Lachlan, who was hitting them baseball style with his sword. They splintered on contact, much weaker than Russell's dogs, who could withstand the hit.

She dropped down to the shiny wood floor, too tired to even care how hard it was. "I'm exhausted. Not the kind I feel after working on karate moves for two hours."

"Using supernatural abilities wipes you out in ways beyond physical exertion. I was always shattered after astral projection." He loomed above her, his hand stretched down. "One more hour. Then we'll break for a meal and rest."

"One more *hour*?"

"Sixty little minutes."

She merely looked at him, not moving a muscle.

His mouth quirked. "You're giving me the same look you had when you sent me that lovely gesture with your finger."

"That's 'cause I'm too tired to make the gesture. But don't doubt for a second that I'm sending it."

"You're not going back until I'm sure you can protect yourself." He tilted his head at an angle. "You don't look very tough at the moment."

"I can't move. I mean, I really can't move. My body is a blob of jelly."

He knelt down, scooped her up and flung her over his shoulder. Then he walked to the door.

"Where are you taking me?"

"To bed."

Her body perked up at that. "Really?"

"You can have a little rest, eat, and then we're back at it."

Rest. Of course. "Thank you."

He walked across the courtyard to the room she was staying in, opened the door, and set her gently down on the bed. "I'll get you in an hour."

Which meant he wasn't joining her. Just as well, all things considered. Maybe she'd scared him a bit, seeing her Become. Maybe it disgusted him or freaked him out, though he didn't look either of those things.

He tucked her in, as he'd done one other time. She felt like a girl, Daddy tucking her in. He made her feel safe, loved, or at least cared about. She grabbed for his hand as he started to back away.

"My name is Ally Jackson. Short for Allyssa."

He stopped, his expression softening.

"I met Jessie at the second foster home. She was a foster kid, too. Remember Mattie Stepanek, the boy in the wheelchair who was on television a lot? He wrote those beautiful poetry books about love and peace? Jessie had the same fatal form of muscular dystrophy."

It hurt to think of her, so pretty, with glossy blond hair and blue eyes the color of a deep mountain lake. "Jessie had been with the Marshes for most of her life. She was already in a wheelchair when I got there. She, more than anyone, taught me that no matter what, you can find joy in life. It was a great lesson for me. I was scared, angry, closed. She was the only person I ever opened up to, though not completely. I told her about my dad killing my mom, and I hated lying like that. But if she ever heard the news story or found it online, it would be my dad who went to prison, so I kept it simple."

He just listened, without any judgment, arms at his sides.

She scrunched the blanket in her hands. "She and I were born on the same day and year. We looked nothing alike, but we told people we were twins. When she died two years later, I was devastated.

"Soon after that, I was waiting to give Mrs. Marsh my report card when I saw Jessie's folder buried under a bunch of other stuff in her office. Mom Marsh had to run to find the ringing phone, and I opened the folder. Copies of Jessie's Social Security card and birth and death certificate were in there. I took the folder and put it in my school backpack."

She shrugged. "I don't know why I did it. Maybe to keep her close. Or maybe I knew I would take her identity someday. I'm sure Mrs. Marsh was supposed to file something with the government, but right afterward, her husband got into a car accident. His injuries made life even more hectic. She probably forgot all about the folder.

"I continued on through school and graduated. I knew Russell would be released someday, and I figured I'd be safe if he couldn't find me through my name. And it was like resurrecting my old friend. Jessie lived! But yeah, I felt wrong doing it, too. The first time I got a paycheck and my new driver's license, I worried. Nothing happened, no one knocked on my door, and eventually I relaxed." She looked at him. He'd stood the whole time she was talking, no expression on his face. "Am I a horrible person?"

"No." He reached down and brushed the back of his hand against her cheek.

He wouldn't judge her. He'd done worse things, in his opinion. Like him, she judged herself more harshly than anyone ever would.

He stepped back. "Get some sleep, Jessie. I want to see your cat. All of it."

CHAPTER 17

Olaf!" Jessie called, standing in front of Lachlan in the living room.

Nothing.

"What if he was sucked into the Light? I haven't seen him since I came back." Panic tightened her throat. She needed him. They'd spent another hour in the studio working on the blobs, and she'd very nearly gotten a *splat* out of them. She hadn't produced her cat, though.

"Olaf," Lachlan said.

Olaf's image shimmered into place. "Ye called?"

She crossed her arms over her chest. "I did, but you didn't come."

"Canna hear ye, lass. Only the laddie, here. Missed me, did ye?"

She smiled. "Yes. Terribly." That smile faded. "I want you to take me back to the Void. I need to get my dad out of there."

He listened with what appeared to be sympathy, but at those last words said, "I dinna want to go back there."

"My daddy's soul is there. I've been an orphan since I was ten, and now I have a chance to get my dad back. I can't leave him there, Olaf." She told him what she'd seen, how the wall was swallowing him. "I have to save him. I'll pay your price."

She wasn't above bribing. She pulled off her shirt and closed the few feet between her and Lachlan. She yanked his shirt over his head, slapped her hands against his back and pulled him against her. On her tiptoes, her mouth connected with his.

"You are killing me," Lachlan managed to say.

She plunged her tongue into his mouth, raking her nails down his back, and felt his body respond. His hands had started bracing her face but now moved back through her hair. She kissed down his chin, his throat, holding onto his hips for balance. Her tongue flicked against his skin, leaving behind a trail of chill bumps. He let out a soft moan, both agony and pleasure as she moved down to trace circles around his hard nipple. She didn't know men's nipples hardened when they were aroused. There was so much she didn't know about men and their bodies. She sucked softly. She'd never done this before either.

All around him was Olaf's ghostly image, but she was tasting, licking, Lachlan. It was all him, breathing in huffs, fingers kneading in her hair. She moved across his chest to his other nipple, doing the same. Then she moved lower, down the ridges of his stomach.

"No, you're really killing me," he said on a tight breath.

She'd hooked her fingers on the waistband of his jeans in front. She had the most delirious urge to unbutton, unzip, taste him. That hard ridge went right up to the top of the waistband.

"Now ye've got it, lassie!"

Olaf. She jerked upright, blinking to bring herself back and trying to catch her breath. "There." She pulled on her shirt. "Was that sufficient?"

Lachlan made a choking sound, but she tried to keep her focus on Olaf, who wore a ghostly grin. "I wasna going to ask you for that again. Ye won me over with the sob story about your dad. Still, I enjoyed it verra much."

She smoothed down her hair, feeling all the blood leave her face before rushing back. "Oh." Cleared her throat. "Well, then. Thank you for helping."

Had she been a bit . . . too eager? Now that Lachlan had woken up her body, she craved sensual pleasure. Craved him.

"Did you come?" she whispered.

"No, I won't be going off like a teenager again. I've got it under control, no thanks to you. Are you trying to drive me nuts?"

"Just paying the price."

She sat on the sofa, the leather cool beneath her. Lachlan still looked flushed and peeved as he sat down in front of her.

"If you didn't come, why was there semen at the tip?"

He raised his eyebrow. "It's charming, really, this mix of sensuality and naiveté."

"No, it's not." She didn't want to come off as naive. "I'm curious, that's all."

"Are we ready?" Olaf said. "Before the sad story wears off and I change my mind."

She reached out and clasped Lachlan's hands. The weird energy flowed through her, like last time, and then she was floating in nothingness, the Void a dark specter above them. Olaf handed her the rope, and she wound it through her fingers and faced the opening.

"Daddy, I'm coming." She whispered it, then shouted it.

Even knowing what to expect, it was no less disgusting and scary when she slid into the folds. How fast was the thing swallowing her father? Would only the tip of his nose be showing now? He'd said time was different here, but she wasn't sure whether it would work for or against her. She was midway in, trying to remember how she'd gone last time, when she heard a woman's voice.

"Ally! Is that you, baby?"

She knew that voice. It wound around her heart the same way the rope twined around her fingers. "Mom?"

"Thank God you're here. I thought I felt you before, but I couldn't believe it. But it's true."

The hope in her voice sailed through Jessie, too. "I'm coming."

"Follow my voice. I can't wait to see you. You're probably all grown up now."

Jessie slid through the cracks, timing the breaths. Her fingers tightened on the rope. She wouldn't drop it this time.

She stepped into a small chamber like the one that held her father. *"Mom."* A word filled with pain and love. The same nausea hit her as she took in the horror of that wall. She rushed forward. "How are you here?" Calista was in the same state, not much of her beautiful face showing, not a strand of the long dark hair Jessie remembered. She touched her mom's fingers, feeling again like that little girl who never got enough of her mommy's love.

"I came when your father's soul did, after I died."

"That was you calling to me the last time I came here, wasn't it?"

A moment of silence passed. "I forget I can't nod anymore. Yes. I could feel you there, just barely hear your voice. How have you come to be here?"

She told her briefly about Olaf and held up the golden rope. "This is my way out. I came back to free Daddy. I'll free you, too." She tugged on the rope to bring it to her mother's fingers.

Hope flared in Calista's eyes for a second. "But I have no body to go back to."

Jessie gasped in frustration. "I didn't think about that."

"But there is a way."

"How?" She gripped the rope as hope surged.

"Do you trust me, baby? Do you trust your mommy?"

She nodded.

"I know you think Russell has been hunting you for revenge."

Her heart plunged. "Yes, he's been hunting me. He killed my dog. He hurt my friends."

"Calm down, sweetheart. He's only been hunting you because he needs something from you. To free me."

She stumbled back a step. "Free you? But he put you here. He killed you—that's why you have no body to return to. He killed you and took Daddy's body."

"Your father killed me. Russell sent him here to punish him. He sent me here to try to find a way to bring me back. He's been working on that, but all those years in prison kept him from doing much."

"No." Jessie shook her head so hard she felt dizzy. "Daddy did *not* kill you."

Calista let out a soft breath, her green eyes filled with sadness. "You've gone through so much, you poor thing. That terrible day . . . fifteen years ago, right? How much did you see?"

"Russell and Daddy fighting. You were . . . already on the floor bleeding. Then Russell sent his Darkness into Daddy's body and banished him to here."

"I'm glad you didn't see him kill me. But you

must know what he did before you try to free him. Russell came to the house to declare for me. He'd been in love with me all those years, and no, he shouldn't have barged in like he did. He was a man driven by passion."

By Darkness.

"Your father became outraged. I knew about the Darkness, but I'd never seen it in him. It was frightening. He became a monster and spent that rage on me."

"No."

"Honey, I'm sorry. I never wanted to take that away from you. But you mustn't free that man."

"If Russell is trying to help you, why are you imprisoned just like Daddy?" None of this made sense.

"Russell didn't know what this would become. He created it, but it took on a life all its own. Your father and I were in different chambers. He was contained. I was not. But eventually this mass began growing. It trapped my feet first, and then the wall came to me, growing inch by inch. It will continue until it swallows me whole. It's growing faster, and time is running out for me." Fear penetrated her voice, her eyes, tearing at Jessie's heart.

She instinctually shifted her feet, looking down at the ridged gray floor. "What does Russell need from me?"

"Your blood. He knew you would never trust him, so he had planned to capture you and take some blood. Not a lot, a pint maybe. He would then release you unharmed. I hated that it would be so frightening for you, but I knew he was right. You fought him." She smiled softly. "Of course you would. You were a feisty girl.

"He felt terrible about your dog, broke down and cried right here. But it was threatening him. And he's growing desperate. He loves me, has always loved me. Your father was a good man, but he hated his younger brother. I became something else they fought over."

Jessie could see how they'd fall in love with a beautiful, fragile woman. "But Daddy loved you, didn't he?"

"I think he did, but in this fierce, territorial way. He was insanely jealous, moving us far away after we married because he thought Russell was looking for me. All Russell wanted was love, acceptance. I loved them both, but I got pregnant by Henry and so I married him. I'm glad I did." She smiled. "Russell had a place in my heart, even after he married, and had a son. I'd heard that his wife died in a fall a few years later. A few months before the end, Russell and I met up. He wanted to heal me. He'd learned Darkness could do that, and he gave me small doses."

Jessie's mouth tightened. "You had an affair, cheated on my dad."

"How could I not fall for a man who loved me that much?"

"So that's why you started getting better."

"He had nothing but his love for me. His son had

turned his back on him. I . . . couldn't do it, too. His devotion has never wavered. He has been coming here ever since my 'death,' trying to free me. But we need you, darling. Just a little of your blood. Please trust him. He won't hurt you, I promise."

Jessie's knees went so weak, she slumped to the floor. Her father a murderer? Russell not so much the bad guy? Her heart hurt, as though this horrible organism was squeezing it.

"I wish I could hold you, darling, like I did when you were a girl. I've missed you so much."

Jessie didn't point out that she had done most of the holding. It didn't matter. The floor pulsed beneath her hands. She lurched up, wavering. "I've missed you, too." All those years of longing for her mother, feeling so pained and envious when she saw mothers and daughters together. "He'll use Darkness to bring your body back?"

"Yes. He'll create a body using your blood, because it contains my DNA. I'll have Darkness, too. We'll be alike, all of us. And maybe someday we can be a family."

"No, I will not be a family with Russell. With you, yes. Not him."

"Okay. You'll need time, I understand that. But he loves me, angel. He loves me so much he's making himself crazy trying to save me. I hate shattering your illusion about your father, but think about this: why was *he* sent to prison?"

"They convict innocent people because of circumstantial evidence all the time."

"Evidence confirmed that he'd done it, blood splatter, fingerprints. Think on it. You'll know in your heart what the truth is. But don't think too long." She wiggled her fingers. "I don't have much time."

The breathing was getting louder.

She walked closer to her mother. "Are you in pain?"

"No. The agony has been watching the walls close in. But it's almost over, one way or the other. You must go. Find Russell, give him your blood, and then come back for your father, if you must. But if you bring your father back now, Russell's soul will be gone, and so will the knowledge of how to bring me back. You must go to Russell first."

The choice twisted inside Jessie. She'd come to save her father, but it would be at the expense of her mother's soul.

"All right."

Her mom sighed in relief. "Thank you, baby. I knew you'd make the right decision. I love you so much."

"I love you, too." The words came out in a whisper. "How do I find him?"

"Put a note on your apartment door with your phone number. He'll call you."

Jessie gripped the rope and walked toward the crevice from which she'd come. One last look at her mom and then she slid in. She followed the rope back through all the pulsing layers, fighting the panic when pressed tight between its breaths.

What if it didn't let go? She felt its hunger.

It eased open, and she slid a few more feet before it closed on her again. Was this how it felt for her parents, being held immobilized? She shuddered, moving again when she could, faster and faster until she broke out of the opening.

She came awake in Lachlan's arms again.

He was studying her. "It didn't work?"

"I didn't even try."

She told him everything, watching the same disbelief she'd felt about Russell's part in it in his expression.

"You're not going to Russell," he said.

"Don't you see, I have to save her? If that's all he wants, then you're safe, too. The only reason he's been so brutal to you is because you're in the way of his saving the person he loves. You said you would kill for me. What Russell's doing isn't so different."

He grunted in disagreement. "You're sure it was your mother? Not some illusion?"

"I'm sure. She's always called me by a lot of endearments: baby, honey."

Lachlan walked over to where he'd propped his sword, never far away. He took it in hand and walked down the hallway toward his room. Where was he going?

He returned a few seconds later, no sword. "When I astral-projected back to that day, I saw it from your point of view. I stayed with you. I want to go back and see it from the kitchen. Olaf!"

The image of the Scottish warrior flickered over Lachlan. "Ye've exhausted me and ye want me again?"

"Believe me, I'd rather do it on my own. We don't have time, or I'd let you rest. I need to go back to the past again. Just a quick trip."

Ah, so that's why he'd put his sword away.

"Nae, canna do any more for a time. Ye ask too much of me."

"We gave you something in return. At our expense, we let you experience carnal pleasure."

"At your expense? Och, ye enjoyed it more than I. Do not fool yourselves, as ye dinna fool me."

"It's not a matter of us enjoying it or not," Lachlan said. He lowered his head. "Aye, she and I lust for each other. But I have honor, or at least I'm trying to have honor."

She walked up to Olaf. "We're only human. Do you remember being human, Olaf? Having weaknesses? Feeling loss?"

Lachlan said, "You threw yourself into battle knowing you could be killed, because you believed in a lost cause. She believes in this cause, and you're the only way for me to find out the truth before she throws herself into a dangerous situation."

She let all of her emotions fill her eyes. "Please?"

Olaf growled. "Ye think ye can tug at me heart with that look?"

She bit her lower lip. "Help me save my mother, Olaf." She put her hands on Lachlan's arm and squeezed, peering into the visage of a face that looked so much older than twenty-six. "We need you."

"All right, all right. Ye've chipped away at me enough."

Lachlan sat on the couch and closed his eyes. She sat next to him. He reminded her of a sleeping cat, fingers convulsing, eyelids twitching. She put her hands on his arm again, thinking of that golden rope that anchored her in the Void.

It amazed her to think that he was going to her past. He'd said he looked like a ghost at the target location. She tried to remember if she'd seen anything strange that day, but the events in the kitchen would have taken all of her attention.

His muscles moved beneath her fingers. If only he could change the past.

He sat up, eyes open, clutching her hand in his. He rubbed his face, as though trying to rub away the horror of what he'd seen. With a deep, shuddering breath, he turned to her. "Your mother was telling the truth. Your father did it."

Her chest caved in, and he pulled her against him. She clutched at him, trying to catch her breath. "What did you see?"

"I came in at the moment it happened. Your father . . . he was destroyed. I could see it on his face as he took the two of them in, I'm guessing just then realizing your mother had been involved with Russell behind his back. He became a wolf and lashed at her. One swipe, like Russell did to Magnus." He held her closer. "I'm sorry."

She sank into his comfort, savoring the feel of his mouth against the top of her head. Her father, a murderer. "That's why he was convicted. The evidence did point to him. So that means, the man's voice I heard, saying he could save Mom with Darkness . . . that was Russell. I assumed it was my dad." She hated to move out of Lachlan's embrace, but she got to her feet. "I have to get in touch with Russell. Mom said to leave a note on my apartment door."

He tried to stand, but his body sagged back onto the couch. "I don't like this."

"Don't you see, it's going to be all right. Russell won't hurt me, won't hurt you. I won't have to hide. And I'll have my mom back."

He took her in. "I hope so. Does this mean you won't have to go back to that Void?"

She shook her head. "I hate the thought of my dad being there, but I can't risk my soul for a murderer's soul." She turned to him. "You look tired." He'd said he was tired after using his abilities. "I'll drive into town—"

"With me." He stumbled down the hall and returned with the sword. "I don't trust Russell. He did say he wanted to talk about your mother the other day. Has he ever tried to tell you what he really wanted before then?"

She thought about it. "Once, he said something about my mother, but I didn't want to hear what he had to say." Now she wished she had. Magnus wouldn't be holding Darkness. "I'll drive, you relax. All I'm doing when I get there is sticking a note to the door and leaving."

"If I fall asleep, wake me when you get there. I'm going up with you."

"All right." She put her hand to his cheek. Her protector. With sleepy eyes.

He dozed while she still tried to process everything. Darkness had turned her father into a murderer. She knew it wasn't in his heart. He was a gentle and loving man. He had adored her mother, coddling her when she fell ill. Yet, Darkness had turned him into a savage beast. She had that beast in her, too. She glanced over at Lachlan. Any man she loved would be subject to it. One false move, one flirtation on his part, and someone would be dead. *Like your nightmares, when you kill the children.*

Not fair. She wanted love, family, the simple things everyone could have. Not her. Never her.

By the time she pulled up to her apartment complex, Lachlan slept like a sweet, innocent boy. The sight of him made her heart swell, filled with an emotion she dared not identify.

She'd run up, tape the note on the door, and come right back down. No need to wake him. She quietly opened the glove box, took out the sticky notes and pen and jotted down her number.

As soon as she reached the top of the stairs, her heart lurched at the sight of her door cracked open. She hadn't notified her landlord of her departure. No one should be getting it ready for the next tenant yet.

Russell moved into the gap, opening the door a little more when he saw her. "Calista said you were coming here. I hope I didn't startle you, but as you saw, time is running out."

Seeing him up close like this, her father's green eyes, his impossibly long eyelashes, twisted her up inside.

He gestured to the living area, where a silver cup, a blood bag, and a needle sat on the table.

She glanced back to the vehicle where Lachlan still slept.

"Your mother was so happy to see you. I haven't seen her with that much hope in a long time."

It was bizarre, being civil with the man she'd been hiding from all this time. "You visit her every day?"

"I hate knowing she's there alone."

"You love her." She could see the agony saturating his expression.

"More than life itself." Genuine emotion seeped into his voice, a love warped by Darkness. "I loved her from the first moment I saw her, and all those years after your father stole her away from me. I could see that she still loved me, too. She had affection for your father, but we . . . we had an overwhelming kind of love. Have you ever loved like that before?"

She glanced again at her SUV. "Only my parents." Was what she felt—the passion, the desire—Darkness?

"Your father and I had a turbulent history. I'm sorry for taking his body, but he killed your mother. I couldn't bear for him to live when she was dead. But she's not dead. She can be here with you again, Jessie. However you feel about me, I respect that. I've done some terrible things to you, but I hope you understand why. I'll stay out of your way, allow you and your mother to get to know each other again."

Her throat tightened at that. "What do I do?"

He stepped back and opened the door more. "Just lie down there. I confess that I have no practice in sticking a needle into one's vein, but I've done a lot of reading on the subject. It might hurt, but I doubt I'll do any permanent damage. In any case, it'll be over in a minute or two. It won't take as much bravery as it took for you to go to the Void, not once but twice. I admire you. I know how scary that place is."

She shivered. "All right." She sent one more glance Lachlan's way before taking a step into the apartment. She saw no weapons, but of course, he *was* a weapon. But so was she.

Before Lachlan even woke, it would be over. He wouldn't have to worry anymore. She'd go back to the car, drive to Sanctuary, and tell him it was over. Or would she wait with Russell to see her mother come alive again?

The door closed behind her.

CHAPTER 18

Lachlan dozed, lulled by his exhaustion and the soft vibration of the car as it moved through traffic. His body was dead tired, but his mind rolled through the possibility of Jessie being safe.

Maybe.

So all this time, Russell had only been trying to get some of her blood.

Maybe.

He didn't like her meeting with him, but he would be right beside her. He summoned Olaf, mentally this time. "I know we just tapped you, cousin, but I need one more favor."

"Och, ye're wearing me out!"

"But I know the hearty stock you come from. You're tough, a Highlander living in the frigid cold, pledging his life to protect those he cares about."

"Hmph. Who says I care about ye?"

"Maybe you don't, but you attached to me because you wanted adventure. Well, now you're getting it."

"This is the last time. I dinna like going to dark places where I canna do anything."

Lachlan breathed in relief. "Just an astral projection this time. Take me to Russell Jackson."

"At the present moment?"

"Take me back a week or two. Let me skim over the past, like an eagle over the plains."

Olaf disappeared, long enough for Lachlan to think he wasn't coming back. Then he felt the familiar sense of astral projection. He saw Russell, in a hotel room, saw him driving past the music store and then Jessie's apartment. Then a flash back to the hotel, a slice of streetlight coming into the room through the drapes over the bed where a woman lay.

The man wasn't as devoted to Calista as he'd said. No, wait. Something was very wrong with the scene. Lachlan pulled the image back, feeling his whole body tighten. Good God, the woman was tied to the bed, gagged, and terrified. Russell stood over her, drawing black smoke all around her.

"Calista," he said, drawing out the name. "Come down, my love. The body is ready for you, the woman a perfect look-alike, wearing your clothing, your jewelry. I think it will work this time."

A thin stream of smoke materialized from the ceiling and spiraled down to the woman. Russell lifted his hands to it.

"Calista, come to me."

The smoke stabbed into the woman's chest like

a jagged knife, making her arch and groan in pain. Russell pinned her shoulders to the bed, his face close to hers.

"Almost there, my love."

That stream of smoke joined his Darkness and lit up like lightning inside a tornado. The woman arched again, her body jerking in seizures. The smoke from the ceiling had almost gone all the way in.

The woman went limp, blood dribbling from her mouth. The line of smoke shot back up to the ceiling and disappeared. Russell fell forward onto the woman's body and screamed in agony.

Lachlan jerked awake, the words "He's killing women" out of his mouth before he even focused on . . . the empty driver's seat.

Disoriented, he looked around. They were parked in front of her apartment building, the engine still running. She was nowhere in sight, not smelling roses or looking at a flutterby.

The sword felt as though it weighed a hundred pounds as he pulled it from the backseat. He didn't even bother to hide it beneath his coat, only holding it to his side as he ran from the car to the base of the stairs.

His legs felt as though they were filled with sandbags. "Olaf, I need your help. You wanted battle. You might get it."

He felt the Scot's energy suffuse him, but not as powerfully as before. They'd both worn themselves out.

She'd be okay, having popped inside to get something she'd forgotten. He turned the doorknob and pushed at the same time. When the door opened, the horror of what he saw hit him squarely in the chest: Jessie on the couch with Russell sitting next to her, pulling her arm out straight.

"Stop!"

"It's okay, Lachlan," she said. "He's just taking some blood—"

"Not if he's going to do to you what he did to that woman a week ago. And not only her." He moved closer as he spoke, sword down but ready to strike. "Remember the newscast about a woman going missing, and the police thinking it was connected to several other disappearances in the area? It's him." He reached for her arm from over the back of the couch, yanking her up. "He surrounds them with Darkness and calls down your mum's spirit. But it hasn't worked. He needs you, Jess, because you have her DNA." The pieces clicked together, making a heinous puzzle. "You're a perfect match."

Russell turned to Jessie, on the couch. "He didn't see that. It's preposterous."

It was clicking for her, too. Lachlan could see horror creep into her expression. "You don't need my blood," she said. "You need my body. Does my mom know you're trading me for her?" He saw the betrayal drain the color from her face.

Russell threw out his hand and a ball of Darkness hit her. She sailed across the room and fell against the wall, landing in an unconscious heap.

"Calista!" Russell called, sending a stream of Darkness toward Jessie.

Lachlan stepped in front of it, feeling it sting him like the blade of a knife. He sliced through it with his sword. The sparks of magic shattered it.

Another stream of Darkness came down from the ceiling above Jessie. Lachlan made to cut it, but Russell spun off his dogs. Four of them sailed over the back of the couch at him, knocking him to the floor. He'd thrown up his sword as he fell, and one of the dogs ran right into it, splintering. If he could work through the dogs, making Russell create more, it would weaken him.

Russell ran toward where Jessie lay on the floor. "Calista! Come, my love."

Lachlan lashed another dog as he ran toward them. Using his hand as a brace, he jumped over the couch and landed a foot away from Russell, sword at the ready. As he brought the blade down, Russell swung his hand, throwing him back against the couch. The dogs had been coming at him, and they flew right into Russell. Lachlan took advantage of the momentary chaos and lunged at the twisted mass of them.

The dogs exploded out of Russell, crashing into Lachlan. Olaf's energy swamped him in rage. He felt the blackness edging in.

Back off! I need your help, not you possessing me.

If ye need my help, ye canna set the terms.

Great. He was fighting Russell, his hell doggies, *and* Olaf. Lachlan swung his sword from side to side, magic crackling along the blade. The two remaining dogs flanked him. As he swung one way, the other dog would move in. Damn, he needed his dirk.

Olaf tried to take over again, and Lachlan's arm jerked out of his control, the sword twisted in a clever way. Blackness throbbed at the edges of his vision now.

Hold fast.

Russell Became, snarling at Lachlan. Another dog splintered as he rotated the sword above his head and delivered a fatal blow. Olaf was good, he'd give him that. But at what price? Lachlan held on, swinging in a full circle, slicing at the final dog, using the momentum to fling himself at Russell. He knocked the wolf aside, ramming it into the wall.

They engaged, sword against claws. He didn't dare spare her a glance, though he was worried sick for her. She'd been knocked out flat.

More dogs emerged from the dark form, like bees from a disturbed hive. *Bring them on, you son of a bitch.* Lachlan backed the dogs away from Jessie.

One grabbed at the back of his leg. He hadn't even seen it. Teeth sank into his calf. He brought the sword round and sliced it in two, then stabbed another one that had come up to join the first.

From the corner of his eye he saw Russell

moving in on him. Lachlan was twisted round, and he bent down and lunged through his spread legs. The tip of the sword sliced into Russell's leg. Unfortunately, he didn't splinter like his creations. He groaned in pain, though, and backed up, electrical arcs still moving over his knee. Lachlan felt the tug as Olaf used his body to run toward the smoke that hovered above Jessie—Jessie's mum. He heard Russell scream, "Calista!"

Then everything went completely black. The rage came on him like a tidal wave, sinking him deep into his subconscious. Just like the day he'd killed his mum.

No! I can't hurt Jessie. Let me back in!

Olaf wasn't letting go this time. Lachlan felt himself move but couldn't see anything. *Focus on my body, the ache of my muscles and the heat on my skin.* The Darkness ebbed, and Lachlan saw a smeary blur. He heard a Gaelic battle cry coming from his mouth and felt himself rush toward a dark figure. He felt a thud as the sword hit something, sending him falling backward.

It jarred him out of Olaf's control. He opened his eyes. The sword handle still rocked from the motion, inches from his face. His gaze flew to Jessie, in a heap only inches below where the blade had jammed into the wall.

"Son of a bitch! You nearly killed her!"

"I knew what I was doing."

Lachlan pulled out the sword, jumped to his feet and searched for Russell. "Where is he?"

"Gone," Olaf said. "When I went for the smoke and it disappeared, he ran out screaming the woman's name."

Lachlan dropped to his knees. "Jessie. Come back."

He tapped her cheeks, making her head rock back and forth. He pressed his finger against the pulse point at her neck. At first, nothing. He moved his finger and finally found it, strong and steady. He pulled her into his arms and stood. Her head lolled to the side. The thought of losing her felt like his half-lang stabbing right through his chest.

It wasn't easy, but he managed to hook his sword at his hip, hidden by the coat. The place was a mess, but he had no time to tidy up. He carried her down the stairs to the SUV.

A man got out of his car, his eyes going to them as he rushed over. "Is she all right?"

Luckily, she bore no lacerations. The goose egg was hidden from sight, at the back of her head. "She's wiped out from the flu. Wouldn't go to the doctor when she first got the fever. And they say men are stubborn."

Go on, then.

The man had backed up at the word "flu," but he was clearly suspicious.

Lachlan's heartbeat tripped when he saw the tip of his sword peeking out between the folds of his coat.

The man said, "Maybe I should call someone.

Ambulance. Police." His gaze started to move down Lachlan's coat.

Lachlan shifted to the side. "I'm taking her to the hospital now. No worries, she'll be fine."

The man must have sensed that something wasn't right. "I'll get the door for you."

Was there anything in the front seat that would further pique his suspicion? Last thing they needed was the cops looking for them. "Sure, that would be great."

The good Samaritan opened the door and was none too subtle about peering inside. Lachlan nudged him out of the way and laid her in the front seat. "Thanks, mate." He closed the door, got in, and headed off.

He watched her as he drove, her chest rising and falling evenly, her face peaceful. Poor Jessie. She would be heartbroken. Let down by her father, betrayed by her mother. And now, possibly suffering a brain hemorrhage? Swelling? God, he didn't know what to do.

"The lassie's all right."

Olaf, popping in just like that. Lachlan held in his fury. For now. "How do you know?"

"Since she and I ha' gone to the Void together, I feel a connection with her, too."

Great. "Will you be possessing her now?"

"Nae, but I get the feel of her. She's having scattered thoughts, like pieces of dreams. She's thinking of ye."

Lachlan didn't want to think about her dreaming of him. "Can you read my thoughts? How'd you know I was worried about her?"

Olaf sputtered a laugh. "It's plain on your expression how ye feel about her."

"I care about her, aye." The sight of her on the floor had crumpled his heart like a balled-up piece of paper. "She might be my sister-in-law someday. I have to see her like that. Like a sister."

Another damned laugh. "If that's what ye want to tell yourself."

"I do." Lachlan's fingers tightened on the steering wheel. He should feel shame for how he lusted for her, but so far he'd managed to do the right thing. He'd keep doing it. Magnus would awake in a day or two, and they'd sort out their feelings.

It hit him then, that Magnus had the same Darkness as her father, who killed her mother over the affair. Russell had sought Calista for years, even though she'd married and had a child. If Magnus possessed that territoriality, he might kill him if he got a whiff of what had already happened between them. He and Jessie would have to squash any last bit of their attraction. Hell, even Olaf could see how he felt about her.

And how do you feel about her?

Not going there. "Olaf, you said you couldn't possess me, but that's what you did back there."

"I hadn't possessed ye, but I can possess ye. Did I not make that distinction?"

"No. That's how I killed my mum, lost control. And I almost killed Jessie. The damned sword was *inches* above her head!" If he'd come to and found that he speared her, he would have run the blade through himself rather than live with that.

"Russell was trying to bring the spirit down into her," Olaf said. "I had to move. Ye weren't doing anything."

Lachlan gritted his teeth so hard his jaw hurt. "Because you'd taken me over! I blank out when you do that. You go crazy, slashing and stabbing without thinking. Never do that again."

"Och, ye only want my help on your terms, is that it?"

"Aye, that's it."

"It doesna work that way. I told ye already, ye canna dictate how I should help."

"Then I don't want your help. I can't trust you. You're a wild card."

"I dinna know what that means, but I take it as an insult." Olaf pulled out so fast, it sucked Lachlan's breath away.

"Hell."

Had he made a mistake? Lachlan glanced over at Jessie. Olaf had nothing to lose. But he had everything to lose. He would live with the consequences, knowing he wouldn't be the one to hurt her. It would have to be enough.

My brain has cracked in half.

That was Jessie's first thought. She took note of her body. *I'm in a bed, cozy and warm, though there's something cold against the side of my head where it hurt the most.* Her second thought. Other than that, it was hard to think. Her mother! She was going to give blood to bring her mother back, and Lachlan burst in, and Russell had thrown her. That's all she could remember.

She cracked an eye open. Lachlan was pacing by the bed, but he turned at that movement and came closer.

"You're alright?"

She nodded, then winced as pain rocked her head.

He knelt by her side, clicking on a penlight. "I'm supposed to check for concussion. I thought about taking you to a hospital, but here seemed the safest place, so I looked up symptoms."

She forced her eyes open, which was damned hard with him shining a light in them.

"You remember what happened?"

"Mostly, up until I hit the wall." She struggled to sit up, and the pieces came together. "You ruined it, Lachlan. I was going to bring my mom back, and you barged in yelling, setting Russell off."

"I barged in because Russell isn't after your blood, Jess." He opened the bottle of aspirin by the bed and took two out. "Think about it. Can he really make a body from Darkness and a pint of blood? His hell doggies are forms, not anything that can pass for normal. But just like he went into your dad's body, he thinks he can bring your mum into yours." He handed her the aspirins and the glass of water he'd already put there.

"No. My mom wouldn't do that. I'm her *daughter*."

She swallowed the aspirins as something hard and cold seemed to break loose deep inside her, like a chunk of glacier breaking off. "You said Russell killed women while trying to bring my mother back." The words moved up her throat like one of those chunks of ice, slowly, painfully.

He related what he'd seen during his astral projection. "He was summoning your mother's soul down into her body, but the woman died before it was completed. I researched news stories while you were sleeping; the four women who disappeared recently all look like you, like your mother might look."

"I remember worrying that a serial killer was targeting brunettes." She wrapped her arms around herself. "Obviously it hasn't worked. He needs me, my body. He was using my feelings for my mom to get me to cooperate." A bigger, darker truth loomed closer. "My mom . . . she knew."

He gave her a sympathetic look. "He was trying to get her to come down into your body. Maybe he's lying to her about how he's going to bring her back. We won't find out, because you're not going back to the Void."

"But if I talk to her—"

"No. It's too dangerous, for one. Besides, I don't know if Olaf will be helping us anymore."

Her eyes widened. "Is he gone? Did he go to the Light? It frightened him so."

"No, he pissed me off. He took me over at your apartment, pushed me right out. Next thing I know I've plunged the sword inches above your head." His voice tightened in fear, at the thought, no doubt, that he could have hurt her like he hurt his mother.

"The hell of it is, we need him." He stood and started pacing again. "What were you thinking, going up to your apartment without me?"

"You were asleep."

"I woke and you were gone. Gone! You weren't supposed to go inside. You said you were just putting a note on the door." He pinned her with a fierce look. "What are you smiling about?"

She curled her arms around her pillow, a soft smile warming the ice just a little. "You care about me."

Now he flung his arms out. "That's all you've got to say for yourself?"

She shouldn't like that he had been so worried, but she did. "I'm sorry. I went up and the door was open. He was inside, and I thought this whole thing could be over before you woke."

"Don't do it again. Ever."

"Fine. I won't." She loved that he'd allowed her the hope that maybe Russell was duping her mom, even if it wasn't likely. She scooted out of bed. "I want to see the women he's killed."

"Why?"

"They're connected to me."

"It's not your fault they're dead."

"I know that, but it's because of my family that they're dead."

He looked at her, releasing a breath. "All right. Then we'll have dinner, if we've an appetite for it."

He led her into his bare room and gestured for her to sit in a hard wooden chair at the small desk. "Not even an office chair?" she said.

"Dad and I once astral-projected to a monastery. This is what their rooms looked like. It seemed appropriate. I even thought about joining one."

"You were going to become a monk?"

"I thought it would ease the pain. But I didn't want to abandon this place, so I stayed."

She shook her head and sat down in front of the laptop. She moved the mouse and the blank screen made way for a newspaper's website.

"That's the last one," he said, coming up behind her. "The woman I saw."

"She's beautiful. Only twenty-seven. Oh, God, and she has two young children." Her heart crushed under that one line. Two children were missing their mother, like she had missed her mother. "Were any of them found?"

"No. And they've started disappearing more frequently. He was getting desperate when he couldn't get you as easily as he wanted. Now he's focusing on you again."

"In an odd way, I can understand why he's so desperate. If you could see her, embedded in the wall, fear in her eyes, knowing she'll be swallowed. He loves her fiercely, insanely. Of course he's getting desperate." She put her hand over her mouth. "If he'd found me, none of these women would have died."

Lachlan clamped his hands on her shoulders. "Don't put that on yourself. This is him, all him. You don't get to die to save anyone. It's not your place. In any case, he's failed with these other women. You're his only hope."

She returned to his initial search, clicking on another link. Another woman. This one also had a child, though he was a teenager. Still, losing a parent at any age had to be devastating.

"Stop," he said when she clicked back to the search results. "No more. You can't do anything to help those women now."

"No, but I can give them closure. I can, some-how, let them know that their mothers, wives, have been murdered and that the man who did it is dead. I can do that."

"And get yourself arrested. Then tossed in the loony bin when you tell them how you know." He tilted his head at her. "But you'll do it anyway. You've got that look about you."

"I'll figure out a way, a good way. But first we have to send the bastard to the Void."

CHAPTER 19

Having Lachlan in the kitchen, helping with the prep, made her feel less alone. He was chopping the onion, bless his heart. Damned things always made her eyes burn.

She sliced up a zucchini. "I have to go back to the Void one more time."

She expected him to argue, but he simply asked, "Why?"

"I need to talk to my dad."

"I figured you'd want to talk to your mum."

"I do . . . and I don't. I'm not sure I could handle her telling me she knew what Russell was doing. I can't bring her back anyway, not at that price. My dad, I can."

"You still want to try, even knowing he killed your mum?"

"He didn't do it; Darkness did. My mom had an affair. Not that she deserved to die because of it, but she sparked it." She gave him a meaningful look. "He didn't mean to do it, and so I forgive him. I need to let him know."

"You'll need Olaf for that, and he probably won't help us now."

Ah, that's why Lachlan wasn't arguing. He didn't think she'd be able to go. "He's pissed at you, not me. I'll get him to help."

"I doubt he'll come when I call him." He scraped the last bits of onion into the pan. "I checked on Magnus while you were sleeping. He's beginning to stir. I want this done before he wakes. I want to be able to tell him that it's over and you're safe."

She crossed her arms over her chest. "Is that where you hand me over to him?"

"It's where I back away. I realized something earlier: Darkness took over your dad, and made Russell into an obsessed killer. Magnus has that now. The last thing he remembers is being with you, wanting you. Darkness isn't logical as far as I can tell. He'll feel territorial toward you. We don't know how he'll react if he suspects there's anything between us."

Mine. The echo of that sentiment, the raw feeling of it as she looked at Lachlan . . . "*Is* there anything between us?"

His mouth moved silently before he said, "Not like that."

"Because the way you said it—"

"We've experienced a bit of lust due to the whole adrenaline thing. But we got off, so that should be out of our system."

"Yeah, that's done." She forced a laugh, waving her hand. "All that craziness."

"Yeah. Madness."

It wasn't just adrenaline. It was everything in him that he didn't see. Honor. Loyalty. Compassion. The way his breath hitched when she touched him, even just a casual touch on the shoulder as she passed him in the narrow space between the island and counter. The way she affected him.

She added the zucchini to the onions and garlic and stirred everything together, feeling the sting of the onion juice in her eyes.

"Here." He took the spoon from her, nudging her aside with his hip. "I'll take care of it. You're crying."

"Onion tears." She watched him stir for a while. "Do you think Magnus forgave you for accidentally killing your mother?"

Her question seemed to take him off guard. "Maybe a little. I think he realized I'm all he has, for better or worse."

She started spooning the sautéed vegetables into the cavities of the two Cornish hens.

"Seems obscene, ramming your hand between their legs like that," he said, watching her.

She wrinkled her nose. "I never thought of it that way, but now that you've mentioned it . . ."

"I've ruined it for you. Sorry."

"It's not the worst thing that's happened to me lately." She opened the oven door, and he slid in the pan.

He closed the door. "We have an hour to kill."

Memories of their time in the guest bedroom

sparked through her body. Okay, maybe she hadn't gotten it out of her system. "At least."

"You work on Darkness. I'll work with the sword. We need all the practice we can get."

Of course. Though she felt disappointed, she didn't fear working with Darkness anymore. She needed to master it. She gestured down to her black, calf-length skirt with wide gray ruffles at the edges. "I'm not really dressed for it."

His gaze swept down her, as it had when she emerged from her room earlier. "You're not working on your karate. That'll do."

She glanced his way as they headed down the hallway. "All this time, Russell has been trying to trap me. Now we have to trap him. I'll use my Darkness to send him to the Void and bring my dad back."

"But remember, Russell can do the same to you. We need to knock him out. First, we need to draw him to us. Time is running out. Desperate men get sloppy. I'm going to have Cheveyo lift the shield. Russell will track us here. And we'll be ready."

"To my apartment. Not here."

"It's too risky to take this fight where others might get involved. You heard his threat at the carnival. Russell will kill anyone who gets in the way. We can't afford for that to be some guy who happens to investigate strange noises. And this is our home turf. We have the advantage."

Our home turf. *Our home.* Though he hadn't

meant them that way, the words settled over her like a warm blanket.

Once in the studio, he set a timer that had probably been used for his bouts with Magnus. He put angry rock music on the stereo.

She didn't want to Become out of anger, though. She wanted to Become out of strength.

He pulled a sword from the wall. "Work on the tiger. That's where your power is."

As though he'd read her mind. She faced Russell there, as powerful as he.

Tiger.

She felt the growl come up from somewhere deep inside her. Saw the room blur for an instant. She ran across it so fast she reached the other end and nearly hit the wall. Human again, she looked for Lachlan.

"You did it." He gave her a proud smile. "You were a gorgeous tiger, and you moved so fast I could hardly see you."

She shivered, from both his pride and the knowledge that she'd become something dangerous.

"Do it again," he said.

She faced the far wall, gleaming with swords and knives, and charged. He'd said she was gorgeous. He hadn't been disgusted or afraid, only impressed. He clapped softly, as though she were putting on a show. She did it again.

Russell sat at the table in his motel room, staring at the laptop screen.

Failure pounded at him, breaking his body out in a sweat. He swiped at his forehead, his upper lip, and flung the drops of perspiration away.

So close. He'd been so close today, and other times. Always, success teased him but stayed just out of reach.

Bastard had attacked his beloved. Afterward he immediately went to her. She was shaken, battered by the magic on the sword.

He had tried in vain to bring Calista back into other women's bodies, when he couldn't find Jessie. The last failure had been the hardest because he had to accept that using another woman wouldn't work. With organ transplants, donor and recipient had to be the same blood type. Maybe in this case they had to share the same DNA. Jessie was ideal, of course, being Calista's daughter.

But Jessie was proving too problematic. He still held hope, though. One last thing to try. The girl with the bright hair smiled at him from the picture on the monitor. The Jessie who had donated blood marrow had to be *his* Jessie. Hayley held part of Jessie, and maybe, just maybe, it would be enough.

Bringing Calista back in a teenager's body . . . *not* ideal. It smacked of immorality. He wanted a grown woman. Hayley would be missed as well. He would hide her away for a while, maybe a cabin in the woods. After having just snatches of time with Calista in the Void, he could saturate himself in her, just the two of them. It would be heaven. Hayley would be a lot easier to grab, too. She wouldn't have some guy with a sword and magic to protect her. The article mentioned the school she attended. He would wait, follow her home.

Calista, soon. Soon we'll be together again.

After forty minutes of working with Darkness, Jessie could Become at will for a few seconds at a time. She was exhausted, though, her legs rubbery.

Lachlan, the big distraction, had stripped off his shirt and worked with the sword. Thrusting. Parrying. She didn't know all those sword-fighting terms, but she did know a thrust when she saw one, and he had such a nice one. He put his whole body into it, all of his muscles flexing. His chest gleamed with the faint sheen of sweat, which dampened the hair at the nape of his neck. Even worse, with the wall of mirrors, she had a view of both sides of him at once.

She felt such a stirring, as powerful as Darkness. As though sensing her attention, or maybe more, he turned to her. The blade caught the light, flashing like a signal. Their gazes locked, and his throat convulsed as he swallowed.

She tilted her head. "Did we, Lachlan? Did we get it out of our system?"

He shook his head, a quick movement that ruffled his hair. He set the sword at his feet. "We could do the back-to-back thing again. Get rid of it completely."

"You think one more time would do it?" She took a step closer, her heartbeat fast and thready.

"Be the safe way."

She closed the distance between them. "And you're a safe kind of guy, aren't you?"

That made him laugh despite himself. "No, but I'm an honorable sort of guy. Or trying to be."

"Yes, you are." She reached up and stroked his cheek, seeing him shiver. "But here's the thing: there is something between us. Not lust." She smiled. "Well, yes, lust, but not adrenaline lust. You're always thinking of how Magnus feels about me, but what about how I feel? My feelings count, too."

She left her hand on his chest. "I didn't have a chance to get to know him well, but I *do* know you, Lachlan. I know your heart. I know you hunger to regain your honor to feel worthy. You'll put your life on the line to save Magnus, or me, because you believe you need to redeem yourself. But that's not really why you do it."

"If you claim to know me so well, then tell me why."

"Because you are a warrior who will go to any length to do what's right. To protect those you care about. And you do care deeply. That you care about me is a complication you tried to avoid. You did your best to erect a wall between us by being a—"

"An arrogant arse," he supplied.

"And you succeeded." She smiled. "I didn't want to feel for you either, because of my Darkness. But here we are." She took a quick breath, talking so fast she'd forgotten to breathe. "Wanting each other. Feeling something for each other." She drew her hand down his throat to his chest, finger sliding against his slick skin. "I like Magnus, but I fell in love with you."

Her mouth dropped open as words she hadn't planned on saying flowed out, mirroring the surprise on his face. "Yeah. I fell for your passion, your loyalty, the way you look when you fight, and the *thing* you do with your eyebrow. So right now I don't want to think about shoulds and shouldn'ts. I want you. The real way."

He kissed her, banging her against the mirrored wall, his body pushing against hers. She felt the hard length of him grinding into her stomach, the pulse of his breath, and the cool smoothness of the glass behind her. Bracing her hands on his shoulders, she wrapped her legs around his waist and ground back, drowning in the lust that consumed her. *More, more.* She dare not say it, afraid of . . .

The thought flitted away like a flutterby, because his hands were moving down her sides, thumbs brushing the edges of her breasts, her sides, then her hips. She'd pushed him too far, past his boundaries. Finally.

He shoved up her skirt, and she sighed at the feel of his hands on her bare thighs. She was caught between the sensations of his mouth against hers and his fingers trailing higher, edging the bottom of her panties and then slipping beneath. She sucked in a breath.

More, more, more.

He brushed her crinkly hairs, stroking back and forth, and then lower. She was throbbing, aching, wanting . . . him.

She shifted, moving against his fingers. Her kisses were getting more feverous, and she let her body move the way it wanted to, grinding against him. His fingers were fully beneath the silky fabric, rubbing over her sensitized pubic area.

"Touch me," she whispered, pleaded.

His finger slid into her folds, brushing her swollen nub and making her gasp. She was that close to the edge. He backed away, just enough so that she didn't go over.

"Do . . . not . . . stop," she stuttered. "You will be much more d-dishonorable if you leave me like this."

He chuckled, low and throaty. "I don't intend to leave you like this." He gripped her behind, supporting her, and walked out of the studio, around the corner to his bedroom, and laid her on his bed. "I want to do it the real way."

Her heart jumped even higher. "The real way?"

He hiked up her skirt, hooking his fingers at the edges of her panties and yanking them down her thighs. He ran his hands up her inner thighs, pushing them apart as he did so. He had a spark in his eyes, devilish and playful. "The real way."

Then he put his mouth on her and the world exploded.

His mouth, warm, soft, playful tongue sliding and swirling around her, making her huff and puff. He tried to tease her, but she was way too gone for him. Hot lava flowed over her as she came.

He kept running his tongue over her, sending electrical shocks through her. The feelings were intense, too much, and then . . . over she went again. He sent her one more time, and when she felt his tongue, she said, "Enough! I'm going to die, honestly."

He pulled off her skirt and panties, then shucked his pants and crawled up beside her.

She shrugged out of her shirt, and when it cleared her head, he was taking her in with amazement and wonder.

"You are so beautiful, especially with the flush on your cheeks."

He ran his fingers across her skin, her breasts, and over her stomach. Her skin trembled beneath his touch.

"Touch me. Everywhere." She needed to feel him.

He slung his leg over hers and ran his hands everywhere, her neck, her ears, over the curves of her face, and then along her hips and even her legs. He touched her like a blind man would, as though absorbing every valley, dip, and rise on her body. Or, she realized, like a man who hadn't touched a woman like this before. She was the first woman he'd touched. The thought of it sent a tremor through her.

His gaze followed his hand, taking in her body as it moved across her. "No man has ever touched you like this?"

She shook her head. "No one but you."

"I don't deserve . . . this treasure."

She put her hand against his cheek. "Yes, you do. There is no one else I want to share this with." The only light in the room came from the hall, barely enough to illuminate the bed and their bodies. She got up and turned on the light. "I want to see you. See us. Everything."

Her gaze skittered from his chest, his erection, his thighs, hungry to see all of him. She sat on the bed and ran her hands over him, no doubt with that same wonder on her face.

"You're the first man I ever touched like this."

He anchored his hands behind his head. "Then touch all you want."

The invitation sank into her, like a sponge soaking in hot water. She did, tracing his nipples, running her finger down the center of his stomach, around his belly button, and touching the velvety tip of his penis. It twitched, making her jump. She laughed, embarrassed by her reaction. "Did you do that on purpose?"

He shrugged. "It's involuntary."

She ran her hands down his inner thighs, feeling the hairs on his legs rub against her palms. His muscles were hard, well defined from all that sword practice, no doubt. She moved back up, cupping his balls, and then wrapping her fingers around his penis.

His body stiffened, toes flexing when she'd put her hand on him. She leaned down and traced her tongue across the tip of him, tasting the astringent drops of semen. He sucked in a breath at that.

She ran her tongue down the length of him. A tremor went through his body. She grinned. His body, hers to explore, all she wanted. When she had brought him to toe-curling status, she worked her way back up, kissing, licking, loving the taste of him. She straddled him, the most intimate part of her pressing against his stomach. She felt powerful, strong.

He, however, was frowning. "I don't have any condoms."

"Well, we know we're clean. And I'm too early in my cycle to get pregnant." She'd worked with a woman who was trying to get pregnant, and gotten an education on fertility.

"Thank God." He rolled her over so she was under him and reached down between her legs. "Mm, still wet. You'll need that."

"Will it hurt? Not that I'm afraid of that, but just wondering."

"I've heard it might. I'll be gentle."

She tightened her fingers on his shoulders. "Don't be gentle."

He kissed her, then trailed down her neck, dipping his tongue into the hollow at her throat. He took his time, loving her with his mouth, even while his erection pressed into her stomach between their bodies. She wrapped her leg over the back of his, stroking with her foot. Her hands moved over his back, down the dip of his spine and over the firmness of his behind.

He shifted and ran the tip of his penis up the length of her thigh. She moved against him, inviting him in. He was gentle anyway; she knew he would be. He slid into her by degrees, pulling out, then nudging in a little farther. He cupped her shoulders, holding her close.

"Breathe," he whispered, giving her a playful smile. "Don't want you to pass out."

She laughed softly. She hadn't even known she'd been holding her breath.

"You okay?"

She nodded.

He slid in all the way, and she took a deep breath then, feeling both a sharp pain and the most incredible feeling of being filled. For the first time, filled from the inside. Not just physically, but spiritually. Emotionally.

She opened her eyes, meeting his questioning gaze with a smile. "More than okay."

"Rotate your hips, clockwise, then counter. Nice and slow."

She did as he instructed, remembering how well he'd gotten her to climax before. He rolled his eyes in pleasure as she moved, and he continued to slide in and out, building a feeling inside her she'd never had before.

Painful, yes, but beneath that pain a building heat, intensity. They moved together for several more minutes, and then the world exploded. Her body shuddered hard, and she gripped him, burying her face in his neck.

She felt him pulse inside her, hot, wet, and he held her just as tight. "Jessie," he whispered in a tight voice. He touched her face, moving his thumb across her mouth. "I fell for you, too."

She smiled. "Sucks, doesn't it?"

He kissed her between each word: "In . . . the . . . worst . . . way."

An alarm pierced the air, followed by the scent of smoke.

"The hens!" she screamed.

They both scrambled off the bed. He grabbed two towels from the bathroom and handed one to her, and they ran to the kitchen. Smoke poured out of the oven, and all the alarms in the house were going off. He opened the door and used his towel to pull out the roasting pan. He dumped it in the sink and ran water over the smoking lumps.

She put her hand over her mouth. "I've never burned anything in my life."

He kicked the oven door closed and then opened the doors near the sitting area. Cool air swept in, stippling her skin. She ran to the dining area and opened the sliding doors there, too.

Smoke tickled her throat as she waded through it to the kitchen.

He came up beside her, watching her pick at the lumps. "I don't think they can be saved."

She wondered if he'd be annoyed, but he was giving her a sympathetic look. A laugh escaped her, at the absurdity of it all, standing naked in a still smoky kitchen with alarms screaming. He laughed, too, and before they knew it they were both bending over cracking up.

It felt good to lose herself like this. And share it with him. When they'd gathered their composure, he said, "We'll throw a couple frozen entrees in the nuker, eat them in the garage." He walked to a panel in the dining room and punched in some buttons on the touch screen.

"Will the alarm system call the fire department?"

"No, Dad didn't want anyone coming here. But if it reaches a certain temperature, the sprinklers will go off. With the doors open and no actual fire, it shouldn't trigger them."

Lachlan put two entrees in the microwave, and they went back to his room to put on clothes. By the time they returned to the kitchen, the entrees were ready. He put them on plates, she filled glasses with water, and they traipsed out to the garage.

"Won't it be cold out there?"

"I turned on the heat from the main panel. It won't be cozy just yet, but it'll be warm enough."

He jammed a knife—his dirk, he called it—into the waistband of his pants, and they walked together to the garage. They sat side by side on the hood of his truck and ate off their laps, facing the skeleton of the car. Lachlan slid off the truck, took her empty tray, and tossed both trays in the trash.

He ran his hand over the Camaro's hood, which had been sanded down to a smooth, gray finish. She watched his fingers slide over the surface and felt a different kind of stirring. She had touched that body, had been intimately connected with it, with him. He'd fallen for her.

Mine.

She swallowed back the thought. *Not mine.*

He wasn't necessarily thinking about the car, she thought. His gaze looked a million miles away. Did he regret making love to her? She knew he wouldn't have if he'd still been planning to hand her off to Magnus, but if they got involved, it would complicate things for him.

He lifted his head. "Did you hear that?"

"What?"

He smiled. "Nothing. The alarms are silent. It's safe to return."

She slid off the truck hood. "I'm sorry."

"For what? It wasn't your fault we forgot."

"Well, it sort of was. But thanks for not blaming me."

He regarded her with that curious look again, but gestured for her to walk ahead of him. The house was chilled now, and they closed the doors.

"Uh-oh, I hear a beeping sound," she said.

Lachlan went to the panel and checked the screen. "No intruders." He cocked his head. "It's my cell phone ringing." He ran to the bedroom, and she followed. He snatched it up. "Yeah? Is Magnus all right?"

He listened, and the expression on his face said that something very bad had happened. Her hand went to her throat and she stepped closer. She could hear a man's voice but not what he was saying.

"All right, we'll be over in a bit."

She didn't even wait for him to disconnect before asking, "What?"

"Magnus isn't awake yet, but he's stirring, mumbling. Just now he said the first intelligible word since it happened." His eyes shadowed. "He called out your name."

She could see self-recrimination in Lachlan's eyes.

"That doesn't mean anything, necessarily. I was the last person he saw before he blacked out. And I was in trouble."

"What if it's not? What if the thought of you is keeping him holding on?" He pinched the bridge of his nose and turned away. "I'm an arse. The biggest arse ever." Now he regretted it, and that stabbed her in the chest. "And if he feels territorial, Darkness could make him hurt you."

She had been selfish, losing herself in her feelings. Because of her weakness, she had created an untenable situation between two brothers. "I'm the biggest arse. Let me take the blame on this one. I threw myself at you."

"Oh no, you don't. I wanted it as much as you did."

She didn't let herself savor those words. "Let's just pretend it didn't happen."

He snorted. "You think we can do that?"

Never. "It'll be okay when I'm gone."

"Gone? Where are you going?"

"I don't know. Admit it, things will be a lot less complicated if I'm not around."

He didn't admit it, but he didn't deny it, either.

He grabbed up his coat, lying over the back of the couch. "We'd better go, in case Magnus wakes up. We have a lot to tell him."

"I want to go to the Muse concert, Mom. Puhleeeze?"

Russell watched through one of his dog's eyes from outside a kitchen window. The teenage girl was pressing her hands into a prayer position.

The woman who must be her mother asked, "What's Muse?"

"Remember the video with the teddy bear rampaging through the city?"

"Oh, yeah. Nice. I'm still saying no. What if something happens? What if—"

"Mom, I have MD, I'm *not* MD. I need to have a life. Remember, I almost died."

"Exactly. I'm not ready to let you into the world,

especially at a place jammed with people, drugs, and who knows what else? They have stampedes at concerts. I'll buy you their CD, but no concert."

The girl stomped off, slamming a door somewhere in the house.

Ah, parental strife, Russell thought. Even when Julian was young, he was incorrigible and defiant. The anger had only come after he had killed his mother.

The dog curled up in the yard, settling in for the night. It would wait until she went to sleep. Then he would crawl into her window.

Music blared inside the room for forty minutes, and he could see her silhouette walking around behind the curtains. The dog stood and stepped closer to the bushes when she walked to the window and pushed aside the curtain. She looked to the right and left and then opened the window. A leg swung out, then a butt, and then the girl herself, landing on her feet. She quietly closed the window and walked right past the dog.

She was sneaking out. What a gift! The dog followed, and Russell ran to his car. She was no doubt going to that concert. He headed in the direction she'd gone. When he came up beside her, she stuck her thumb out for a ride.

He slowed to a stop beside her. "Where are you going?"

She took tentative steps toward the open passenger window of his car, perhaps trying to judge whether he was a pervert. "To the arena. If you could give me a lift to the entrance, that would be great."

"Who's playing?"

"Muse."

"Oh, yeah, the group with the video of the teddy bear."

Her face brightened. "Yeah. You like them?"

"They're great. How about if I do one better? I'll go with you. See, my girlfriend just dumped me, and I'm at loose ends tonight. A concert will be the perfect thing to cheer me up, and I can make sure you get there and back safely. I'll even buy your ticket."

She thought *she'd* gotten the gift. "Really? You don't have to buy my ticket—"

"You made my night so much better. I want to."

She opened the door and slid in. "Thanks. I'm sorry about your girlfriend."

"It's for the best. She's been a pain in the ass from the beginning. Now, my dear, direct me to the concert venue."

CHAPTER 20

Lachlan pushed the doorbell button of the town house in downtown Annapolis. He hadn't said much on the drive up, and that worried Jessie. He grimaced when a big hunk of a guy opened the door.

"Well, look who's here." He had a playful gleam in his eyes as he took in Lachlan. "Should I check you for possession of a wrench or some other potentially deadly tool?" He laughed, then thrust his hand at her. "I'm Eric Aruda. I'm sure you've heard an earful about me."

She shook it, thinking of nothing else but that he could set fires with his mind. "Not all that much. I'm Jessie."

"That's shocking." Eric released her hand and gave her a grin that smacked of mischievousness. "Lachlan and I are practically related. I'm married to his half sister."

She looked at Lachlan. "You have a half sister?"

Eric gestured for them to come in, leaning

close to Jessie as she passed. "Doesn't he tell you *anything*?"

"Apparently not."

Eric shot Lachlan a glance. "Funny, he didn't strike me as the strong silent type."

Lachlan's mouth tightened in annoyance as he took her hand and followed Eric up stairs that led to the living area. "Didn't expect to see you here."

"I'll bet. Fonda and I came over to check on Magnus. As you pointed out, that guy saved my arse. It was the least I could do." Eric glanced back. "You helped, too, and reluctant though it was, I still appreciate it."

A petite blonde with soft waves flowing over her shoulders stepped out of one of the rooms. She linked her arm through Eric's, taking them in with big brown eyes. "He's still pretty out of it, but his pulse is good." Her eyes sparked with recognition. "Oh, yeah . . . Lachlan. Last time I saw you—"

"I know, I was being an arse. Sorry about that."

Jessie knew that apology hadn't been easy. She really wanted to hear about the wrench, but there were more important things to deal with.

"This is my wife, Fonda," Eric said, gesturing to her.

Jessie introduced herself and shook her hand, and then Eric and Fonda led the way down a short hallway to a bedroom on the right. Pope, Cheveyo, and a beautiful, tall blond woman stood near the bed where Magnus lay. He looked calm and peaceful.

She felt a hand softly touch her back and turned to see Fonda. "I've been there, watching someone I care about lying in bed for hours, what felt like *days*, wondering what he'd be like when he came out of it." She glanced at Eric, and love sparked in her eyes. "Magnus'll be okay, too. He's a good guy."

Lachlan moved to the side of the bed, pain and worry on his expression. "He hasn't done anything more than say Jessie's name?"

The tall blonde stepped away from a chair at the side of the bed. "No, but I think he'll come out of it soon. He's moving around more." She walked over to Jessie. "I'm Petra, Cheveyo's wife. Are you the Jessie he was asking for?"

"Yes, but we're not . . . I barely knew him, really. He was just in the wrong place at the wrong time. My trouble became his trouble."

Pope stepped forward from his place at the far side of the bed. "You all right? You look like you've been through hell."

"We know what Darkness is," Lachlan said.

They told the group what they knew, but she and Lachlan had agreed not to involve them. Looking at Magnus made her even more resolute in that. No one else needed to get hurt . . . or worse. Having Lachlan at risk was bad enough.

Cheveyo put his hand on Petra's shoulder. "It sounds like Darkness there is like dark magic here. People tap in because they need more power. But it always backfires."

Eric nodded to Magnus. "And it's in him now?"

Jessie nodded, her mouth tight. "He should seem normal when he wakes. Darkness will only take over if he's triggered. I can't imagine you all would do anything to trigger him."

Lachlan obviously trusted these people, despite their troubled history. And rightfully so, as they'd come together to help Magnus.

Petra clasped Cheveyo's hand and led him toward the door. "We'll leave you alone with him."

Lachlan reached out and shook Cheveyo's hand. "Thank you." He met all of their eyes, even Eric's and Fonda's. "Thank you for taking care of him."

She knew it was hard for him to ask for their help, and she understood why a little better now that she knew about his solitary life. That he had some antagonism with Eric made it even harder, she was sure, but Lachlan would do what it took to take care of his own.

Everyone but Eric had filtered out to give them privacy. He lingered in the doorway. "If you need help—"

Lachlan shook his head. "No, but thanks. I don't want to drag anyone into this."

Jessie stepped closer to Lachlan. "Too many people have already been hurt."

Eric took the two of them in. "Yeah, I know exactly what you're thinking. I was there." His gaze flicked to her hand on his arm, and a grin broke out on his face. "Totally been there. But Fonda and I had some help or else we would have been burnt craters in the grass. Don't be too proud to ask. I won't rub it in." He handed Lachlan a piece of paper. "We're heading back to our place in DC now, but here's our info if you need it."

Lachlan accepted it with a nod, and Eric walked out, closing the door behind him.

"Why were you threatening them with a wrench?"

"Not Fonda, just Eric. He's the guy who set the house on fire where my father was being held. He's a hothead, and he overused his abilities like I did, to the point of nearly losing it. When they came to us for help, I was still angry about the fire. But Magnus helped me to understand that it was my father's doing, ultimately, that got us all into this. Blaming Eric or my father wasn't going to change anything, so I let it go."

"But you haven't let go of your part in your mother's death, have you?"

His gaze slid to Magnus. "I want to. It's a start, right?"

"A start, yes." Her heart swelled in happiness for him. But he wasn't smiling, because he was thinking about her and Magnus. She could tell by the shadow in his eyes.

She stepped up next to the bed. Magnus was beautiful, but the difference was clear between what she'd felt for him and what she felt for Lachlan. "You can't control how people feel. Not him, not me. Not even yourself."

"That's for sure." He looked at her. "And if he hates me, is that what I'm supposed to tell him?" He scraped his fingers across his scalp. "As screwed up as this is, as bad as I feel, I still want you. That's what an arse I am."

His words twisted inside her. She would make it easier on him. "It's over between us, so you don't have to agonize over it or thrash yourself anymore. He doesn't need to know."

"You think it'll be that simple?"

"Yes. Easy . . . no." Her phone vibrated in her pocket, and she pulled it out. "Hayley's home number." She touched the screen and engaged the call. "Hello?"

"It's Carol Adams. I hate to bother you at this hour, but is Hayley with you?"

Jessie's hand went to her throat. She mouthed to Lachlan, *Hayley's mom.* "I haven't talked to her since the carnival yesterday."

"She wanted to go to a concert tonight, and I was being overprotective. We had a tiff, and she stomped off to her room. I just went in to check on her, and she's gone." Panic stretched her voice. "She's never done this before, and I'm scared. I know what's out there."

No, she didn't. She had no idea.

"You've tried her cell phone?" Jessie asked.

"No answer. I'm going to ground her for a hundred years when she gets home."

"Maybe she'll answer for me. I'll let you know

as soon as I hear something. It's okay. Lots of girls sneak out and they come home fine. So will Hayley."

Jessie disconnected, meeting Lachlan's concerned gaze. "Hayley snuck out of her room. She's a smart girl—strong, even with MD—but sheltered. It's just a little rebellion thing. She's probably at a girlfriend's house. She knows not to go to my place."

Magnus shifted to his side, mumbling, and then calling out, "Jessie!" His eyes twitched beneath his lids.

"He looks like he's reliving those last moments, fighting Russell all over again." She touched his arm. "I'm here, Magnus. It's okay. We're all okay."

Lachlan's face darkened as he hovered, waiting for signs of Magnus's awakening. "Come out, Maggie."

After a few seconds Jessie said, "I need to get hold of Hayley." She stepped away, and a moment later the girl answered. "Hayley! Thank God."

"Jessie!" She heard the same relief in Hayley's voice. "Is everything all right?"

"That's what I was wondering about you."

"Uh-oh, you talked to my mom, didn't you? She knows I snuck out. Shoot. Well, I'm not going back yet. I'm tired of being coddled. I'm with a very nice man who's taking me to a concert."

"Man?" There went the relief.

Lachlan looked at her, probably because of the way the word had torn out of her throat.

Hayley said, "Hold on, he wants to talk to you."

"Hello . . . Jessie, right? My name is Henry, my dear. Don't worry about your friend. I'll take the utmost care of her."

Jessie's blood drained from her head so fast it left her dizzy. Lachlan was looking at her, but hopefully the soft lighting in the room camouflaged her paste-white face. She gestured to him that it was all right and walked farther away. Was Russell using Hayley as a hostage? Or worse, another experiment?

It clicked, in one horrible moment. He'd seen the newspaper article about her donating blood marrow to Hayley. If he couldn't get her, he'd take the next best thing: the girl who held her blood.

"You understand?" he asked.

"Yes."

"Good. You are most welcome to join us, but there's only room in my car for one more. Shall we come pick you up? It will take but a minute, and it's done."

He meant that bringing Calista into Hayley would take a minute. If Jessie tried anything, all he needed to do was subdue Hayley and it would be done.

On the other end, Russell said, "Hayley, if your friend Jessie comes, we'll be late to the concert. Will that be a fair trade-off?"

She heard Hayley say, "I'd love that. Please come, Jessie."

He wasn't talking about being late. He was

talking about a *trade*: her for Hayley. She wouldn't have to know. Russell was using double talk to keep her in the dark. They would go to the concert, where it would be loud and dark and chaotic, and Hayley wouldn't even know anything bad was happening. He had no reason to harm her if he got what he wanted. He'd take her home, and all she'd know was that Jessie was acting differently. Maybe she was just tired.

Jessie peered at Lachlan from the corner of her eye. He was tapping his brother's cheeks and talking softly to him. She could spare him, too, from being involved in this. Magnus wouldn't feel territorial because there would be no more Jessie.

"Hayley, I don't want you roaming around by yourself. I'm in downtown Annapolis. There's a coffee shop around the corner on Main Street. Pete's Java. I want you to meet me there. We'll talk, figure this out, okay?"

"Well done," Russell said, getting that she was putting on an act for Lachlan. "I'd be delighted to pick you up. I know it would mean a lot to Hayley. We'll head over right now."

Jessie disconnected, composed herself, and turned to Lachlan.

"Everything alright?" he asked.

She rolled her eyes. "Teenage drama. I'm going to talk her down."

Lachlan stepped closer. "You said a coffee shop near here?"

"Just me. You being there will keep her from talking openly."

"You're not going alone."

"We'll ask Cheveyo to put a shield over the shop so Russell won't be able to find me." Her words seem to float out of her mouth into an airless room. She had a hollow feeling in her chest, the odd sensation that she didn't really need to breathe. "Magnus is going to wake up any minute. You need to be here when he does. I'll have my phone with me. I won't be long. I need to calm her down so her mom can come and get her."

She hated lying to him, especially when he looked so concerned.

"It's just around the corner."

"Alright. But if you're not back in twenty minutes, I'm coming."

That should be enough time for her to be long gone. "Deal."

Lachlan's phone sat on the nightstand next to the bed. She took it, tucking it beneath the folds of her coat. Downstairs, she slid the phone between the couch cushions. He would eventually find it by having someone call his number, when the time was right. But she didn't want him to hear any audible indication that he'd received a text message.

It seemed to take forever to reach the bottom of the stairs. She turned to find Lachlan watching her. She waved and walked out.

Maybe her mom didn't know what it would take to come back, Jessie thought. She hoped not, but she'd probably never know.

She felt separated from her body already, as though floating somewhere above it. She pulled out her phone and called Carol. "I've talked to Hayley. She's fine, and she'll get home safe. She's on her way to a concert, and I'm going to meet up with her. Give her some space tonight, 'kay? Afterward, you can ground her for a hundred years."

Sadness tinged Carol's laugh. "I know I'm too strict and overprotective. I forget how I was at that age. No, the problem is, I remember too well. But you'll be with her tonight?"

"Absolutely." For a while anyway. But Russell wouldn't hurt Hayley if he got what he wanted. The last thing he needed was to be connected to a hurt or missing girl, especially one who was the darling of the community. "I'll make sure she calls you as soon as the concert is over." She finished the call, turned on the video camera, and held it up.

"Lachlan, it's me, Jess." She rolled her eyes. "Well, of course you know that. You're seeing me. I hope you understand I had no choice, and that there was nothing, absolutely nothing, you could do. Russell has Hayley. I'm trading myself for her. I know you would throw yourself into danger to prevent it, and I can't let you do that. You need to be there for Magnus. Love him and know how lucky you are to have him. Tell him I'm sorry. You know everything about Darkness that I do, so you can work through it together. By the time you get this, it'll be too late. If you see me, it won't be me, so don't do anything stupid to put yourself in danger."

Don't cry. She swallowed tears that wanted to spill out. "You are a great guy, Lachlan. Forgive yourself. That's what you can do for me." She wanted to tell him how much he meant to her, but he would no doubt show this to Magnus. No, let that be. What would be the point anyway? She ended the recording and sent it to him. She hated that he'd go crazy for a bit, but he knew her, knew this was what she'd have to do in this situation.

He knew her. The only person who really did.

She reached the warm lights of the shop as a sports car pulled up to the curb. Russell hadn't been lying about the size; it had one of those barely there backseats.

"Jessie!" Hayley jumped out and hugged her. "I can sit in the back. I'm so glad you're coming."

Clearly, she had no idea how terrible this man was, just as it should be. As they stood outside the car, Russell peering at them from inside, one desperate thought of running flared in her mind. But he was Darkness. He would catch them in an instant, and Hayley would know how dangerous and awful the world could be, if she survived. Once she was a witness, he couldn't let her live.

Hayley crawled into the back, and Jessie sat in the passenger seat and closed the door. She turned to the girl as the car pulled away. So innocent, so beautiful. "Who are we seeing in concert?"

Jessie thought her voice sounded odd and disconnected. Hayley didn't seem to notice.

"Muse. I hope you like alternative rock."

"You do realize how dangerous it is to get into a car with a stranger."

The girl's expression fell. "I know. But it was so cold, and I had a while to walk yet. I promise I won't do it again."

"Ever. And don't sneak out of the house again either. I know you want to stretch your wings. You'll have time for that." Her breath hitched, making her heart hurt. "Plenty of time."

Russell watched in his peripheral vision, a small smile on his face. Bastard. He'd found her biggest vulnerability. He'd ripped out her heart and now the slowing blood flow was shutting down her organs.

They pulled into the jammed parking lot of the auditorium, hearing the throbbing bass right through the closed windows. Only a few people remained outside. Hayley's face lit up the moment she crawled out of the backseat and looked at the large building. "My first concert!"

"Shall we go, ladies?" Russell gestured toward the entrance.

Jessie took Hayley's hand and they walked together, though the girl's pace was much faster. Hayley was going to a concert, and she was going to her death.

"You don't look well, Jess," Hayley said. "Are you okay?"

"I may be coming down with something. I'll be alright." Would she? Where would her soul go? To the Void?

"I'm sorry I dragged you out here."

"Just enjoy yourself. And when we get out, call your mom and have her come get you. She's worried."

"She's going to be pissed."

"Yeah, and deservedly so. You have to earn her trust, and she has to give it to you. Work on that together." Jessie wanted to give her all the advice she could think of, but they were approaching the box office.

Russell bought the tickets but held them in his hands. "We need to stick close together."

Hayley gushed in gratitude. Jessie did not.

They walked in, his hand on each of their shoulders. Jessie shook it off, but he only put it back and squeezed gently. *Cooperate*, he was telling her.

She moved away again. *Get your hand off me. I'm not going anywhere.*

Bleachers went way up all around the sides, but Hayley led them straight into the crowd in front of the stage. The music was hard, pounding, and loud. Blinding white lights flashed and swept over a mass of heads and arms. Hayley became one of those people, moving to the music next to her. Russell stood right behind Jessie, his body brushing hers ever so slightly. He was smiling, eyes glittering with anticipation. The song was about being victorious. The bass pounded right through her, making her eardrums itch.

She leaned next to Russell's ear. "What if I die like all the others?"

That, at least, stole the smile away. "How the hell did you know about them?"

"That doesn't matter. What if I collapse right here in front of everyone? You can't hide my body like you hid the others'."

"It will work. You're a part of her."

"Does she know you're trading me for her? That you're sacrificing her own daughter?"

"Shut up."

Maybe she could somehow talk to her mother before the exchange and get her answer. That was her only hope, that Calista would be horrified and refuse. Mothers sacrificed for their children, not the other way around. Well, in theory.

Hayley screamed. Jessie jerked around, imagining a column of black smoke coming down into her head. But she was frantically waving at someone.

"My friends!" she said. "I'll be right back."

She weaved through the crowd to a group of teens. One girl hugged her and both girls jumped up and down and squealed. Hayley gestured toward Jessie, clearly trying to get her friends to come her way. They shook their heads, pointing to the spot they had near the stage.

Russell pointed to a section way up high and nearly empty. "We're going up to the bleachers."

Most people were either on the floor or midway up.

A few minutes later Hayley returned, looking letdown.

Jessie leaned closer. "We're going to sit up there. It's too crowded down here."

Hayley's face reflected even more disappointment. "But I like it here. Can I stay with my friends? No, then I'd be leaving you, and you came because of me."

Leaving her.

She looked at Russell. "Hayley's going to stay with her friends." It wasn't a request.

He considered it, then nodded. It would probably work better in his plan anyway.

Hayley hugged her. "Thank you, Jess."

"Why don't you plan on staying with them the rest of the concert?"

"And leave you with some strange guy? No way."

"You were comfortable enough with him to get in his car. Besides, I'm a grown-up. I'll be fine. I don't want to stay for the whole concert anyway. Now that I know you're safe with your friends, I'm good with leaving early." When Hayley hesitated, Jessie said, "It's okay, really." Yes, get away from Russell.

"Well, all right. Text me when you get home."

Jessie smiled. "Yes, Mom."

Hayley rolled her eyes. "I did so totally sound like her, didn't I? I guess I can see why she worries."

Jessie pushed back a strand of Hayley's pink hair. "It comes with caring. It's a small price to pay, believe me."

The girl dashed off to her friends, merging with the group. Jessie followed Russell through the crowd to one of the stairways that led up toward the cavernous ceiling. Her heart tightened into a tiny ball with each step. He wouldn't wait much longer. He had a couple of hours to do what he needed to do and give her time to recover. Or leave her there and escape if she died. Would he try again with Hayley? Probably not. If she didn't work, Hayley wouldn't either. And Hayley would now be with her friends.

She told Russell that. "She'll be expecting a text from me when I get home tonight. Otherwise she'll be worried." And investigate. "Text her that I have to leave town now. Assure her that it's not her fault."

Jessie wanted Hayley as far away from who she'd be. She was sure Russell would take his love—her body—away as soon as the exchange was complete. The girl would be hurt by her distance, but Hayley would go on.

Thank God.

She would go on, too. She just didn't know where.

CHAPTER 21

From the window, Lachlan watched Jessie walk down the sidewalk. She was on the phone, probably calling the girl's mother to assure her she was all right.

Cheveyo stepped up beside him. "You're still worried about her."

"I trust your shield. It's kept Russell from finding my home so far. But . . ."

"You love her." That wasn't a question either. Cheveyo smiled. "I've seen the look before, and I've felt the same resistance you feel now. I had my reasons, too. Good ones. But you know, reasons, codes of honor, don't fill your heart, don't warm your bed or slake your desires. They're cold and lonely when it comes right down to it."

Lachlan only grunted in answer. How did the guy know so much? He wasn't a normal guy, that's why.

"Go on, follow her. She doesn't have to know you're there. I'll watch over Magnus. The second he wakes, I'll call you."

He gave Cheveyo a nod of thanks and went to grab his phone. He searched the floor, under the bed, everywhere. Then he looked downstairs. "Where the hell is my phone?"

"Give me your number and I'll call it."

Lachlan traced the ring tone to between the cushions of the couch down in the living room. Odd. He pulled it out and saw a text message notification from Jessie. Even odder. He opened it. No message, but a video. Tightness pulled at his chest even before he could think of why she'd be sending a video.

Her words plunged his heart to the depths of despair. That's why the phone had been hidden. She hadn't wanted him to find it before she had a chance to do something really stupid.

Lachlan turned to Cheveyo, standing behind him. "Where's the nearest coffee shop? She said the name of one on Main Street . . . it had a name, Jack, Peter—"

"Pete's Java?"

"That's it."

"Follow me." Cheveyo ran down the stairs to the door, Lachlan steps behind him.

It wasn't far to what looked like the main drag. Their shoes pounded on the pavement, his blood pounding the same way in his head. Lachlan saw the lighted sign, PETE'S JAVA, no one standing out front. Was she inside? He tore through the entrance just as a couple was coming out. He slammed right into them, but his gaze scoured the space, the woman in the corner with her laptop, not Jessie, a woman at the counter ordering, not Jessie. No Jessie anywhere.

"Hey, man," a voice said next to him.

A cup lay on its side on the floor, coffee spilling.

"Sorry." Lachlan dashed back out to the side-walk where Cheveyo was still searching, shaking his head.

"She's not here."

Lachlan's heart was like that cup, all of his blood spilled right out. "I've got to find her."

"Let's get Pope."

They raced back to the town house. Cheveyo called out for Pope the second he opened the door.

Lachlan grabbed his sword. He hated asking for help, but there was no room for pride when Jessie's life was on the line. "Olaf, now would be a good time to have your help."

No answer.

Cheveyo and Pope rushed back in. Pope said, "To Jessie?"

"Yes. Now."

Pope grabbed his arm and Lachlan felt a *whoosh*. He heard Cheveyo's outraged, "Hey! What about me?"

Lachlan and Pope materialized in a dark, loud place that smelled of sweat and smoke. It only took a second to orient himself. Concert.

Lachlan searched the crowd. "Where is she?"

"My ability hasn't come back precisely. She's here somewhere."

They pushed their way through the mass of

people in the smoke-filled space. Twenty minutes later, he spotted Hayley.

"Where's Jessie?" he asked, startling her.

She pointed up. "She and the guy who gave us a ride went up there. She's not, like, *with* him—"

Lachlan turned, finding Pope and gripping his arm. "Up there!"

In a flash, they transported to the top of the bleachers.

Jessie! Lying limp across Russell's lap, his hands hovering inches above her, his head thrown back as he looked at the ceiling. Bringing down Darkness, though in the murky smoke-filled air Lachlan could hardly discern it. Russell looked up, and his expression fell.

Nothing like I feel, you bastard.

Lachlan lunged at him, but Russell stood, holding Jessie's body in front of him.

"You don't want to hurt her, because there might be a chance she's still in here."

Was there a chance?

Fury burned through Lachlan. "You're going to hide behind her, you coward?"

Russell's gaze slid beyond him to where Pope stood. He Became, dumping Jessie on the floor between the rows of seats. The dark wolf blended in with the black walls behind him. An occasional flicker of light reached them, flashing on the churning interior of the wolf. Several dogs emerged like a visible belch from the wolf's mouth, and two turned toward Pope.

Lachlan removed the dirk at his waist and called, "Pope!" He tossed it to him, handle first. Pope caught it a second before the dogs hit him. Then he disappeared, reappearing behind Russell.

Russell spun, baring his teeth and snarling at Lachlan, who brought the sword down, scraping the wolf's chest. No magic. No arcs of electricity. The wolf yelped in pain but didn't back up. Lachlan could see the realization in its eyes: it knew he didn't have the power.

But he had skills. He took a second to check on Pope, who was leading the dogs on a chase, disappearing and then reappearing. He pushed out his hand, and the dogs fell back as though hit with an invisible force, only to leap at him again.

Lachlan saw movement and swung around, sword slicing through the air. The wolf stumbled back. They fought in the small space behind the last row and the wall. Damn small spaces again. He thrust, the wolf advanced, then retreated.

Back and forth, until Lachlan's back slammed into a wall. Hell. He was cornered. The wolf smiled and prepared for a final strike. Lachlan jumped to the top edge of the seats, then to the next row, running along the top of that one, and pounced on it.

He landed on the wolf's broad back, bringing the sword round and cutting its throat. Russell should have died right then. Far from dead or severely wounded, it howled and twisted, sending Lachlan to the floor. He couldn't win, he realized, not without magic.

Olaf! Now is not the time to hold a grudge.

No response. Bastard was ignoring him.

Russell tore back toward Jessie. Knowing he had to keep himself between them, Lachlan leaped to the top of the seats again, keeping her in his sights. The wolf had been solid enough when he landed on it. He knew he could hurt it. There was a slash in its throat, but the beast had no blood to spill, no skin to split. He was weaker, though. As Lachlan watched, the split mended.

Russell's gaze shot behind Lachlan, where Pope smacked the dogs back with some unseen force. The wolf's mouth moved, uttering the words, "Who the hell is that?"

"You're not the only one from Surfacia."

Russell's eyes widened as he turned back to Lachlan, who was charging toward him. Russell sent him flying backward, slamming into Pope and scattering the dogs like bowling pins.

Pope whispered, "Get to Jessie. I'll get us out of here."

Russell, much closer to Jessie than they were, bounded toward her again. Pope clamped onto Lachlan's arm, and with a *whoosh* they were next to Jessie. Pope put his other hand on her leg and they left again. The last thing Lachlan saw was Russell's shocked face.

The three of them popped into his living room. Lachlan, on the floor beside Jessie, set his sword aside and pulled her onto his lap. "Jessie. Wake up, baby. Wake up."

It hit him then that if she woke, she might be Calista.

She looked just like she had when she went to the Void. An enormous hole opened inside, threatening to swallow him. The thought of Jessie being in that horrid place she'd described, being devoured by it . . .

Pope put his hand on his shoulder. Out of sympathy, Lachlan realized.

He turned to the man. "You left Cheveyo behind. Why?"

"I care about him and his family deeply. They have been through a lot, but now they are happy, settled, and raising a son. Cheveyo would throw himself into your fight without a second thought. It's his nature. If he was hurt, Petra would heal him and end up dying. If he was killed, she would kill me."

Lachlan nodded. "They've earned their rest, as have you."

Pope knelt down, waving a hand over Jessie. "She's not in there. Something like this happened to Petra. She had healed too many mortal wounds, and Cheveyo warned her not to heal again for some time. Unfortunately, as you know, when you love someone, logic does not prevail. Nor self-preservation. When Cheveyo was shot, and she healed him, her soul left her body. He used their soul connection to go after her."

Lachlan looked at Pope. "He obviously succeeded because she's here."

"Yes, but he almost got lost himself."

"I can bring her back."

Pope shook his head. "I do not sense the kind of psychic connection that bonds Petra and Cheveyo."

Lachlan's heart opened. "I love her. Isn't that enough?" He did love her, he realized. He hadn't just fallen for her, but loved her with everything that was in him.

"You must have a way to get to where she is," Pope said. "Their bond allowed that connection."

Lachlan lifted his head. "I have a way. I just have to convince him." Something occurred to him. "The girl! There's a girl at the concert who got some of Jessie's bone marrow. Russell lured her into trusting him, figuring if she had Jessie's DNA, it might be enough to use her body to bring Calista back. Russell might go after Hayley again. She doesn't know she's in danger, and we want to keep it that way if we can."

He set Jessie on the couch and ran to the kitchen to find the initial article about the carnival. His gaze went to Jessie's picture even as he pointed out Hayley. "This is her. She's down in the pit."

Pope vanished. The man wasted no time, that was for sure.

Lachlan rushed back to the couch, pulling Jessie into his arms. "Olaf!" Desperation and fear saturated his voice. "Please."

He felt the Highlander's energy. "Och, *now* you ask nice. What happened to the lass?"

"Russell sent her soul to the Void to bring back her mother's soul." He tore his gaze from her, looking at his reflection in the glass. He and Olaf both looked opaque, ghostly. "I need you to take me to the Void, like you did with her. I have to go in and bring her back."

"Nae, I'm no' going back there. Ye took me to task before, and now ye beg for my help. I'm done helping ye."

"Yes, I'm begging."

Olaf made a grunting sound. "Ye dinna even know if ye can go there. She holds the same as that place, the Darkness. Ye dinna have that. And the Light, it gets closer e'ery time I go. As angry as ye make me, I'm no' ready to go yet."

Lachlan looked at that grizzled face, weathered and old even at a young age. "This isn't about you or me. It's about her. She's done nothing to make you angry. Can you let her be trapped in that place? Swallowed?"

The ghostly image looked down at Jessie. "It's a terrible thing, aye. But so is the Light."

"I thought the Light was supposed to be warm, welcoming, full of joy with loved ones coming for you."

"No' when ye've done the things I done."

Lachlan remembered something he'd said earlier. "You let your men down."

"Och, rub it in, why don't ye?"

"I'm not rubbing it in. You said you let your men down, that it haunts you. You have a chance to make up every wrong you've ever committed. Redemption. You ache with the need for it, the hopelessness of ever getting it. I know that ache well, and I know that sometimes we're given a rare chance to hold it in our hands again. This is your chance. Help me save her."

"You're killin' me, cousin. Aye, it sounds honorable and brave, but it's a lost cause. Ye willna get in, or ye'll get trapped yourself."

"Scots always embrace a lost cause. That's what the Jacobite rebellion was. When you ran across the heather, sword in hand, you knew that, didn't you? But you ran anyway, with your battle cry and your rage, knowing you were fighting for the right side. You lost that time."

"Och, there ye go, rubbin' it in again."

"You get a do over."

"A what?"

"You get to do it again, only this time you're going to get it right. We're going to win."

Silence for a few seconds. Good. Lachlan put his hand over her heart, feeling the beat of it. "We can save her. Remember her laugh, the soft smile on her face, and her adventurous spirit." He remembered, and it hurt and soothed at the same time. "She wasn't afraid of anything." Not even of him. "We can save her, Olaf. You can save her."

"And what if I go to hell?"

"There's no hell. Hell is here, on earth. It's what we make of our lives. I've made my own hell. You probably made yours, too. A lot of us do. When you go to the Light, you leave this hell behind." He didn't know where this was coming from. Maybe out of desperation. But it felt right. "All you take are your triumphs and joys." Olaf's energy ebbed. "Don't you slink off like a coward!"

"Now ye're getting mean again."

Ah-hah. Being called a coward poked an old wound. A deep one. "That's what you did, isn't it? When things started going bad, you ran. That's how you let your men down."

Olaf vanished, as wholly as Pope had. He'd pushed the Highlander too far.

Lachlan touched his forehead to Jessie's. "I'm sorry, Jess. I blew it."

This was like those moments after he'd come out of the blackout to find his mother dying on the floor, feeling so damned helpless. He wanted to throw something, break something. But he clutched Jessie to him, not wanting to let her go.

Where was she? He couldn't abide it, thinking of her in that place she'd described with fear and disgust in her eyes. He couldn't sit there and do *nothing*.

Her words echoed in his mind: *You are a warrior who will go to any length to do what's right. To protect those you care about.*

How they'd filled him then, how they tore at him now. He laid her down, pulled up her shirt and stretched out beside her so that his head rested on her stomach. He traced the symbol there, then pressed his hand flat against it.

Everything he felt now, for her—all the loss, his guilt—swamped him. He'd never released any of it, not his mother's death and his part in it, not his father's death. Like Jessie with her tears, he'd held it in, thinking he was stronger for it. When he'd held her, and encouraged her to let loose, he'd only felt her strength. Losing Jessie ripped open the floodgate. He heaved in great breaths, pressing his face against her soft skin, feeling moisture slide down his temple.

CHAPTER 22

Jessie felt the Darkness seep into her, and then suck her soul through what felt like a long dark pipe. Suddenly she stood in a chamber in the Void.

No, not the Void!

She looked down at herself. Thank God not buried in the wall. The gray, pulsing folds shuddered. No, not the folds; the whole place shook in violent tremors. The chamber was so small now, there was barely room for her to spin around. She did turn, expecting her mother to be gone.

Calista was still in the wall, even less of her face visible. She didn't say anything for several seconds. Because she was waiting to go. Then a hesitant smile. "Baby."

Jessie narrowed her eyes. "Were you expecting to be zapped into my body?"

"Wh-What?"

"You knew, didn't you? It wasn't going to take a pint of my blood to bring you back. You needed all of my blood, my bones." She spread her hands. "Everything."

"Don't be preposterous, darling. I would never come back at your expense."

Jessie wanted to believe her, ached to believe her, but the heaviness in her heart and heat behind her eyes told her that she didn't. She had her answer, but a new question as well: why hadn't her mother disappeared?

Calista must be wondering the same thing, but her puzzlement morphed to panic when another tremor shook the place. "What's happening?"

"Don't you mean, what's not happening?"

"This place is falling apart."

Was the heartbeat louder? Faster? Yet another tremor shook, sending Jessie off balance.

Calista's gaze shifted to someone behind her, and she spun to find Russell.

"Russellmylove," Calista said, mashing all the words together into an endearment. "Why didn't it work? I started coming in . . . it was supposed to work this time."

So she knew. It hurt, God it hurt. Jessie waited for Russell's answer.

His glare speared Jessie. "You *are* here. I had only just begun the soul transfer when your boyfriend popped in out of nowhere. And I do mean *nowhere*. And he brought a friend."

Lachlan. But how had he found out so soon and gotten there so fast? Pope, the one who could teletransport. Had to be.

That hard look in Russell's eyes softened as he neared Calista. "I'm so sorry, sweetheart. As you can see, I'm halfway there. The boyfriend didn't have magic this time, but the man with him is from where I'm from. He can teletransport, and in the blink of an eye he took Jessie's body. But I will find it. If I can't, I still have a backup plan."

Jessie turned to her mother. "He's talking about a teenage girl! Did you know that? Would you steal her life away, too? Or does it matter, as long as the two of you are together?"

Her mother's face contorted. "Don't throw that moral crap at me. What about *my* life? Does that not count? I've spent fifteen years in this purgatory. It's my turn to live again!"

Maybe this hell, and her desperation, had driven Calista crazy. Jessie backed away, disgusted by both of them. "If you don't care about taking your daughter's body, or all those other women, or a teenage girl, then know that Hayley has muscular dystrophy. So you'll have it, too." She had one last chance to save Hayley.

"I don't care. Look at me. Anything is better than this."

Anything. Jessie turned to Russell. "Make it work. I don't want you touching that girl." *Damn you, Lachlan. You had to go and be a hero, didn't you? Everything would have been fine if you'd found your phone just a few minutes later.*

The room shook, harder this time, and Calista let out a scream. "What's going on? Why is the Void shaking?"

"I don't know," Russell said. "Maybe it's overloaded with both you and Henry in here, almost swallowed up. There's too much emotion, yours, his, hers." He pointed to Jessie.

Calista's voice pitched into a high screech. "It's going to explode! We'll all die here."

Jessie slid in between the folds, escaping the chamber and the horrible people inside it.

"Can she get out?" she heard her mother ask.

"No."

The organs breathed, pressing against her and muffling their conversation.

". . . last time she had a rope. It's what helped her to get out of here. But she doesn't have it this time."

Squeezing her eyes shut at her mother's—her own mother's—callousness and selfishness, she pushed on as soon as she could. What if she never found her dad? What if he was gone by the time she got there? Panicked thoughts flitted through her mind. She endured the press of flesh against her and the horrid sound of the breathing. So much scarier navigating without the rope.

Better get used to it. You're never getting out of here.

Olaf wouldn't come. She'd seen his fear of the place, felt it herself. She was not worth coming in for as far as he was concerned. Lachlan had messed everything up, and now both he and Hayley were in danger again. Unless the Void destroyed itself first.

She felt her father's energy, as she had before.

She pushed through, faster, and finally stepped into the chamber.

"Daddy!" She ran to him, touching the tip of his fingers. All she could see of him now was the area that included his eyes, nose, and mouth. "Oh, God."

"Allybean, I told you not to come back." He looked behind her. "Where's the rope?"

She opened her mouth to tell him everything. Words stopped in her throat, and she just shook her head.

She felt an odd tingling sensation above her right hip. Blindly, she felt the ridges of the cross, blazing as though it had been touched by a low voltage wire. She pressed her hand over it. "You gave me this symbol to protect me. And it did. But it was never about the symbol, was it?"

"No. It was easier for a child to believe in a symbol than in some scary thing inside her. But it was all you. Ally, tell me what's going on."

The place trembled again. "Russell thinks the Vuld is overloaded with our emotions. My mother's afraid it'll explode."

"Your . . . you saw her, didn't you? I didn't want you to know she was here."

"She was trying to trade her soul for mine." Her voice broke on those words.

"That can't be." He saw that she was serious. "No. I can't believe she'd do that."

Jessie tried to take a step closer to him. Her legs wouldn't move. Panic clawed at her. The floor had clamped onto her feet! She pulled, hardly able to breathe.

"Oh, Allybean, I wish I could help."

Another violent shake made her stumble and fall to the floor. The gray mass grabbed onto her knees, her hands. She fought, crying, screaming, but it had her. Exhausted, she rested her head near the tips of his toes. "It will be over soon, Daddy. Do you remember when we used to cook together?"

He didn't answer for a second, probably confused as to why she was bringing that up now. Then he obviously got it. "Yes, I do. What was your favorite meal?"

"Fried chicken. We made such a mess, but it was so good." She smiled. "What was yours?"

Connected to the floor, she felt every shudder even more. She kept her focus on her memories, though, and her father's words. That would get her through until it was over.

Lachlan traced tracks through the moisture on Jessie's stomach. His tears. So foreign to him, so useless. Because they couldn't bring her back. Thirty minutes had passed and they'd changed nothing.

Lachlan felt Olaf's energy return in a rush.

"Och, ye're killing me, cousin."

"Unless you've changed your mind about helping, I'm not in the mood for you."

"Ye pulled me to ye. I've never felt anything like what you're feeling. It's . . ."

Lachlan could see his beefy hand ball into a fist as he tried to find the right words. "Bone-deep grief," he supplied. "Muscle-tearing frustration. Gut-wrenching—"

"I got it, I got it. For the lass. She's permeated your thoughts and everything about ye."

"She's gone."

"Dead?"

"No, in the Void. Her soul is trapped there for God knows how long."

"Love."

Lachlan moved his hand to her chest and could feel her heartbeat, still strong and steady. "What?"

"That's the strongest feeling I get from ye. More than all that other dreck. Love. I had lassies, aye, but never felt like this."

"Me either." His voice came out hoarse, raw.

Silence hovered between them for several seconds.

"You're right," Olaf said. "I did run. I was a coward."

Lachlan stroked across her skin with the tips of his fingers. "We all do cowardly things. It's part of being human."

"I let them down. Left them to be slaughtered."

"If you'd stayed, would it have made a difference? The enemy had artillery, you had swords. Your men would have died anyway, likely. You would have died."

"Then I grabbed onto you to avoid the Light. Another cowardly act." Olaf gave a ragged sigh.

"At least I got to fight with ye, got to feel a woman's body again, got to fall in love. It was worth it."

"Now you get to feel what it's like to lose someone you love."

"That part's no' so good." Olaf rubbed at his eyes. "I didna think I could cry in this state."

"I'm surprised you were brave enough to come back."

"Nae, ye dinna understand. Feeling your pain . . . ye let me cry."

"Glad I could oblige." Lachlan's voice sounded hollow to his own ears, devoid of emotion now. But Olaf was still here. Hope flickered in the darkness of his soul. "Maybe you could do something for me."

"Go to the Void? Ye dinna know what that place is like."

"No, but she did. She went anyway to save her father."

He grunted. "Aye, she's the bravest warrior I've ever known."

Lachlan knew better than to poke at Olaf's ego or the sore that was still so raw, especially if he had any hope of getting him to help. Neither bullying nor begging had worked before. He let those words settle instead.

"An' I had my moments, in clan clashes. I took heads. I faced death and wasna afraid. Only at the end, and I paid the price for that."

"If you could go back to that battle, would you stand?"

"I would fight to the end."

"You have another chance to hold fast. Right here." He tipped Jessie's face so Olaf could see her. Her innocence. Those apple cheeks. "You can save this brave warrior. You don't have to go in the Void. Just take me there."

Silence. Lachlan held back any more words. He'd never been good at finessing people. Now Jessie's life depended on it.

"Ye said there was no hell up there."

The light flickered even more.

"Look at your life. Constant battles. Treachery. Wasn't that hell?"

"Aye."

"But that was the way of it back then. No matter what you've done, you can make it right."

"What if it doesna work? Or ye canna find her or bring her back? Or ye get stuck there, too?"

"Then you come back here. With my soul gone, maybe you can come back into me." As soon as the words were out, he regretted it. What if Olaf cut him loose in the Void intending to take over his body? "Or you go on. It's time, Olaf. So do this one thing before you go."

Another few seconds of silence. Every cell in Lachlan's body froze, waiting.

"All right. I'll do it."

Lachlan wanted to shout in joy but kept it in. Olaf was still a wild card. He would have to put his ultimate trust in an entity who hadn't always been trustworthy. He'd do it a hundred times if it meant bringing Jessie back. He sat up, cradling her in his lap.

"Thank you."

"I'll come back and haunt ye if I end up in hell."

"Deal. How does this work? Do we clasp hands?"

"Nae, we're attached already. Just hold on."

Everything disappeared, including Lachlan's physicality. His stomach churned, which was strange since he had no body. They spun blindly through chowder-thick, dark fog. Then, up ahead, light filtered through, and he felt Olaf's anxiety tingle through him as they veered away from it. The Light, then.

What they headed toward, as the fog thinned, produced even more anxiety. A black sphere floating in nothingness. It shook and flickered as though it contained a great lightning storm. *That* was hell right there. She never said she'd been afraid, but if he felt fear, she probably had, too.

"It wasna doing that before, the shaking business."

That wasn't good.

Olaf pointed to a place that looked different from the rest of the sphere. "There, that's how she went in." He rolled out a golden rope. "Tie it onto ye. It's the only way ba—" He looked behind him as light washed over them, like sun streaming through a break in the clouds. "Hurry. I'll no' be waitin' here if ye take too long."

What would happen if Olaf went to the Light while he was in the Void? *Don't think about that.*

Remembering Jessie telling him how the rope came loose as she tried to free her father, Lachlan wrapped it around his wrist several times and floated toward the opening. As he reached it, the sphere trembled again. He pushed his way inside. She'd said she could feel her father's energy and followed it to him. Lachlan tuned in and felt her. He knew about timing his progress between breaths, about the fleshy folds. Seeing them made him admire her even more for going back the second time.

He heard a woman screaming but knew it wasn't Jessie. Her mother, then. He followed Jessie's energy to the left, impatient with each breath he had to wait through. Finally, he broke through into a room barely big enough to contain him . . . and Jessie, lying on the floor with a panicked and now shocked expression. Relief rocked him.

But she didn't look at all relieved. "No! Please, go, Lachlan. It will suck you in. Now I know how my dad felt when he saw me here. Please, go."

"Not without you."

"I'm already stuck. You can't get me out."

"Hell I can't." He pulled her arms, struggling to free her. She was right; the gray mass on the floor held her tight.

"I've already tried everything possible to free Dad. Just go."

He shook his head. "I'm not leaving you, Jess."

That's when he saw the man, or what was visible of him, in the wall. It was more gruesome than he'd imagined.

"Get her out of here," her dad whispered.

Lachlan stared into his desperate eyes. "I will."

A violent shake made him stumble.

"Don't fall!" Jessie screamed. "It'll grab you."

He righted himself and pulled at her again.

"That's love, Ally," her father said.

"No, it's insanity. Lachlan, please go!"

Lachlan studied how the gray muck, hard as dried glue, mired her legs.

Her father said, "Russell and I loved your mother for the wrong reasons. Love isn't the right word for it. I wouldn't go into a place like this to rescue her. I wanted her because Russell wanted her. He had taken something precious from me, or at least that's how I saw it. I wanted to punish him. For Russell, she represented someone to love him, to love. He would possess her because he had nothing else. It became a war over Calista."

Two brothers loving the same woman. Look how that had ended. Lachlan kept working. Was her leg coming loose, just an inch?

"So you killed her. And him, too," Lachlan said.

"I don't think I would have killed her just because she had been having an affair. It was the twisted, dark nature of it, of their intention. Russell was dying. She brought him to our home so that he could take over my body. When I figured out what they were up to, Darkness overtook me."

"Oh, Daddy, that's terrible. How could she . . ." Jessie's face shadowed. "Because she's a selfish, callous person."

"She knew, didn't she?" Lachlan asked her.

Jessie nodded, seemingly unable to say the word. Tears glittered on her cheeks.

Lachlan wanted to kiss them away, but he needed to free her more than he wanted to comfort her. He grunted with effort, but his mind went back to two brothers fighting over one woman, becoming insane over it. Killing the object of their obsession. The rope squeezed his wrist, tight as a snake.

"That's not you, Lachlan," she said, watching his face. "Don't even go there. You and Magnus have an entirely different relationship. You love each other. You would never hurt him on purpose."

He was distracted by the sucking sound coming from beneath her legs. "You're coming out!"

He started to put his hands down to brace against the floor.

"No, don't touch the floor!" her father yelled. "Dammit, I feel so helpless."

"Don't beat yourself up for what you can't do," Lachlan said under his breath as he put every ounce of his strength into pulling her. He kept shifting his feet, feeling the suction every time he moved.

She screamed in agony but pushed out, "No, don't stop. I'll be . . . okay. What happens to our bodies here doesn't affect our real bodies."

He pulled again, and again. Finally, he was able to yank her leg partially free. "Oh, God . . . Jess." What he saw turned his stomach. The gray muck was stripping the skin off her calves. And by her screams, she felt it. He could hardly breathe, seeing her raw flesh, bloody skin still attached to the floor.

"Just keep . . . going." Pain contorted her face and tightened her jaw.

He did, because he couldn't do anything else. The tearing of flesh, her gasps, killed him, stole his breath away, and still he played a life-threatening game of tug of war. With one final tear, one guttural scream, he wrenched her free.

She fainted, falling heavily into his arms. The sphere shuddered, sending him crashing to the floor. He jumped up, gathering her, and looked at the man in the wall.

"Go!" her father said. "And thank you."

With a quick nod, Lachlan turned. Using the rope, he pushed his way through the gray masses, feeling the whole thing shake and tilt. They had to get out before the damned thing exploded.

"Help me!" Calista's terrified screams echoed from far away.

He feared he'd taken a wrong turn somehow, but he had the rope. It felt loose, as though he could pull it all the way in.

Hell, had Olaf taken over his body? But Jessie could still go back, couldn't she?

With another shudder, the sphere belched them

into the openness. Lachlan breathed, looking down as her eyes fluttered open. "We're out," he told her.

"My father . . ."

He shook his head, looking to Olaf. All he saw was the end of the rope floating freely. And Olaf, or more specifically his silhouette, floating toward the Light.

"Olaf!"

"Nae, it's alright." He was smiling. "You're right, laddie. There canna be a hell when I feel such joy and love."

The Light burst brighter, blinding, and then it rocketed into the distance like a shooting star. In that same moment, Jessie and Lachlan plummeted.

Lachlan came back with a gasp, feeling dense in his body. She woke in the same violent way.

"I've got you." He held her tight, then looked at her legs. No missing flesh, no blood.

She trembled, running her hand over her calves. "It felt so real." She put her hand to her stomach and realized it was bare.

"I lost myself," he said, pulling her shirt back down. "Buried my face against you, wanting to feel you, to know you were alive."

She lifted her fingers, rubbing her thumb against the tips. "I'm wet." Her eyes widened, then softened. "Your tears." She touched his cheek, her fingers sliding across more moisture. He took her hand and pressed it to his mouth, because he hadn't lost her after all, and he never wanted to feel that cutting sorrow again.

She put her other hand over her scar where it was wet. "I felt you. It tingled. We were connected, even when I was there and you were here." She punched his arm. "I can't believe you went there, risked everything—"

He kissed her, bracing her face with his hands.

She held his face, too. "Lachlan, did you save me for Magnus? Or to redeem yourself?"

He swallowed hard. "No. I saved you for me. Selfish bastard that I am. I did it for me."

She hugged him, and he held her for a second. "And we're going to save your father."

She pushed back, gripping his shirt. "How?"

"We don't have much time. We have to find Russell, trap him somehow. Can you walk?"

"I can run, if it means saving my father."

They jumped up, and Lachlan grabbed his sword. "I don't have Olaf anymore."

"Which means the dogs will tear you apart. But I have Darkness. And desperation. And anger. I'll make my own damned dogs."

"Remember, he has desperation, too. If he gets hold of you, he can still bring your mother's soul in if the Void hasn't exploded yet."

She held out her hands, palms up, and focused on them. Harder. Gritting her teeth, groaning with the effort. Defeat racked her expression. "Nothing. It's gone. I don't even feel it. Oh my God. I've lost Darkness just when I need it most."

They were out of luck.

The door burst open and two dogs raced in, followed by Russell. His manic gaze shot right to her. "You did get out!"

No, they were dead in the water.

"I looked on the satellite view of the area where the dogs became confused," Russell said, looking satisfied with himself.

The dogs rushed Lachlan. He backed against the wall, swinging his sword. "Get over here, Jess. Stay away from him." He cut at the dogs, but the magic was gone. All he could do was nip at their shells. They backed off and then came at him again and again.

She didn't move. Was she so afraid she'd frozen? He shoved his way toward her, feeling the dogs' teeth at his ankles.

Russell's eyes narrowed, and he smiled. "You don't have whatever it was that helped you before. No sparks. No aura." His gaze shifted to Jessie. "And you don't hold Darkness."

She reached out to him. "Russellmylove. It's me. I . . . I don't know how it happened, but I came back, not my daughter."

Her fingers wrapped around Russell's arm, and she stepped closer.

"Calista?"

She nodded, a beatific smile on her face. "It's me, sweetheart." Her voice was choked up, her hand against his chest.

Russell was so captivated, the dogs paused at

the lack of direction. He studied her face, flicking a glance at Lachlan, but then back at her. "It's really you?"

She ran her hands down her body. "I'm back!" She wrapped her arms around him, pressing her cheek to his chest. "We're together at last!"

For a second Lachlan felt time suspend. The sight strangled him. She'd just been here. He was sure it was her. So how . . . ?

She turned just slightly and winked.

Then he could breathe. She was pretending to be Calista to get close to Russell. And putting herself right in his arms. It was brilliant . . . and bloody dangerous, because if he suspected . . .

Russell wrapped his arms around her. "My love, my love," he murmured, still keeping an eye on Lachlan.

Lachlan had to fight not to move between them. He had to play the game. He had brought back the wrong soul. *Go back to that moment when you thought it was Calista, dredge up how you felt.*

"No. Noooo."

Russell's gaze pinned him. "You've lost. Let her go. The Void is gone now, or will be any second. You won't hurt her body because you love her. I know that kind of love."

"What I feel for her is nothing like your kind of 'love.' I would kill to protect her, but I would never kill innocents to bring her back. Because she would never abide that."

She turned to him. "Don't you dare judge me.

You don't know what it was like in that purgatory for fifteen years."

She was good. Damned good. Is that what the crazy bitch had said to her?

"It's done." Russell was backing toward the door, his arm around her shoulder. "Should I kill him, honey?"

"*No.*" Had she given herself away with that shocked word? Quickly, she added, "I mean, we don't need to. We won."

Russell's hand tightened on her. "He knows the truth. He could be trouble later. He's caused so much already." He looked at her. "I want to kill him."

He knew. Or suspected and was testing her. He raised his fist toward Lachlan.

Something was happening around her hand that pressed against his chest. Where his heart was. Darkness, in a smoky mist, surrounded it. Had she gotten it back?

Russell stumbled, looked down. "Wha . . . what are you doing?"

"Daddy!" she screamed as the mist burst forward. "Daddy!"

She pushed Russell, and they both fell to the floor. She kept her hand on his heart the whole time, gripping his arm to stay in place, calling her father over and over.

Russell struggled, hitting her. She didn't fall away, though. He reached out again and opened his mouth to say something. Only a groan emerged.

He shuddered, his eyes rolling back. Lachlan knelt at their side but didn't dare interrupt her. The dogs exploded into puffs of black mist. Russell's body convulsed, fingers clutching at the floor.

"They're fighting," she whispered. "Daddy, you can do it."

Because if Russell came back, he would kill them.

"You still have Darkness," Lachlan said, watching the blackness cover her hand.

She shook her head. "I'm using Daddy's. I realized that if I could feel you touching me, we were connected. And if I touched Russell's heart, my father would feel it. Maybe it will open a connection between them, since it's my father's body. But I'm afraid it's killing him."

Russell seemed to have trouble breathing, thrashing about and gasping. Lachlan put his hand over hers and held Russell's shoulders down. She closed her eyes and seemed to pour every ounce of energy into her hand.

The thrashing stopped. Russell fell still, breathing raggedly. Lachlan squeezed her hand but reached for his sword.

Russell's eyes opened and he sucked in air. Someone had come back. But who?

"Exploded," he said. "Void exploded."

Lachlan knew he should be watching the man, but he was watching her face. Because she would know first who it was. Hope and fear mingled on her expression, in her eyes.

"It's over," she said.

The man reached out with a shaky hand and touched her face. "Allybean."

"Daddy!"

She threw herself down on him, but Lachlan still didn't trust it. She'd used that trick on Russell, after all. His fingers tightened on the sword. The man put his arms around her. Tears rolled down his temples and he heaved in great sobs.

Lachlan couldn't stand it anymore. He pulled her to her feet, maybe a bit too hard. "You'd better let your father up, let him breathe."

She met his gaze, the joy seeping away. "You don't think . . ."

"I don't know." He leaned down and clasped the man's hand. "Welcome back, sir. Here, let me help you up."

The man stood, wobbly on his legs. "It's been so long since I've been able to stand." He didn't let go of Lachlan's hand, his body swaying. "Thank you. You saved my daughter. And even better, you love my daughter. Because no way would you have gone into that disgusting pit if you didn't. I'm Henry, by the way. We weren't properly introduced."

Lachlan shook his hand. "Lachlan."

She was studying her dad. She glanced at Lachlan and smiled. "It's him. I can see it in his eyes. That's how I knew it wasn't him right after it happened."

Henry laughed, though he leaned against the

arm of the couch for support. "He's still looking out for you. Yes, it's me." He took her in with love, not the desperate, manic so-called love in Russell's eyes, but genuine love. "My little girl."

She rushed forward, and this time Lachlan relaxed. He still held the sword, but he enjoyed their reunion.

Finally, she backed up enough to take Henry in with the same love. "What happened?"

"I was shocked to see Russell appear in the Void, especially in my chamber. The place was really breaking apart. He looked terrified. I felt heat in my chest, and I could feel you calling to me. And suddenly I was free. He lunged at me, and we fought, while the whole place was tilting at crazy angles. I felt stronger than I've felt in years. I pushed him at the wall, and it grabbed him. Swallowed him. I woke up here." He took them in, a warm smile on his face.

"Daddy, can you feel if you still have Darkness?"

He looked at his hands, then patted himself. "I feel different. Lighter."

She was nodding. "Yeah, me, too."

He flexed his fingers. "And I can't bring it out."

"But how?"

"The Void sucked it out of us. I could feel it, drawing the Darkness into itself."

She looked at Lachlan. "I'm free!" She hugged him, holding him tight. Just as quickly, she backed away and her joy dimmed. "But Magnus isn't."

"Magnus?" Henry asked.

She told him what had happened.

"No, you can't go to him. Not together. If he feels any attachment to you, he could kill Lachlan. Or you."

Lachlan's phone rang at that moment. It was Cheveyo's number on the screen, which meant Magnus was waking up. He answered.

"Hey, it's Cheveyo. Is everything all right there?"

He looked at Jessie. "Couldn't be better. Is Magnus . . ."

"He's been mumbling, shifting around, trying to open his eyes. I think he's going to come out any minute."

"Thank God." Lachlan felt his chest lighten and simultaneously get heavy. "I'll be right there." He looked at them. "I'm going. Magnus is coming round."

She walked closer, her hand on his arm. "I should—"

"No. I'll tell him."

She stood right in front of him. "Tell him what?"

"About Darkness. And us."

Relief suffused her smile. She put her hand on his cheek. "When you tell him—and you'll be thrashing yourself while you do—I want you to remember that you are an honorable man."

"Honor is all I have."

"No, you have value and . . . you have my love. You didn't set out to steal me away from Magnus. You wanted to scare me *away* from him. But I never belonged to him or to anyone. Until you. I belong to you, Lachlan. You have my heart now. It's not a gift you can return, by the way. Or give to someone else." She slid her hand to the place over his heart. "I told you that I know your heart. It's a good heart. Worthy of being loved."

Her words filled him with warmth, with strength to do what he needed to do. "A wise man recently told me that honor doesn't fill a heart, doesn't warm a bed or slake desires. He was right." He cupped her cheek. "You do. I'll do anything to help my brother to get through this. Except give you up. I won't do that."

He kissed her, soft and sweet, because he had to leave, because her father was standing there watching them. "I'll call you." He rubbed his thumb across her lower lip and pulled away.

He'd held onto his honor because he thought that was all he had. Now he had much more. He hoped he had a brother who would forgive him, because finally, he had forgiven himself.

RETURN TO THE HOLLOWS WITH
NEW YORK TIMES BESTSELLING AUTHOR

KIM
HARRISON

WHITE WITCH, BLACK CURSE
978-0-06-113802-7
Kick-ass bounty hunter and witch Rachel Morgan has crossed
forbidden lines, taken demonic hits, and still stands. But a new
predator is moving to the apex of the *Inderlander* food chain—
and now Rachel's past is coming back to haunt her . . . literally.

BLACK MAGIC SANCTION
978-0-06-113804-1
Denounced and shunned by her own kind for dealing with
demons and black magic, Rachel Morgan's best hope is life
imprisonment—her worst, a forced lobotomy and genetic
slavery. And only her enemies are strong enough to help her
win her freedom.

PALE DEMON
978-0-06-113807-2
After centuries of torment, a fearsome creature walks free,
craving innocent blood and souls—especially Rachel Morgan's,
who'll need to embrace her demonic nature to survive.

HAR2 0811

*At Avon Books, we know your passion
for romance—once you finish one of our
novels, you find yourself wanting more.*

May we tempt you with . . .

- **Excerpts** from our upcoming releases.
- Entertaining **extras**, including authors' personal photo albums and book lists.
- Behind-the-scenes **scoop** on your favorite characters and series.
- **Sweepstakes** for the chance to win free books, romantic getaways, and other fun prizes.
- Writing **tips** from our authors and editors.
- **Blog** with our authors and find out why they love to write romance.
- **Exclusive content** that's not contained within the pages of our novels.

Join us at
www.avonbooks.com

AVON

An Imprint of HarperCollins*Publishers*
www.avonromance.com

Available wherever books are sold or please call 1-800-331-3761 to order.

FTH 1111

Give in to your Impulses!

These unforgettable stories only take a second to buy and give you hours of reading pleasure!

Go to *www.AvonImpulse.com* and see what we have to offer.

Available wherever e-books are sold.

AVON**IMPULSE**